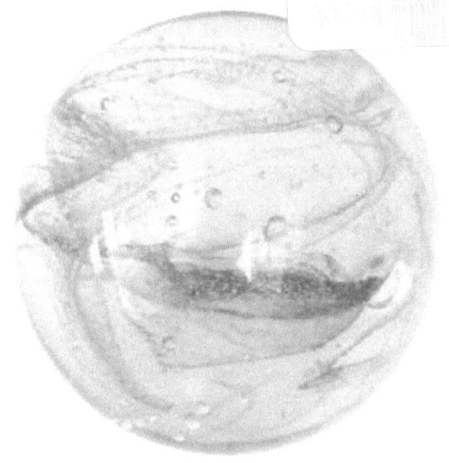

SECTOR C
THE BRIDGE

by Nina Soden

This is a work of fiction. All of the characters, organizations, businesses, and events portrayed in this novel are either products of the author's imagination or are used fictitiously.

The Bridge is the third and final book in the SECTOR C Series.

http://www.ninasoden.wordpress.com
Editor: Ula Manzo, Ph.D.
Beta Readers: Clara Tapaninen and Karen Mullins
Cover Design by Nina Soden and Amanda Orneck

DEDICATION

I dedicate this novel to my amazing beta readers. I value your time, your suggestions, and your passion for these characters. Thank you for helping me find my voice to bring these characters to life.

ACKNOWLEDGEMENTS

A special thank you to my amazing editor, Ula Manzo, who once again helped me bring Zelina, Ciara, Merick and all the others to life. Your attention to detail, professionalism and passion continue to help me create the best stories I can.

1

I have always been taught that every being has a purpose, and I believe this to be true. In Sector C, where I grew up, life is organized and efficient, and although it is not completely predictable, it is intentional. Every meal is scheduled, every birth is preordained, every task is monitored, and every relationship must be approved by the High Council. I was taught from earliest childhood that life in Sector C was a gift. I was taught that I was fortunate to be allowed to fulfill my purpose in Sector C, whatever that purpose proved to be. In Sector C, I was safe, cared for, and...as I would soon find out...asleep.

When I woke up in the holding cell, I knew instantly that something was different, although I couldn't pinpoint exactly what it was. It would take time for me to be fully awake, but the change had already begun. My eyes had been opened to understanding the possibilities. Although I didn't know it at the time, I would soon realize how I had been deceived. We had all been deceived into believing that the powers that be, those who ran Sector C, had our best interests at heart and protected us from the evils that roamed freely in the wastelands beyond the sector walls.

It was not a comforting realization, knowing that things were changing yet not understanding how, but it was one I now knew I had to accept—and deal with.

I woke up to the thought that the "monsters" outside in the wastelands—the humans—the discarded and desperate ones, the angry ones, and the deserters who had fled of their own accord, were just that—humans—and not truly monsters. The fears of the generations who came before me had kept me caged. Fear had kept us all caged, in slumber. Although, that didn't mean real monsters didn't exist. They just weren't who I thought they were.

There were so many unanswered questions that had plagued me since Selection Week, and now they had solidified into one clear "need to know": Why? Why had I been injected with not one but two viruses that changed my genetic makeup? I had heard the lies: all about how I was to be the mother of a hybrid race that would bring peace to the lycanthropes and vampires. But that wasn't how they treated me. They treated me like some kind of guilty secret, not a redeemer or a liberator. That one clear question challenged everything I had ever been taught. It was the question we had been taught never to ask: Why? To what *purpose*? And yet, I had begun to question everything. I was finally ready to find the answers. I was finally ready to wake up.

2

I gasped for breath as I sat straight up in bed. The question burned in my brain. *Why?*

"Another nightmare?" Ciara asked, popping her head up on the side of my upper bunk.

Nightmare?

"A, are you, all right?" she asked, quietly leaning in so no one else could hear.

"I'm…" I glanced around, surprised to find myself back in the selection student barracks. "Where's Merick?"

"Merick? Who's that?" she asked, looking more confused than I felt.

No, no, no—this isn't right, I thought. *Merick is still "M" here, and I still need answers.* I closed my eyes, wishing it away.

When I opened my eyes again, I was back on the cold hard floor of my holding cell. The sirens in the hallway had been triggered, and the deafening blast brought me wide awake instantly. There was no one in any of the other cells, and the guards seemed to have deserted their posts.

"Hello?" I shouted. But my voice was drowned out by the sirens.

I wasn't in a holding cell because I had been arrested. It wasn't that kind of holding cell, not that it was any less barbaric. In fact, it was probably more primitive than what someone would typically imagine, hearing the words "holding cell".

In Sector C, new lycanthropes are kept in holding cells during their first few moon cycles. Each cycle is a three-day period: the days before, during, and after a full moon. The new lycanthropes are kept there until they can learn to control their transformations and their actions. For some lycanthropes, it only takes a couple of moon cycles, and for others it can take years. The newest lycanthropes are held in the primary cells, away from the older lycanthropes. I can't say with certainty why this happens, but I've heard rumors that it is because they feed us differently. We younger lycanthropes are given raw meat—livestock. The older lycanthropes, those who have taken longer to adjust to their transformations, are fed fresh living "meat"— castaways brought in from beyond the wall. I'm not sure how true these rumors are, but if they are accurate, I'm glad they keep us separated.

The Council says the cages are used to keep us safe, but after all I've witnessed—all I've experienced—over the last few days, I'm pretty sure they're used to keep everyone else safe.

Transitioning, transforming, shifting, whatever you want to call it, isn't pretty. In fact, it is downright scary.

Until your beast has matured, you can't really control what you do while you're in animal form, and you don't remember it either. Or at least you're not supposed to remember it. Unlucky for me, I remembered everything: the sound of my bones popping in and out of place, the smell of blood as my claws ripped through the skin of my hands, the feel of my muscles growing and stretching to accommodate my new form, the odd tingling sensation as hair—no, fur—grew and spread across my body, even the cries of pain coming from my own lungs and the burning in my throat as my screams became overwhelming.

I remember watching as the others around me shifted, and wondering if I even would. I was only in the holding cells because the Council was afraid I *might* shift, not because they knew I would. I watched as the others shifted and then devoured the raw meat that was thrown into their cages, tearing it apart with their teeth like savage beasts. They *were* beasts— animals. *It's no wonder the Council locks us up,* I thought, watching and listening to the chaos going on all around me. The thought sent chills down my spine, and I could taste the vile presence of vomit threatening to come up.

They turned us into beasts, and we let them do it. And I am the freakiest of them all, I thought.

But now all the other holding cells were empty, and the hallway alarm still screamed. *Where is everyone?* I wondered.

When the alarm abruptly stopped, I expected someone to come in and tell me what was happening, but no one came. The deafening silence brought with it a throbbing headache that I hadn't realized I had. When I reached my hands up to my temples, clasping the sides of my head, I realized my long chestnut brown hair was matted and knotted. My hair, along with the rest of my body, was covered in a thick layer of mucus that had already begun to harden and crust over. Just one of the many disgusting side effects of the transformation process. I managed to peel most of the dried secretion off my arms and legs, but as I pulled at my hair, trying to smooth it out, I eventually gave up, declaring it a lost cause. Naked, and more uncomfortable than I had ever been in my life, I tried to get my thoughts together.

I'll shower. As soon as I get out of here, I'll shower, I told myself. I was sure I looked even worse than I felt, and I felt disgusting.

How long have I been asleep? I wondered. *And why am I alone?* I stood up, slowly stretching my stiff legs and arms. *Where could they have taken everyone?*

"Hello?" I yelled, hoping that someone might be passing by in the hall and hear me, but deep down I knew there wouldn't be an answer. I paced the width of the cell more times than I could count.

"What the hell?" I muttered to myself, starting to get more than a little upset. Even William and Haden, my personal security team assigned by the Council to watch over me, were gone.

William was a vampire, the largest one I'd ever seen, even bigger than most of the lycanthropes, though not quite as tall as Haden. He had blue-black hair with just a hint of gray at the temples, sky blue eyes, and a long scar that ran down the left side of his face. You'd think with all that he'd be scary, threatening, or even gruesome, but he wasn't. At least, not to me. Somehow, he seemed more approachable than his sidekick and long-time friend,

Haden. Haden was a lycanthrope, a werewolf to be exact. The first time we met, he had threatened to eat me as a snack. I'm sure he was joking, but I still wouldn't want to be left alone in a room with him if he really was hungry.

Sector C is run by a joint Council of vampires and lycanthropes. William and Haden work directly for their respective Council leaders. They had been assigned to watch over me by the Sector Leader, the head of the Vampire Council, Remy. It was a glorified babysitting duty for William and Haden, and they knew it, but they did it anyway. They didn't really have a choice. The Council was worried. No one knew what to make of me or what to expect from me. There had never been a hybrid vampire-lycanthrope until me.

With both William and Haden gone, along with everyone else, I could only imagine that something really bad had happened, forcing every available sector security guard to assist. Or maybe it was just that the moon cycle was over, and they had simply forgotten about me. Or maybe Remy had written me off as no longer a threat. However, considering the fact that I had shifted, proving that my lycanthrope capabilities were real and no longer just theoretical, and the fact that the sector alarms had been going off when I woke up, I was betting on the former.

"Hello?" I yelled again. "Why am I still locked up?" The only answer was the echo of my own voice bouncing off the concrete walls, not that I really expected anything else.

I glanced up, remembering that the Council is always watching, and scanned the ceiling for the familiar blinking red light of the security camera, and sure enough, it was there. "Hello!" I yelled, waving my hands in the air hoping someone on the other side of the video footage would see me.

No luck. Or, if they did, they didn't come.

Not finding answers to any of my questions, my thoughts turned to an assessment of my health. When I woke up, despite needing a long hot shower and feeling a little stiff, I had actually felt thoroughly rested. I was surprised that after everything I had experienced, aside from the headache, I wasn't in any real pain. I was, however, naked.

I looked around the cell and spotted my clothes neatly stacked in a corner—and a memory flashed through my mind. I was slowly undressing in front of William and Haden, and they were staring at me like I had gone mad.

"What are you doing?" Haden had asked, looking confused yet intrigued.

"Well, I don't really have an endless supply of clothing, so instead of ruining this set even more, I'm taking them off before I shift." I had told him.

Where have they gone? I wondered.

I pulled on my clothes, realizing that taking them off may have prevented them from getting torn up, but it hadn't stopped the mucus from spattering all over them. Dried splotches covered the front of my shirt and down the left pant leg. *At least I'm not naked anymore,* I reassured myself. When I was fully dressed, I went back to pacing. Walking helped me think. *I don't want to be here,* I mentally whined. *Why am I still here?*

I felt something in my pants pocket—it was a note from Uma that I had almost forgotten about. Uma and I grew up together, although I had known her as C65U277 at the time—U277 or U for short. She hadn't taken the name Uma until after Selection Week, the same time the rest of us got to pick our names. Uma had wavy brown hair, that hung just below her shoulders, and sun-kissed skin that seemed to glow even when she was indoors. We had been in the same selection class, and I guess you could say we were friends. Uma was sweet: and she always got along with everyone, never wanting to make waves. She was smart, too. She even got accepted into one of the advanced education programs. She was training to be a medical assistant, and would eventually go on to become either a nurse or a doctor, which I think was the perfect fit for her.

The advanced education programs are extremely demanding, at least that's what I've been told, and I hadn't seen Uma since Selection Week. Then, unexpectedly, she had shown up at the holding cells during the moon cycle with Amelia, one of the sector doctors. I suppose she was there just doing her job, but it seemed strange that they would allow a vampire, who had only just begun her medical training, to assist in treating young lycanthropes during their first moon cycle.

During Selection Week Uma had selected vampirism, and I…well, I never made a selection. My choice was made for me. Uma had gone on to work as a caregiver in the infant unit at the sector medical clinic as part of her training. I'm not sure how she did it. The cravings a fledgling vampire experiences are violent and intense. I can't imagine trying to control them in the presence of helpless human babies.

The note I was holding had been given to me by Amelia the last time she examined me here in the cells. She had been in and out of the cells throughout the moon cycle, examining not only me but the other lycanthropes as well. She secretly slipped the note to me when she came to visit my cell the last time.

A ~ You'll never believe what I've discovered. We need to talk. This is huge. ~ U

'Huge' was a word that Uma threw around about a dozen times a day. In other words, what may have seemed *huge* or important to her wasn't always huge or important to anyone else, but that didn't mean I wasn't curious. She finished the hastily written note with:

P.S. Good luck with the moon cycle. You've got a lot of people rooting for you out here.

I chuckled at the thought: not because it was funny, but because it was far from believable. I didn't really have faith in the fact that there were all that many people rooting for me. Maybe some of my selection classmates, but that was about it. There weren't many others in Sector C who liked me, let alone who would be crossing their fingers that I would even survive my transformation.

I remembered it well. You could have cut the tension with a knife when Councilman Remy, the Leader of Sector C, introduced me at the release ceremony at the end of Selection Week. All the other students had been announcing their name selections with pride, and their respective communities, vampires or lycanthropes, had cheered for them as Remy proclaimed their affiliations. However, the announcement he made for me was different. It started out fine enough: *"As the firstborn of her class, A53 has proven herself a leader..."* He told them how I had excelled both mentally and physically far beyond any of the other students, and how I ranked at the top of the charts on the fighting mat. He surprised and shocked the crowd with the announcement that I had fought a castaway and survived, something no other selection student had ever done. I had almost felt a weight lift off my chest, allowing me to finally breathe, when it all came crashing back down as he announced to the listening crowd that I had been exposed to both the lycanthrope virus AND the vampire virus, and that both were active in my bloodstream: also a first for any selection student. In fact, as far as the Council knew, it was a first for anyone ever.

I couldn't have known what to expect. No one could have. The crowd went silent, and all eyes were on me. My heart pounded harder than any vampire's scarcely-beating heart had ever pounded. Sweat trickled down the back of my neck and gathered in the palms of my hands. In a few short words, he had single-handedly turned my life upside down, labeling me a freak—a being that was unheard of— unthinkable—and everyone in the crowd knew it. I wondered why he hadn't just banished me to the wastelands. It would have had the same effect.

In that moment I felt the same way I feel right now, standing here alone in a locked holding cell: confused, scared, frustrated, angry, and betrayed. I should have been safe—welcomed by my community like all the others—but he had taken that away from me.

I have to get out of here, had been my only thought as I stood on that stage, completely exposed.

Here in the cell, alone and cold again, a sense of déjà vu struck me. *I have to get out of here.* I needed to find Merick, Ciara, Uma, anyone.

I paced the length of my cell, trying to push back the memory of that day as I looked for a way out, already knowing there wasn't one.

The bars had been repaired where Merick had spread them apart to get through to my cage. Merick had also been a member of my selection class. If I'm honest, we were more than classmates, and we were more than friends.

Merick had been protecting me, and somehow he had managed a partial transformation. While in animal form, he had shifted just his paws back to human hands in order to grip the bars of his cage. I wondered, at the time and again now, how he had done it during his first moon cycle. How had he managed to spread the steel bars of the cage apart? They had to be at least two inches thick. It should have been impossible. But I knew: the power of a lycanthrope during the moon cycle is incomparable.

As I ran my hand down one of the smooth steel bars, the cold metal sent a chill up my arm, and a memory floated into my mind's eye as if I were watching it through the lens of a camera. I had been standing in just this same spot at the edge of my cage, gripping the bars, and suddenly they were moving apart, spreading open for me. At first, I wasn't sure if it was real or something I was imagining, after seeing Merick do it, but then I heard Haden in my mind, asking, *"You really think that's a good idea?"* and I knew.

"Where did they take him?" I asked.

Shortly after Merick had broken into my cage, they had carried him out on a stretcher. He had been trying to protect me. Amelia had wanted a blood sample while I was in animal form. She managed to trick me, luring me to the bars of my cage with meat. Even though I knew it was a trap, my lion couldn't resist the bait. William had grabbed me through the bars, pinning me down. Haden had made his way into my cage, climbing on top of me, making it easier for Amelia to get what she wanted. I guess Merick didn't like it, because he came to my rescue in a way that should never have been possible, not for a new lycanthrope.

"Leave her alone," he had said, just before lunging through the open bars and attacking Haden and pulling him off of me. I remember only bits and pieces of the fight that followed, but what I couldn't get out of my head was the image of Merick, lying there on the floor of my cage covered in blood, with his abdomen clawed open.

When Haden didn't move, I asked again, *"Where did they take him?"* I had been standing at the bars, about to step through the opening I had created, when Haden stepped in front of me with every intention of stopping me. He would have used any means possible, too. Normally I would have done it anyway, without second guessing myself—without worrying about the consequences. However, Haden was easily six and a half feet tall, towering over me, and although he was slender for his height, he was in no way thin. His shoulders were at least twice the width of mine, probably three times, and I'm sure he could have easily picked me up with one hand. His light brown hair hung over one eye as he glared at me through the opening in the bars, waiting for me to make a decision. He seemed almost excited at the thought that I might actually try something. I thought twice, then stepped back away from the bars.

Haden wasn't there anymore; no one was. I stepped forward again, reaching for the bars in front of me and wondering if I could do it again—if I could bend the bars and get out of here. Glancing across the room, I saw that the door at the far end was closed tight. I was alone. The metal was cold against my palms as I grabbed two of the bars. I pulled them with all my might, first trying to spread them apart and then trying both hands on one bar. It didn't work. The steel was too strong, or I was too weak—too tired to muster up enough energy.

"There is little that can compare to the power a lycanthrope feels—the strength they gain during the moon cycle," Professor Gunner had explained during one of his many lectures. *"But like everything else in life, actions have consequences. The more power a lycanthrope exerts during their transformation, the longer his or her recovery process takes once they have transformed back."*

I knew I had used up my supply of energy, so I let go and stepped back from the bars. There was no point in trying again, at least that was what logic told me. Suddenly, though, I felt an irrational and persistent urge to try one more time. I was tired physically, yes, but I was even more tired of allowing others to dictate my life. Locking me up...locking me out...injecting me against my will...keeping me from the people I loved most.

Love? I thought, questioning my own feelings. *Do I really love him?*

I was getting angry, angrier by the second, angrier than I had ever been. That was when the bars parted for me. That was when my lioness came forward and empowered me with the strength I needed to set myself free. I stepped out of my cage and into the small aisle between the cages, but before I made it any further, before I had a chance to process what I'd done, I heard the familiar, heavy footsteps of William and Haden, and I knew my personal security team was on its way.

Instantly, I knew I had a choice. Trust William and Haden to keep my strength a secret, which was doubtful since neither seemed to like me very much, or hope that no one would have any reason to review the monitors and see me put myself back in the cage, pulling the bars back into place as well as I could. It was a no-brainer.

I stuffed Uma's note back into my pocket, grabbed the thin standard-issue blue blanket they had given me when they locked me up, wrapped it around my shoulders, and sat back against the wall of my cell to wait. I closed my eyes and heard her voice—the voice of the woman with the long red hair. *"I'm your mom,"* she had said. I knew it couldn't be true, I didn't have a mom. No one in Sector C has a mom. But that was what she had said. *"I'm your mom."*

"I'm your mom."

"I'm your mom."

I knew it wasn't possible, but there had been something about how honest and sincere she sounded that had almost made me believe her. I found myself zoning out and entering another bizarre vision.

3

"Hey, what are you doing in here?"

"What?" My voice was hoarse, and barely audible. I cleared my throat and rubbed my eyes. I guess I had fallen back asleep. I leaned forward, away from the wall which was much too cold against my back and a shiver ran through my body.

Where did my blanket go? I wondered.

My eyes stung when I opened them. I could barely see Amelia's blurry silhouette in the doorway. The light in the hallway behind her just barely lit her delicate features and glistened off her soft brown hair. "I've been looking all over for you," she said, as she made her way over to me, and leaned forward to help me up. She was wearing a long white lab coat over a black skirt, and a red button-down blouse.

Red?

The color was striking on her, but it was against sector regulations.

"Why have you been looking for me?" I asked, my voice still hoarse. "I've been here the whole—" I glanced around. The bars of my cell were gone, and I was crouched in the corner of what looked like one of the patient rooms in the sector clinic. The lights were off, but my vision was starting to return, a benefit of the vampirism that ran through my blood. I could make out the outline of a bed. The mattress was bare, and the window blinds were drawn and dusty.

"Yes, I can see that now," she replied. Her head was tilted just slightly, her lips curled up at the sides, and her eyes were soft, almost sad. "But you're not supposed to unhook your leads, and you aren't supposed to be in here. You know that, right?"

"I…" I didn't answer. I had no idea what she was talking about or where *here* was, so how could I know that I wasn't supposed to be here? I didn't tell her that, though. I was afraid it would make me sound crazy.

She crouched down in front of me, keeping a little distance between us, as if she was afraid I might attack. She kept both hands visible as she slowly reached out to take my hand. "Do you remember me?" she asked, hesitantly, in a soft whisper.

"Yes," I said, cringing as a sharp pain ran through my neck and down my spine when I nodded.

"Are you OK?" Amelia quickly asked, grabbing my arms to steady me.

The initial burst of pain subsided, but a subtle soreness in my neck remained, and I realized my head was throbbing, and my throat was burning. "I… I don't know."

"A little pain is normal. Your body has been through a lot…"

That's an understatement, I thought, as the memory of my transformation came back to me in a rush.

"…If it gets worse, you tell me right away. You don't need—"

"I'm fine. Really," I said, interrupting her. "I can handle it."

"Good. That's good," she said, but I didn't think she believed me. She remained cautious, almost vigilant in the way she watched me. "Do you remember my name?"

This one I didn't have to think about. "Of course, it's Amelia," I said confidently, but I also felt slightly relieved when she confirmed it.

"That's right," she said, her smile growing as she nodded. "Do you remember anything else? Do you remember how you got here?"

I thought about that for a few seconds, not really sure how to answer, or what she was hoping I would say. "You work at the clinic—"

"The hospital," she corrected me, but she was still smiling.

"Right, the hospital," I said. "I'm not sure how I—"

"It's OK. Just think. Can you remember anything else?"

I looked around, but I didn't recognize the room. The last thing I remembered was being in the holding cell. I didn't remember leaving there, let alone winding up alone in a dark hospital room. I decided to stick with what I did know. "I remember waking up. I was the only one there. Everyone else had already left." She was staring down at me, her smile completely gone now, and she looked confused— worried. "I remember you visiting me, checking on me and the others. You're a doctor. But why are you—?" I was about to ask why she was out of uniform when she interrupted.

"I told you the last time," she said, reaching out and placing her cold hand on my forehead as she pinched her lips together in a tight line. "I'm not your doctor. I'm a nurse, and you're burning up."

"But..."

"No buts. We need to get you out of here." She glanced back over her shoulder toward the door. I could hear people bustling about, but I didn't see anyone. When she looked back down at me, her smile had returned. "Do you think you can stand, if I help you?" she asked.

"I think so." My hands were trembling, my legs felt weak, my head wouldn't stop throbbing, and I wasn't sure what moving would do to my neck, but I wasn't about to stay on that floor any longer.

"Good, then I want you to come with me," she said, as she helped me to my feet. "You know, you scare the staff when you disappear like this. Besides, you shouldn't be up and about so soon after waking up, and certainly not wandering the halls alone. We need to get you back to your room."

"My room?"

She didn't answer. Maybe she hadn't heard me. I felt her arm slide around my waist to help support some of my weight as she guided me out the door and down the hall.

"How you keep getting past the nurses station, I'll never understand," she mumbled under her breath, half to me and half to herself. "One day you'll have to share your secret," she said, a small smile touching the edge of her lips.

She led me turn by turn into a more active section of the clinic—hospital. I kept my eyes down, but I could hear people talking, doors being opened and closed, and the squeaky wheels of hospital beds being pushed through the hallways. I could feel people staring as we passed by them—I could hear them whispering, but I couldn't make out what they were saying.

Things were different. Even through my blurred peripheral vision, I could tell that things seemed brighter somehow. Men and women were wearing clothing in styles and materials I'd never seen before, in colors the Council had never allowed. I wondered how long I had been asleep and what had happened after I woke up in the cell. I tried to focus on a face here and there, but it didn't work. My vision was still too blurry. I listened to the voices, listening for someone, anyone I recognized, but there was no one.

Where am I? I wondered. *What is going on?*

"Where are you taking me?" I asked, trying to sound calm. My head had started to spin from the strong smells of bleach and other cleaning supplies.

"Just back to your room. You need to rest. I would think you'd be hungry, too," she said. She slid her arm out from around my waist and took my hand.

"But, I…" I was lightheaded, and it felt like the room was spinning. I ran my free hand along the wall in an effort to regain my balance, but it wasn't working. *Maybe I* am *hungry,* I thought.

Ring—Ring—Ring. The ringing of a phone at the nurses station stopped me as we passed.

Ring—Ring—Ring.

I turned just as the nurse answered. "Hello?" There was something familiar in her voice, but I couldn't pinpoint where I had heard it before.

She had shoulder length brown hair and a roundish, youthful face. Her eyes locked on mine and I couldn't turn away.

"Yes, I can connect you to her room," she said to the person on the other end of the line. "Just one moment please."

Then it hit me. It was Calliope, Remy's assistant—although she seemed younger somehow. I watched as she hung up the phone. She leaned forward, mouthing something in my direction. I couldn't hear what she said, but I noticed that the scar that runs down the left side of her face, the one she always hid behind her hair—wasn't there.

"What? What did you say?" I tried to ask, but my voice came out in a raspy, muffled whisper. The burning in my throat had gotten worse.

I could feel Amelia trying to pull me forward, farther down the hall, but I couldn't lift my feet to follow. The room was spinning, and all of a sudden, I felt sick. "Amelia, I think I need to sit down." There was a bench along the wall across from the nurses station, and I reached for it, trying to pull away, but she wouldn't let me.

"You can sit and rest when we get there. It's not that much farther. I promise." Finally, Amelia looked back. She must have seen something in the way I was looking at her, fear maybe, because she stopped and pulled me into her arms. She supported my fall as I sank to the floor. She didn't say anything for a long while, and the noises around us seemed to fade away, melting into the background. When she finally spoke, her voice was softer and more comforting. "It's all right. Just breathe," she said, stroking my hair as if petting an animal. "You're going to be all right. Just stay with me. You're just a little disoriented. That's completely normal."

And once again a complete understatement, I thought to myself.

"Would you like to use a wheelchair?" she asked. "I can get one." Before I could even answer she had pulled away from me and darted down the hall to grab an abandoned wheelchair, and she was back with it in seconds.

I held my hand up to wave it, and her, away. The dizziness had passed, as had the nausea. I'd manage on my own. "No," I protested, using the bench to pull myself back up onto my feet. "I don't need it. I'll be fine." Using the wheelchair would have been seen as a sign of weakness, and I didn't know who was watching. You never know who is watching in Sector C.

"Are you sure?" she asked, sounding more surprised than I had expected.

"I'm sure," I answered. I tried to smile, hoping she wouldn't see through my charade, hoping she couldn't tell how much pain I was in—how scared I really was.

We moved slowly, but we made our way past another nurses station and down another hallway, then another and another, and another after that. They all seemed to blend together, and the hospital seemed to go on forever.

My legs were just about to give out again as we turned the last corner. And in the hallway just ahead—there she was. A young girl, standing near the wall, looking right at me. People passed by her in both directions without even so much as a glance down at her. When she saw that I had noticed her, she grinned and waved, and then she turned around and walked away, her long red hair bouncing behind her.

I must have stopped to watch her go, because Amelia was tugging at my arm, this time more impatiently. "We have to go. It isn't that much farther," she said, still pulling on my arm.

"Wait, please just wait for a second." She finally stopped tugging at my arm. "Who is that little girl?" I asked.

"What little girl?" she asked.

"That one, in the yellow dress." I pointed toward the girl who was skipping down the hall, weaving in and out of the people passing by.

"There's no little girl," Amelia said matter-of-factly.

"But, I—. She's right there," I said, pulling away. This time my hand slipped right out of hers, and she didn't even try to stop me. I wasn't sure why, but I needed to follow the little redhead. I looked back over my shoulder as I headed down the hall after the little girl in yellow, but Amelia wasn't following me. I could see her calling to me, even reaching out to me, but I couldn't hear her. I couldn't hear anything anymore.

4

"Wait!" I called to the little girl as I pushed my way through the silent crowd. No one turned to look at me. Everyone was going about their business as if they couldn't see me—couldn't hear me. I weaved left and right, staggering to keep my balance as I dodged people at every turn, trying to get a clearer view of the little girl up ahead. When I finally neared the end of the hallway, she was there, just a few yards away. "Where are you going?" I called out to her, but she didn't answer.

She turned her back, giggling, then rounded the next corner and disappeared. I raced to the corner and skidded to a stop, but she was gone. This hallway was secluded and dark. I looked back down the hall I had just come from, and all the people had vanished. Most of the lights were out, and some of the ceiling fixtures were broken, hanging haphazardly by wires. What had been a vibrant, bustling hallway just seconds ago was now an abandoned ruin.

"Where did you—?" my voice came out in a rasping whisper.

What is happening to me? I wondered.

I wasn't afraid, at least not yet, but I was starting to get a little worried. It didn't feel like any of the visions I had had before, but it didn't feel real either. I reached for the vision stone that I always wear around my neck, but it was gone. I felt panic welling up inside: my heart started pounding, and I was breathing hard, like there wasn't enough oxygen in the air. If I didn't have the vision stone, this couldn't be real, right? Or did that mean it was real and I was somehow trapped in this deserted hospital? I tried to hold down the rising terror, to force myself to focus—trying to make myself think of a solution.

When nothing came, I scolded myself, "Think damn it. Think!" I said aloud, and I paced the short width of the hallway only twice before it came to me.

I had a decision to make. I could continue down the hall hoping to find the little girl, or I could go back hoping to find Amelia; or, if I believed this was just a dream, and not a vision—not astral projection and not teleportation—then I could try to wake myself up.

I pinched myself hard enough to hurt—hard enough to leave a bruise. But even as I was doing it I knew it wouldn't work, and it didn't. I knew it wasn't just a dream or even a vision. Still, I had to try anyway. Astral projection? Maybe. Teleportation? I wasn't sure. But not just a dream.

Over the last several months, I have started to learn the difference between my dreams, visions, astral projections, and teleportation travels. Although I can't always differentiate among them, I am getting better. Dreams are simple: they are the messages my subconscious mind sends me while I'm sleeping. Everyone dreams, even if they don't always remember what they dreamed. Truthfully, dreams don't always make sense, at least not to me, but I do try to figure out their meaning when I can. Visions are actual events, either from the past, the present, or the future. I don't actually experience a vision like I'm there—it's more like I'm watching it being projected on a large screen. Astral projection is cool. It's as if I'm physically there, in the event as it's happening, but it isn't a corporeal experience. I'm not there in my own physical body. During astral projection traveling I either take over the body of someone else, or I'm there but can't physically affect anything. Teleportation is actual corporeal presence at a past, present, or future event. I still don't understand how it works, or why, but I associate teleportation with Councilman Ash. He is the only person I've ever seen do anything that I could remotely equate to teleportation, although I'm not sure if Ash can do more than teleport from one location to another.

Whatever this was, or wherever, or whenever, I needed to find that little girl in the yellow dress. I needed to know who she was, and why I was being drawn to her, or she to me. Finding Amelia wasn't going to give me those answers, so with my mind made up I headed down the new hallway.

"Hello?" I called, as I walked into the darkness. My vision had returned, and I could at least see, despite the darkness that surrounded me—one of the perks of being a vampire, or maybe it was the lycanthrope virus, I'm not sure. When I try to sort through my powers, to pinpoint them as vampire or lycanthrope, they tend to get blurred—intermixed. The reality of what I am isn't as clearly defined as the textbooks we studied as selection students. Hybrids weren't part of our curriculum.

The air was heavy with dust and smelled like dirt after a hard rain. At first, every door I passed was closed and locked, but I continued to try them one by one, making my way slowly down the hall and deeper into the bowels of the seemingly abandoned hospital, not willing to give up. Eventually the doors started to open, but the rooms behind them were all empty, save for a few broken beds, empty cabinets, and discarded hospital supplies. Where there were windows, these were either boarded up, too dirty to see through, or cracked and ready to send jagged shards of glass in my direction if I got too close. The farther I walked, the worse it got. There was a pungent smell, like rotten meat left too long in the hot sun. The paint was peeling, dirt and graffiti covered the doors and walls, and the occasional wheelchairs and gurneys that littered the hallway were old and rusty.

The silence was deafening. I could have heard a pin drop from a mile away, but the only sound was the whisper of my own footsteps. Except once, when a small mouse scurried across the hall ahead of me and disappeared under another closed door. For a moment I wondered how it had survived and what it had been living on. I forced myself to keep moving. One step at a time.

I went on, turning left and then right, and almost stumbled over an old teddy bear laying on the floor just outside one of the rooms. As I bent down to pick it up, a memory took shape in my mind. I was lying on a blanket in the middle of a field, clutching the teddy bear tightly to my chest and watching the clouds float across the sky. The image was so strong I seemed to smell the grass around me and, from the teddy bear in my arms, a hint of lemon laundry detergent.

Then I heard a faint giggle coming from inside the room. When I turned the doorknob, it fell off in my hand, corroded through, but the door eased open, the rusty hinges creaking. At first glance, I thought the room was as empty as most of the others had been, but then I noticed an old blanket lying in the corner. Something didn't feel right. Something was out of place. I wanted to turn and leave. Every instinct I had was telling me to run—to just keep looking for the little girl—but I didn't. Something drew me farther into the room. Pulling me, like a mouse to a trap.

I picked up the dusty, tattered old blanket, and slowly stood up. The ragged old teddy bear was still clutched in my other hand.

"Well, well, well, you're finally awake," Haden said from somewhere behind me, startling me out of what I knew in that moment had been only a vision.

The hairs on the back of my neck stood up, and I could feel my wolf react to his voice. She didn't like him. Or maybe she just didn't trust him. I turned, dropped the blanket, and quickly hid the stuffed bear behind my back.

"Whatcha got there?" William asked, stepping forward toward the bars of my cage. The scent of fresh blood was all around him, as if he had just bathed in it. I knew better, I knew he had fed recently.

My fangs sprouted, ready to feed, and I quickly covered my mouth with my free hand. *Stop this,* I scolded myself silently.

"Nothing. It's nothing," I said, and I felt my fangs slowly retract. I ran my tongue across my teeth, just to make sure.

They were watching me from the other side of the cell bars. I felt like a prisoner, my every move being scrutinized and judged.

"Nothing, huh?" His eyes felt like they could see right through me.

I didn't think he believed me, but it really was nothing. When I realized it wasn't actually the stuffed teddy bear I had found, but just my flat blue pillow, I tossed it aside. "See, just a pillow, no big deal." But it was a big deal. Something about that raggedy old teddy bear was important. Something about that little girl in the yellow dress was important. I just needed to figure out what. "What time is it?" I asked.

"Just after eleven," Haden said. "You should have been at work hours ago."

"Leave her alone," William said, smacking Haden on the back of the head.

Haden swung back, the back of his hand connecting squarely but playfully with the side of William's face. "It was just a joke, dude. Lighten up," he said. "I get it, the poor little pup needed her beauty sleep."

"I'm not a—"

I was cut off by the low growl of Haden's wolf, but his eyes never fully met mine. The wolf in me clawed up and I growled. Haden flinched, and my wolf howled in delight. I felt a shift that puzzled me. I sniffed. Something was different in an important way, but my animals were too new—too young—for me to understand how important.

I took a deep breath, calming my wolf and waiting for her to settle down. Haden didn't scare me, not at that moment anyway. *Maybe not ever again*, I thought. "If you're done already," I said, as I made my way to the cell bars that separated us, trying to act casual, "…maybe you can tell me where the two of you have been? I woke up when the sirens went off, but you guys were gone, along with everyone else."

"We were called away," Haden said. "Nothing you need to be concerned about."

"Why the sirens?"

"Like he said, nothing you need to be concerned about." William said, reaching through the bars to hand me a tall dark glass.

"Why the sirens?" I asked again.

"Just some outcasts caught outside the walls. Now take the glass. You should drink. You haven't fed in a while."

Outcasts? I wondered if he meant Ciara. *Did they find her? Have they brought her back into the sector? If so, where was she and what were they doing with her?*

I swallowed back about a thousand questions I knew I couldn't ask them about Ciara. But I could ask about the other lycanthropes. "Where is everyone else?" Then, because I really didn't care about everyone, but about one, I asked, "Where is Merick?"

"Drink."

"What about Merick? Where did they take him?"

"Zelina, drink," William commanded.

"I'm not hungry," I said.

"You are, trust me."

"I'm. Not. Hungry," I said again, but it was a lie. The burning had already started in my throat, and there must have been something about the way I was staring at them that gave it away. "I just want answers. Just tell me where they took Merick, and I'll drink the stupid blood."

"We're not going to answer any of your questions, and we're not going to let you out until you drink it, so you might as well just do it," Haden said. The side of his lips twitched, turning up for only an instant, but I could tell he was enjoying himself. He was reveling in his power over me, and that thought woke my wolf again. My wolf was having a visceral reaction to Haden's, and his snarky attitude towards me wasn't helping.

The sweet scent of the blood seemed to fill the air around me, and before I knew it I was grabbing the glass out of William's hand. "Fine." I quickly realized that one glass wasn't going to be enough, and when I was finished, William was ready and waiting with a second glass. That one was gone in moments too. "There, happy?" I asked, not looking either of them in the eye as I used the back of my hand to wipe away the few drops of blood that had escaped due to my haste.

"You're welcome," William said, flatly.

At that, I did look up. I figured he'd be smirking, quietly laughing at me—the young vampire who can't control her hunger—but he wasn't.

"Thank you," I finally said. That earned me a smile, a genuine one. "So, can I at least ask why I'm the only one still locked up?" I asked.

"You were the last one to wake up," said Haden.

"Wow, thank you Captain Obvious," I said. He and William shared a confused glance. Even I wasn't sure where I had come up with the nickname or why, but it seemed to fit the situation perfectly.

"Councilman Ash said to keep you here until you woke up on your own," Haden offered, as a better explanation. "It was the same with all the others, they just happened to wake up before you."

At the mention of Ash's name, I remembered him standing behind me in my cell, just before I felt a stabbing pain in my neck and passed out. *Did he bite me?* I wondered. My hand flew to my neck, but I couldn't feel anything to indicate I had been bitten. There wasn't a puncture wound, or if there had been it had either already healed or it was too small for me to find. The skin didn't feel bruised; it wasn't tender to the touch.

I felt them watching me even before I looked up. "What did he do to me? Did he bite me?" I asked, not really expecting an answer.

William laughed, as if the idea was comical. "Why would Councilman Ash bite you?"

"I... I don't know, but—" I couldn't explain the feeling I had had, the sharp stinging pain. "You were here," I said, turning to Haden. "You saw it. What did he do?"

He stared down at me, and he actually looked concerned. I thought for a moment he was taking me seriously, then he answered. "I guess he wanted to be sure you weren't going to wolf-out again," he said, a sinister smirk spreading across his lips.

"Wolf-out?" William asked, more mocking him for his lame dig then actually asking the question.

"What. Lion-out doesn't sound right," Haden replied, chuckling as if he thought he was funny. He wasn't.

"You're an idiot, you know that, right?" William asked, taking the words right out of my mouth. He smacked Haden across the back of the head for the second time in as many minutes.

"Whatever," I said, rubbing the back of my neck. It wasn't sore, but I couldn't get the idea of Ash doing something amiss out of my mind.

"Just let me out. The moon cycle is over, so I can't *wolf-out* again anyway," I said, in my best Haden impersonation.

"I'm not so sure about that," Haden mumbled under his breath. I let it go. Even if I had asked what he had meant, he probably wouldn't have told me.

"And I'd appreciate a robe. These clothes are a mess, and a shower would be nice."

The guys exchanged glances, and Haden produced a full set of clothes, instead of one of the standard-issue after-transformation robes. They both shifted uncomfortably. And before you think the awkwardness had anything to do with the fact that I would have to change my clothes here in the cell, trust me, there wasn't anything sensual about it at all, in any way. Nor was being fully naked in a room full of lycanthropes during the moon cycle. It was a little uncomfortable at first, sure, but that didn't last long.

Lycanthropes understand that nudity isn't the same thing as intimacy. But that didn't mean I didn't want to get cleaned up and back into my own clothes.

"Yeah," Haden said, as William slid the key into the lock. "About that. Suit up. We've got places to be and things to do."

"Why clothes?" I asked. "I'm just going to ruin them. You know what..." I started, completely exhausted with the entire discussion. "Hand them over. I don't even care anymore."

I changed clothes as they turned away to give me some privacy. Weirdly, I realized something that apparently, they already knew: being naked was less intimate than watching someone dress. As I slipped through the half-open cell door, I stepped on something sharp, and bit my tongue in surprise. I was even more surprised when I looked down and saw my vision stone. The shoelace I had been using to wear the stone as a necklace was gone, and the stone was cracked down the middle, split evenly into two pieces, and only held together by the wire casing Merick had made for me. The necklace must have fallen off, or been torn off during my transformation. I was lucky no one else had found it.

"What's that?" Haden asked, reaching to grab it, but I got it first.

I quickly stuffed it into my pocket and out of sight. "Nothing...just a rock." I turned and headed down the row of holding cells toward the door. I wanted out of that room and as far from those cages as I could get.

"You'll want to wait," William said, as I was reaching for the door handle.

No, not really, I thought to myself, but what I said was, "Oh yeah, and why is that?"

"Remy and Ash have requested to speak with you to discuss what's going to happen next. We'll need to escort you to the Council offices. You probably shouldn't be out alone."

I hadn't heard of lycanthropes going through counseling after their initial transformations before, much less meeting with the Sector Leader. So, why me?

"What do you mean, 'what's going to happen next'?"

No response.

"At least tell me why you need to escort me. I know my way around the sector by now. I'm sure I can get to the Council offices on my own."

They exchanged a look that I couldn't read.

"What?" I demanded. "I thought you two only had to babysit me until after the moon cycle. Well, the moon cycle is over. You can go home now, wherever that is."

It was William who spoke first. "It's just that…" But, for the first time since I met him, he was actually having trouble getting the words out. He cleared his throat. "Well, seeing as you're… you know…" William shuffled his feet and ran his hand through his thick dark hair. I had never seen him at a loss for words, and I didn't like it.

"You're no longer *just* a vampire," Haden blurted out, cutting William off. "You're a wolf—you're a lion."

"Yeah, what does that matter?" I asked. "I was never *just* a vampire to begin with. Wasn't that the whole reason you two were babysitting me in the first place? You were assigned to me, for whatever reason, to make sure I behaved myself during the moon cycle. Well, the moon cycle is over. I behaved myself, right? So, your job should be over too, right?"

"That's not exactly the... Besides, that was before they realized your lion was a Leaena."

"A Leaena?" I asked, unsure of what he meant.

"A Leaena is the leader among lions. It means, you're meant to lead a pride. The way you commanded that young lion's change, that doesn't just happen."

And Merick's, I thought to myself. *I forced Merick to shift too, don't forget that.* My heart gave a lurch. Merick. Everything would feel better as soon as I got to see Merick again.

"Not to mention the fact that the Council is calling you the first female Alpha wolf," Haden said, rolling his eyes. A low growl started in his throat—a silent threat. I could feel my wolf responding in kind, ready to fight if it came to that. "Personally, I think it's ridiculous, but if you thought people were afraid of you before, you've—"

"Afraid of me? I get that they don't like me because I'm different, but everyone has known what I am for weeks now. It's not like the Council kept it a secret. Remy made sure to blurt it out in front of the whole sector after Selection Week. Nothing I have done could be taken as threatening. So why should that change now? What would make people be scared now if they weren't before?"

I wondered how I could use this new knowledge to my advantage. Because one thing was for sure, I wasn't a scared, blind little girl anymore. They may have created my beasts, but now they were MY beasts. And we wanted answers.

"Of course they were scared!" Haden said. "You know they were. Why else would you have been the first person the Council accused of murder when one of your selection classmates was found dead? Why else would we have been assigned to watch over you? Why else do you think the Council assigned you to live with Britt and then Iris instead of at the vampire community center with all the others? Why do you think—?"

"That's enough Haden," William said, stopping him before he could finish his next question.

I took a deep breath. A breath I didn't really need, but it did help to calm my nerves—and my beasts. A breath taken purely out of habit, from, you know, back when I was human. Hello bitterness. When I looked back up they were both watching me, waiting. I stepped forward, closing the gap between Haden and myself, taking a page right out of Professor Gunner's playbook for offensive attacks. I could feel Haden's breath on my face as he looked down, refusing to back away. "Are *you* afraid?" I whispered.

"What?" he asked, almost startled.

"Do I frighten *you*?" I asked, this time slowly enunciating every word. "Do I send chills down your spine and make your wolf claw at your insides, begging to be let out?"

He leaned in, sliding his nose across my neck, moving from one side to the other, and then sniffed the air around me. His hair brushed across my face before he stood up, a little straighter than before, his shoulders pulled back. "No, I'm not afraid of you." He said the words, but he didn't sound convincing.

I followed his lead, sniffing the air between us. "Hmmm. So you're not worried I could command your transformation too? Just like I did Hudson's?"

"No."

"Just like I did Merick's." It wasn't a question, and I didn't expect a response. I was pushing him emotionally, not physically, and it was working.

He swallowed. It was subtle, but I noticed. "You're not my Alpha, Zelina," he said, stepping back. "I'm the only Alpha of my pack." There was a slight tremor in his voice, so subtle I don't even think he realized it, or if he did he wasn't going to show it.

He didn't answer my question, not directly, and not answering was an answer in and of itself.

I stepped forward, again, sniffing the air around him, this time slowly circling him. There was something about the way he smelled. It was different than the other lycanthropes, but I couldn't put my finger on how or why. Beneath the scent of his wolf there was another more pungent odor that filled the space between us—sweat—which I knew signaled fear. "Are you sure?" I asked. "You know I can smell it, right?"

He didn't answer.

We stood there staring eye-to-eye for only seconds, but it felt like forever. William finally broke the tension, with a hand on my shoulder. "We should go," he said, handing me a small backpack with what felt like a couple of bottles inside. "You're probably going to need this."

I took the backpack and slung it over my shoulder. "Fine, then let's go." I turned to the door and walked out. I didn't look back; I knew they'd be right behind me. And all my instincts told me that was exactly where Haden belonged.

5

It was less than a twenty-minute walk from the holding cells to the Council offices, but it felt longer. I could hear Sector Leader Remy's voice in my head, as if he was standing right next to me. *"Once the moon cycle is complete, and it's safe, you'll be let out with all the others. Life will continue as it has been,"* he had said. *"Your family will be notified of your release and…"*

Wait, no. My family? That isn't right, I thought to myself. *What had he said?* I thought about it, trying to remember his exact words.

"Word of your transformation will be released, but to keep you safe, any information concerning the forced change you commanded from Merick and Hudson will be kept confidential until we know more."

"Until we know more," I said, stopping in the middle of the street.

"What's wrong?" William asked, stepping up beside me.

"Nothing. It's nothing." I continued toward the Council building, not looking back.

"Until we know more," he had said. That should have been my first clue. I should have known something was wrong when I woke up alone in the

cells. He had said it was to keep me safe, but I was starting to wonder if that was his real intention.

I should have known something like this would happen. I should have known he had been lying, that he would have William and Haden take me into custody the minute I woke up. But I had trusted him. I had stupidly assumed that because of his relationship with Councilman Iris he would let me go on living with her. That things would actually stay the same. With my eyes now opened to the reality of my life—the reality of our sector leaders—I wasn't going to be blindsided again.

Trust no one. That was going to be my new motto, at least until *I* knew more.

It had made sense, my delusional way of thinking. Councilman Iris is in charge of the selection student resources, and therefore is the one Council member who really gets to know each and every one of the selection students. Besides, she told me that Remy had wanted to bring the vampires and lycanthropes together, to find a way to stop the fighting. She had said I was his answer—the key to his plan. If that were true, why wouldn't he want her to be there for me? Was he lying to her, too?

If not with Councilman Iris, then I at least expected to be able to live somewhere else within the sector, under supervision of course, until I had my bloodlust fully under control—which I felt I was making real progress on.

I should have known it was all just a lie.

An internal conflict was brewing in my mind. I wanted to believe Councilman Iris, and trust that Remy was on my side. I wanted to believe I was safe within the walls of Sector C, but something was nagging at me. The idea that I had been deceived.

But if he wanted to get rid of me, why not banish me after Selection Week? Why wait this long? Why make me this way in the first place? I wondered, but I already knew the answer. Until the moon cycle, my beasts were just theoretical—they weren't real. Now Remy has to face the fact that I'm no longer just a vampire; I really *am* lycanthrope too. Now that he had what he had always wanted, maybe he had regrets.

Be careful what you wish for, I thought. *You might just get it.*

We passed the dining hall, and I saw Counselor Teagan leaving. She was alone and looking down at a book she held open, flipping through the pages as she walked. It's rare to see anyone in Sector C with an actual book, anyone other than selection students that is. Most sector residents use downloadable books, or choose not to read at all. I wondered what she was reading, and called out to her without thinking.

"Counselor Teagan," I said.

She looked up, turning in my direction, and when she saw me she stopped, but she didn't say anything.

"Counselor Teagan?" I called again, this time more apprehensive.

She appeared to be struggling with a decision, but finally she snapped the book closed and made her way down the walkway to my side. "Zelina, how have you been? How was your first moon cycle?" she asked, hugging the book tightly to her chest. I could see her knuckles turning white as she gripped the book tighter. I wondered what book it was, but didn't ask.

"It was hard, but I survived," I said, glancing back at William and Haden who were quietly waiting behind me. "Can you give us a minute?" I asked.

They didn't move.

Teagan exchanged a look with Haden. "She'll be fine," she said, more curtly than I had ever heard her speak.

They still didn't move. They were beginning to get on my nerves.

"I don't think it's me they're worried about," I said, trying to sound casual.

Her expression was innocent, and confused, until what I meant sank in. She took a deep breath, relaxed her shoulders, and lowered the book to her side. She glanced at Haden and smiled. "I will be fine," she said.

At that, they nodded and stepped away. I had hoped I was wrong, but they had just confirmed that I wasn't.

They didn't go far. They waited just down the street about twenty yards away, giving us the illusion of privacy without the actual benefits.

Hesitantly, Teagan reached for my hand. "Are you really OK?"

Her hand felt warm around mine. Comforting.

I opened my mouth to tell her that of course I was fine, but that's not what came out. "I don't know," I said honestly, before I had a chance to stop myself. "I think so, but everyone seems to be keeping things from me. I woke up in the creepy holding cell all by myself with the sirens blaring, and no one will tell me why the sirens were going off, let alone why I was the only one still locked up. William said something about outcasts beyond the wall, which doesn't explain the sirens, because there are always outcasts beyond the wall, that is where they live. The last time I saw Merick…" I could picture him lying there in my cell, bleeding out from where Haden had attacked him "…he wasn't doing well, and they took him away…to the clinic I think…but those two…" I nodded toward William and Haden, who promptly looked up as if I had called out to them. "They won't tell me what's happened to him." I was about to go on. My list of injustices was about a mile long, but she stopped me.

"Merick is fine," Teagan said, but her eyes didn't meet mine.

"You've seen him?" I asked, eager to know more. When she didn't answer I asked again, "Teagan, have you seen him?"

"No, but if anything had happened to him, or any of you, during your first moon cycle, or even afterwards, I would know. They would tell me."

"Anything?" I asked.

"Yes."

"Then you know that Haden…" I said his name loudly, spitting it like poison from my mouth, "attacked him?"

She swallowed, allowing time to come up with a response. "It is not uncommon for an older lycanthrope to have to tame a younger lycanthrope in that manner, Zelina."

"Tame? Are you kidding me? He could have killed him."

"Lycanthropes heal very quickly while in animal form. There are very few things that can harm us in a way that we cannot heal."

I knew she was right, but that didn't explain why they had taken him away or why they wouldn't give me any details other than that he was OK, whatever that meant.

I tried to push away the images: images of Merick pulling the cell bars apart, of my forcing his transformation, and Hudson's transformation. I wondered if Teagan really did know everything. And, if so, had that been the cause of her hesitation when she saw me? What must she think of me? Was she afraid? "Did they tell you why Haden attacked him?"

"Yes," she said, and her eyes met mine, confirming what I already knew.

"Oh."

"Zelina, the first transformation is different for everyone. There was no way either of you could have known what you were capable of, and you can't blame yourself for—"

"Blame myself?"

"I only mean… Never mind, it's nothing. Is there anything else bothering you?" She reached out, resting her hand on my arm. It was a comforting gesture she had used many times over the years, but in that moment it felt different, more important, like there was a deeper meaning that I couldn't possibly understand.

"I…" I took a second, trying to decide what was really important. Merick. But she couldn't or wouldn't help me on that front. "I've been summoned to the Council offices to meet with Sector Leader Remy and

Councilman Ash, and I don't know why. I'm worried that they might…" I wasn't sure how to finish my thought. "What if I'm being banished? What if…what if I don't even have *that* choice?" I asked, exposing my worst fear as a single tear traced its way down my face.

Even though I knew I wasn't safe in Sector C, not the way they had promised us when we were children, and definitely not now that they had turned me into an anomaly, the idea of being banished to the wastelands still unnerved me. I was finally seeing the world around me without the blind acceptance of an unenlightened child, and it was frightening, but was it more frightening than the unknown of what was beyond the walls, or the possibility of death? I wasn't sure.

"Remy and Ash have called you in? That's where they're taking you? Not home to rest, or shower?" she asked.

"Yeah," I started, "I need a shower, believe me I know. I feel disgusting."

"No, Zelina, It's just that… They've called you in to meet with just the two of them. That's what you're saying, right?" Her voice sounded strained, and the muscles of her jaw clenched: she was getting angry. "Without Councilman Cruz or any of the other Lycanthrope Council members there to represent you?" she asked, louder now, and looking over my shoulder at William and Haden.

"I don't know. I guess so," I answered. "What do you mean, represent me?"

"I know your transformation was successful, we all do. That makes you a member of the lycanthrope community now. You shouldn't be called to meet with a member of the Vampire Council, let alone two of them, without a Lycanthrope Council member being present. It goes against Council law." I had never heard or seen Teagan this angry.

"Yeah, but I'm also a vampire," I reminded her. "Besides, I work directly for the Vampire Council."

"You might work for the Council, but if this were about Council business you wouldn't have two security guards escorting you in. And you would have been allowed to shower and change before the meeting. I understand that you're no ordinary lycanthrope, I do. You're a vampire, no one can argue that, but you're also a wolf, and that me—"

"And a lion," I added, cutting her off.

"Of course, and a lion," she said, correcting herself as she glanced down at her feet then back up at me, making sure to make eye contact. "The fact that you are both vampire and lycanthrope means that you fall under the laws of both Councils. Councilman Remy knows this."

I wasn't sure what I was supposed to say, or how what she was saying should affect me other than the sinking feeling of fear that had started in my gut.

"Your lion," she continued. "I've been told she is a Leaena." She stood a little taller, straightened her back, and lifted her chin. Her reaction was almost identical to what Haden's had been, but he had hidden it better. Teagan's hazel eyes flashed a fierce, almost savage gold for a fraction of a second.

"That's what I've been told," I answered, not taking my eyes off of her. I knew she had been the only Leaena within Sector C, and I wondered what this information meant to her.

She's afraid, I thought, *or maybe she feels threatened.* I knew it was the blood of her lion that ran through my veins. If I really was a Leaena, I wondered what that would mean for her—for our relationship.

"You should be very proud," she continued.

Proud? Selection students are not permitted to show pride, but I'm not a selection student anymore. I needed to keep reminding myself of that.

"I suppose," was all I could think of to say. "Well, I'd better be getting back. They aren't the most patient guards in the sector," I said, nodding over to William and Haden, who hadn't taken their eyes off of us since they walked away. "Thank you for stopping and talking to me."

"Of course, any time, Zelina." I turned to walk away, but Teagan stopped me, "Zelina, I just wanted to say…" She hesitated, glancing back toward the dining hall.

"What is it?"

"It's just that, I'm sorry for everything that happened during Selection Week. Selection Week is hard enough without having to deal with everything you went through. If I had known…" she pulled me close, whispering. "I promise you, I didn't know. I had no idea they planned to—"

I grabbed her hand. "It's OK, really. I'm fine." Teagan had had nothing to do with the way they had treated me. It wasn't her fault I had been infected by Merick during our scheduled fight.

Where is Merick, I wondered briefly. *Is he really ok, like Teagan says?*

I knew it wasn't Teagan's fault they had chosen to infect me with her blood. She couldn't have stopped them even if she had wanted to—a new truth that was revealed to me. Even as a Council member, she was powerless. I yearned to know who had the true power. Remy? Ash? Or were they pawns too?

"Do you want me to come with you? Or I could find you someone else, if not me," she said. "You really should have a representative there." I told her no, and could almost see her body relax as if the thought of going had been a heavy weight upon her shoulders. How had I not seen this before? The fear? The defeat?

"I'll be fine. Besides, I have William and Haden to watch my back." I let the sarcasm show a little bit, and they shifted uncomfortably.

She nodded. "Of course you do," she said, but her eyes didn't seem to agree as she stared off in their direction.

"Do me a favor—if you can, just check on Merick at the clinic. Tell him I'm... Just check on him for me please." She nodded and I let go of her hand. As I turned away she held out her book to me. "Take it, it's meant to be yours anyway," was all she said.

There was no title on the cover, but I could tell it was old, because the plain black leather had started to dry out and crack along the spine. When I opened the cover, a single line of print had been hand-written inside: *The Lineage of a Lioness.* I assumed it was the tile, and wondered why Teagan had been reading it, and more importantly, why she had chosen to give it to me.

"Meant to be mine?" I asked, looking up, but she was already gone, heading down the walkway behind me.

I tucked the book into the backpack and started toward the Council offices. William and Haden quickly stepped in line behind me.

I could see the Council offices up ahead. "Where did they take Merick?" I asked, turning and almost bumping into William and Haden who were walking closer behind me than I had expected.

"He's at the sector clinic, with Amelia," William said. "Councilman Ash ordered that she keep him under observation until his wounds are fully healed."

He hasn't healed yet? It's been over twenty-four hours.

I opened my mouth to ask if I could see him, but Haden stopped me before I could get even a word out. "Before you ask, no you can't see him."

"Can I just ask one thing? I promise it isn't to see him."

They stared at me, Haden finally nodding.

"Why would Councilman Ash care about Merick healing? As far as I can tell, Ash doesn't care about the lycanthropes at all."

"No, he doesn't," Haden said, under his breath. "Honestly, I'm not sure what his interests are, but he is a Councilman and he has certain rights—or privileges—within the sector. If Ash said for Merick to be taken to the clinic, then that's where he'll be until he is released." Haden and William exchanged a quick glance and my stomach churned. Something was wrong and I knew it.

"Now turn around and keep walking," Haden said. "People are starting to stare."

Starting to stare? They've been gawking at us—at me—*since we left the holding cells,* I thought to myself. But I did as I was told: I turned around, kept my mouth shut, and headed for the Council offices.

I don't need to give them any more ammunition or motivation to banish me to the wastelands. At least not before I'm ready, I thought. Which surprised me. Since when had I considered leaving Sector C?

They took me to a small white room in the vampire section of the Council offices. There was a plain metal table in the center of the room with one chair on the far side, and two chairs on the side near the door. Decorated differently, it could have been an office, but as it was it felt more like an interrogation room.

"So, is this the part where you tie me up and stick a needle in my arm, or will they send in a nurse for that?" I asked, as I took the seat I already knew was meant for me.

"You are not a prisoner, Zelina," William said. "They simply want to talk."

Yeah, without any witnesses, or 'lycanthrope representatives,' as Teagan called them.

"And they couldn't have done that in a more comfortable location? Like, say, a dungeon for instance?"

Ok, maybe the office wasn't that bad, but still, I think he got my point, or at least he decided not to argue with me. I was beginning to regret telling Teagan not to tag along. I probably could have used her support.

"They will be right in. Is there anything we can get you while you wait?" William asked as he followed Haden to the door.

"No, I'm..." I realized they were leaving. "Hey, aren't you going to stay?" I called out, with not a little bit of panic in my voice. William gave me a look that I couldn't even begin to interpret, and the door closed. *Guards, my ass. Who was supposed to be guarding me now?* I leaned back in the cold metal chair and shivered. I looked down at my arms and noticed chill bumps. *Am I cold?* I wondered. Being a vampire, my body temperature is naturally low. Cold shouldn't affect me anymore. *Hello Fear, meet my good friend Anxiety.*

The metal chair dug into my back, and after what felt like an hour, but was probably only ten or fifteen minutes, my right leg started to fall asleep. I stood up, pushing the chair back so I could move freely. Pacing the length of the back wall helped, but the longer I was in there the more tired I began to feel. Not only was I exhausted, I was experiencing an adrenaline crash from my earlier panic.

Focus, I told myself. *They'll be here soon, and you can't be asleep at the table.*

I remembered the book Teagan had given me, and I took it out. I sat back down and started flipping through the pages, hoping to discover the reason she had chosen to give it to me, or maybe what she had been looking for in its pages. Anything to distract my mind and calm my nerves.

The first several chapters were all about lions throughout history, and the symbolic meanings that different cultures had assigned to them. I skimmed the pages, reading short passages here and there.

"...Nemean Lion, believed by the ancient Greeks to be a supernatural lion, was so powerful he could not be killed with mortal weapons. His claws were sharper than swords, and his golden fur was impenetrable."

"...The symbolism of the lioness's strength dates back to early Egyptian cultures. While the Egyptians ascribed such attributes as power, vitality, strength, courage, and ferocity to their gods, the physical representation of those traits was always portrayed in the form of a lioness."

"...Egyptian pharaohs often hunted down and kept lions as pets. Controlling and oftentimes caging a lioness was seen as a symbol of the pharaoh's power and sovereignty over the people."

"...The spirit of the lioness is deeply ingrained in Buddhism. Seen as religious guides, the lioness was known to escort Buddhist devotees through their journeys toward spiritual enlightenment."

"...The Jewish culture ascribes the qualities of promise and redemption to the lioness."

"...Christians have, for centuries, the role of humanity's judge and teacher has been bestowed upon the lioness."

Another passage caught my attention. I wasn't sure why or how, but I knew it was important.

"...From as early as 3000 BC, the lioness is fabled to have been granted the promise of majestic protection by the ancient Egyptian gods. With the death of Egypt's last pharaoh in 30 BC, as the civilization began to crumble, and corruption and ignorance invaded the people, the lioness was once again given a sacred gift from the gods. The prophecy states that the gods gifted the lioness with the last remaining fragments of the creation energies: the elemental power of divinity and conception. These powers remain today in the DNA of the lioness, passed on from generation to generation, waiting to be awakened, within the chosen, at a time when humanity is ready to reclaim its rightful dominion and take back the power it once possessed."

A surge of energy ran through me, and my vision went dark, as if a black screen had formed in front of my eyes. I thought for sure I was slipping into another vision, but instead, a series of images appeared, each coming into focus and then receding as the next one came into view. The first thing I saw was a stone—no, an orb of light, swirling with colors that I'd never seen before—bright, neon, mesmerizing. Next came one golden eye, the eye of a lion. It faded back, to return as the face of a majestic lioness. The next crystal-clear picture was the bones of a human hand, which then gave way to an entire human skeleton. And finally, there was a cross, the symbol of the Christian religion.

I heard footsteps approaching, and I was pulled out of the vision. I snapped the book closed, sneezing at the little cloud of dust that raised, and tucked it into the backpack.

6

"Bless you."

"What?" I asked, turning toward the door.

"You sneezed. I said, bless you." It was the woman with the long red hair. She was standing in the doorway holding a plate of food out to me. "Are you hungry?"

"I…" I looked around, and the metal table and chairs were gone, replaced by a hospital bed with white linens and two flat pillows. There was a window on the far wall, but the curtains were pulled closed, so I couldn't tell if it was day or night.

You've got to be kidding me, I complained internally. "Yes please," I said turning back.

I was getting good at this scene-shifting, jumping in and out of reality. *Is this going to be my new normal?* I wondered. I made a conscious decision to play along with whatever unfolded— knowing that anything else would make me appear crazy and weak, which were two things I couldn't afford to be in any situation if I expected to survive. Besides, in my experience, Crazy and Weak got me about as many answers as Fear and Anxiety.

She moved closer, setting the plate on a table next to the bed. "Did you want to sit down so you can eat?"

I did as she asked, pulling myself up onto the bed and arranging the pillows behind my back. "What is it?" I asked skeptically, as I looked down at the plate. "It smells—" I would have told her that it smelled foul, as if someone had butchered a cow and left it in a field to decay, but she stopped me before I could finish. I'm glad she did; I think it probably would have hurt her feelings, and that hadn't been my intention.

"Lasagna," she said. "You don't remember?"

"Remember what?"

"It used to be your favorite food. When you were little."

I had no recollection of ever eating lasagna, let alone it being my favorite food. This woman who had called herself my mom in a previous vision was sweet and kind, but she must be confusing me with someone else. I think part of me was disappointed, but another part of me was a little relieved. I had started to question my life, and everything I had been raised to believe, but now I didn't have to. It wasn't me that was confused, it was her.

"I'm sorry," I said, pushing the plate away and moving toward the edge of the bed. "I don't remember."

"It's all right," she said. "Would you like to try it?"

"No," I said, moving farther away from the foul-smelling dish. The odor was starting to nauseate me, and I realized that although the lasagna didn't appeal to me, I did in fact need to eat. "You're a donor, right? I mean, I was told that you used to be a breeder, but now you're a donor?"

7

"Do you need a donor?" Sector Leader Remy asked from the doorway.

I quickly glanced around the room, trying to regain my grip on reality, my hands holding tight to the arms of the cold metal chair. The bed was gone, and so was the red-haired woman and the lasagna she offered. *Just a figment of my imagination,* or so I would allow myself to think, for now.

"Are you still thirsty from your transformation? How much blood did you drink before you were released from the cell?" he asked.

"I'm sorry, I—" I took a deep breath. *Calm and relaxed, Zelina, calm and relaxed.* "I had two glasses, and I have others in my bag. I'm fine. Really."

Remy waved his hand toward the door; it was a simple gesture but proof of the power and control he holds over people. Moments later, as if planned, his assistant, Calliope, walked in carrying a glass and stood near the door waiting for everyone to settle in.

Remy was one of the oldest vampires in Sector C. He had dark blue eyes and slight streaks of grey through his dark brown hair. He was tall, lean, and fit. He took his seat directly across from me while Councilman Ash took the seat to his left. Calliope placed the glass on the table in front of me. I knew what it was without looking; I had smelled the blood before she even came into the room.

"Thank you, but it isn't necessary," I said.

"Drink it," Remy said, politely but commandingly. "It's fresher than the bottled blood you carry in your bag."

I nodded and picked up the glass, trying not to seem too eager, then downed the sticky sweet contents. *Better to get it over with*, I thought. I didn't particularly like feeding in front of people.

"Would you like another?" Calliope asked through clenched teeth.

I considered asking for a steak. It was already past lunchtime, and I hadn't eaten anything of real substance all day, but I held back. I wasn't sure how Remy would respond. Vampires don't crave solid food, and even though Remy knew I wasn't the average vampire, I didn't need to highlight my lycanthrope tendencies around him.

I must not have answered quickly enough for Calliope, because when I looked up her eyes met mine with a dark expression that told me to speak up or starve. I could tell that she didn't care which, and I was betting she was hoping for the latter.

"No thank you," I said in my sweetest voice. I knew Calliope didn't like me, William had told me as much, but I didn't really understand why. She had a superiority complex, I knew that much. Calliope, like many other vampires, believes vampires are somehow better than lycanthropes, but I wasn't just a lycanthrope, I was a vampire too. Shouldn't that count for something?

Calliope turned and walked out of the room without another word, and closed the door behind her, leaving me alone with Remy and Ash.

"You have had a very eventful few days, haven't you?" Ash asked.

"I suppose."

"How did you find the moon cycle?" Remy asked.

How did I find it? As if it were something I was looking for… or as if we were just having a casual conversation about a book we had both read. How did I find it?

"How did I find it?" I repeated aloud without realizing it. "As in, what were my thoughts about the moon cycle?" I asked. "Well, let me think. I guess it was slightly embarrassing, seeing as I had an audience the whole time," I said, the sarcasm rolling off my tongue.

"I am sorry about that, but William and Haden were a necessity. I'm sure you can understand why we had—"

"No, not really," I interrupted him. "I mean I was locked up. In a steel-barred cage, no less. It's not like I could have escaped. Besides, how do you think you would have liked being in my shoes? Being stared at as your body betrayed you, transforming you into something you'd never imagined being? How would you like to—?"

"Watch your tone," Ash cautioned quietly. I had almost forgotten he was there.

When I glanced in his direction, I could feel his eyes on me like lasers, trying to burn their way into my mind. *Not gonna happen,* I thought to myself, and

I pushed back—mentally, not physically, but he felt it just the same.

"The fact of the matter is, you could have escaped. Couldn't you. If you had really wanted to. You and the boy. I've seen the video footage," Remy said, pulling my attention away from Councilman Ash and back to him. "I know both he and you were able to bend the steel bars of the cell. Without the guards there to watch over you, what would have stopped you from escaping?"

I could have denied it, but there was no point. It was true, Merick and I had both bent the bars of our cages. I'm not sure how it had happened, but it had. And if William and Haden hadn't been there to stop us, maybe we would have escaped. And yes, I did notice that he used the word "escape." He wasn't even trying to pretend I was in the cell for my protection anymore. Only prisoners escape.

But I reminded myself that escaping had never been my intention. *It was all Haden's fault that Merick broke through his cage in the first place. If Haden hadn't been there, maybe the moon cycle would have gone by uneventfully.*

"Merick was provoked. He never would have done that, not on his own. He thought he was protecting me."

"So, you admit it?"

"I… I admit nothing, but like you said, you've seen the video footage. I'm only stating a fact, if Merick hadn't felt that I was in danger there would have been no reason for him to attempt to protect me."

I didn't say anything else for a long time, and neither did they. I didn't want to get Merick into any more trouble than he might be in already, and I wasn't about to drag him down with me. Nor did I want to play the blame game with Remy.

"It was painful," I finally said, changing the subject to answer his original question. "If you really want to know, the whole experience was painful."

Painful, embarrassing, scary, frustrating, exciting, even thrilling, I thought to myself, but I wasn't going to share all that.

Remy sat quietly watching me for a while before speaking again, still thinking about the bars of the cage, I'm sure. "Yes, I have heard the pain can be quite excruciating."

"It is," I said. "I know the others won't remember it, and I'm thankful for that. No one should have to endure that pain month after month, afraid of the pain of their next transformation and the one after that. The pain is bad, but the anticipation, knowing it will happen again and again, month after month, year after year. I think that is even worse." I leaned forward, my arms on the table, and again a chill ran through my body. "But I'm sure you already knew that, or at least suspected it. You've lived around lycanthropes far too long not to know a thing or two about what happens during the changing moon."

"I suppose I do," he said, a small smirk flashing across his face then disappearing as if it had never been there. "I've seen a shift or two in my time."

"You've seen more than that and worse, I'm sure."

He nodded.

"You didn't bring me here to talk about my transformation. Like you said, you saw it all on film. William and Haden told me that you wanted to speak with me about what would happen next." I was trying to remain calm, reserved, and in control. I had to take charge of the conversation, lead it. I needed them to see that I was in control of my vampire cravings, my wolf, and even my lion.

"We did."

"And I thought I already knew what would happen next," I said. "You said life would go on. You told me nothing would change. But if that is the plan, I wouldn't be here, would I?"

His silence was the only answer I was going to get.

"If I had it my way…"

If I had it my way, I'd run. I'd leave this place and run as far away as possible. My own thoughts betrayed me, surprised me once again. I brushed it off and finished the way I knew I was supposed to.

"If I had it my way," I resumed, "…nothing would change. Life would go on just as you said it would. I would return to Iris's apartment, or preferably one of my own." They were watching me—judging me. "You would allow me to go back to work as the Council liaison, and life would continue, just as you said it would, here in Sector C."

"Is that what you want? To return to the lycanthrope quarters?"

"I…" I hadn't expected that response. I had thought that was what he wanted me to say. I knew he trusted Councilman Iris. Why wouldn't he want her watching over me? *Could I dare suggest that Merick and I room together?* "No," I quickly responded to my own thoughts without realizing I was speaking aloud. "I just mean—"

"It is what the girl wants," Ash answered for me. "Her beasts are strong. I can smell them on her as if she had rolled in a pile of filth."

"Excuse me?" I said. "The only reason I have *beasts* to speak of is because of you. Because of this Council. It isn't my fault that I'm both vampire and lycanthrope. And yes..." I said, turning back to Remy. "Respectfully, sir. I am a vampire. I claim my vampire just as much as, if not more than, I claim my *beasts*— as Councilman Ash refers to them.

"I don't know where I should live: the vampire quarters or the lycanthrope quarters. Maybe you can tell me. Maybe you can give me some guidance where this is concerned. You brought me here without a member of the Lycanthrope Council to represent me, or at least stand witness," I said confidently, and also subtly pointing out that I knew he was breaking the rules. "I can only assume you still see me as one of your vampires. If you wish for me to live in the vampire quarters then that is what I will do. But it is no secret that I'm also—"

"One of them," Ash finished for me.

"Yes, one of them," I said, standing. "What you made me. What I was told you both hoped I would become, or maybe that was all just an act. Maybe you never intended to bring the vampires and the lycanthropes together by creating a hybrid race. Maybe it was just a ploy. A way to win over the heart of—" I stopped myself, my eyes locked on Remy's and I knew I had said too much.

I sat down and leaned back, resting my hands lightly on the metal arms of the chair. "I'm not sure where I'll be accepted, or even if I will be accepted anywhere," I said, trying to calm myself down. "But I do want to stay here in the sector..." *Liar, liar, liar,* I thought. "...and I do want to continue working with the Council, if you'll still have me." *Liar, liar, liar.*

I took a deep breath, a breath I didn't need, but one that gave me the courage to continue. "You said, it's what you had always hoped for. That I was what you had always hoped for, a vampire-lycanthrope hybrid. If that's really true, then you won't fear me. You won't be afraid of what I can or might be able to do," I said. "You might be intrigued by me," I said, turning my attention back to Ash. "I might even amuse you, like a plaything you would keep in a cage until you're ready to eat it, but I want the same thing that you want. I want to understand what I am." I looked back at Remy: he was leaning in just slightly, but enough to notice. "Iris said it would take time, but that you believe that with time I could lead—"

"She should not have shared so much," he said cutting me off and standing up abruptly. "You will return to work in the morning. You can remain at Councilman Iris's apartment for now, but only temporarily, until your blood lust is under control." I started to argue that I already had my blood lust under control, but I thought better about it and stopped myself.

"At that time," he continued, "you will be given your own apartment within the vampire quarters. You work for me, so it is not appropriate for you to remain in the lycanthrope quarters. Do you understand?"

"I..." *What would that mean for Merick and me,* I wondered.

I glanced from Remy to Ash, and it was clear that Councilman Ash didn't agree with Remy's decision, but he wasn't speaking up. There was something about the way Ash watched me that made me feel uncomfortable. The way he always seemed to be focused—listening—and controlling others like puppets on a string, without so much as a word.

"Yes, I understand. Thank you," I added.

"William and Haden will still be assigned to watch over—"

"Wait. What? Why? I can protect myself. I am not a child."

"You are still young," Remy said, leaning forward and folding his arms on the table in front of him, in a posture of command. "And frankly, you can be as aggravating as a child." He shook his head. "Until others have accepted you, you are in danger. You think you can protect yourself, but you don't know the monsters of our world," he said, with a quick glance toward Ash. It was subtle, I hardly noticed and at the time it meant nothing to me.

"Monsters?" I asked. I had never heard of anyone referring to the vampires or even the lycanthropes as monsters, at least not out loud. The castaways, those beyond the walls, sure, but not those living within the sector.

"You've read about them in textbooks, if by a different name. You cannot begin to protect yourself, not yet. And until that time comes, until I have determined it to be so, either William or Haden will be with you at all times. I suggest you accept that." He stood back up, smoothed out his shirt sleeves, and crossed to the door.

"Councilman Remy," I called after him.

"Yes?" he said, without turning around.

"About Ciara," I said. He didn't turn around, but his posture straightened, stiffened. "Has there been any progress?" I needed to know if the alarms had anything to do with her, but I couldn't ask about that, not directly anyway.

He slowly turned to face me. He didn't look angry, but his eyes held a warning. "The hunt is still on."

The moon cycle was over, and they hadn't located her. That was a good sign.

"And if she comes in on her own, will you honor our agreement?" I asked.

His eyes narrowed to thin slits, and if I hadn't known he was a vampire, I might have likened him to a feline. "I said I would not kill her." His voice was controlled, too controlled. He was hiding something, I was sure of it. He turned back, not waiting for me to respond. He knocked twice on the door, which opened immediately, and Haden stepped in as Remy exited.

"You said, NO harm would come to her," I roared after him, and I could feel my wolf and my lioness pacing just under the surface, begging to be set free.

There was a moment of silence, as both Haden and Ash stared at me. When Remy stepped back into the room I thought I heard Haden gasp. His wolf growled as he took a single step toward Remy then quickly stopped himself, stepping back toward the door.

"Excuse me?" Remy asked.

"You told me that no harm would come to her. Not just that you wouldn't kill her."

More word games. More questions. Never any answers, I thought to myself, annoyed and angry.

Remy stood glaring down at me. My throat started to tighten, and my eyes began to burn. I opened my mouth to speak, but nothing came out. When he seemed satisfied, he turned and walked out. His vampire was stronger than mine, and he was making it a point to show me.

After Remy left, the tension in the room faded. "I've got first watch," Haden said. "I'll escort you home." He still stood beside the door, looming over me from afar, attempting to draw me out of the room with sheer willpower, or maybe intimidation. But I didn't move. I think I was in shock; I hadn't realized Remy was so powerful. When I looked up, Ash was still sitting across from me, patiently watching—waiting to see what I would do next.

"I know what you can do." His voice echoed in my mind, but his mouth never moved.

"And what is that?" I thought, turning back to him.

"You're aware—awake—when you want to be. Remy might see you as the answer, but I see you as—"

"Competition," I finished for him.

He laughed out loud, as if the mere thought of me actually being competition for him was a joke, but I knew better. Councilman Ash thrived on being the best, on being the only one of his kind, but he was no longer the only one with special gifts that Remy was interested in. Ash knew I was different. He had proof that I was the first vampire-lycanthrope hybrid. He may have even figured out a few of my special talents, but he didn't know everything. He was no longer special, and I believed Remy was starting to notice that, or maybe Remy already knew.

"Be careful what you wish for," Ash said in my mind, and then he stood up, scraping the chair across the floor and leaving me there alone at the table. He crossed the room and only paused for a second as he passed Haden. He didn't turn back; he didn't have to. I didn't need to see the look on his face to know I had upset him.

In that moment, a single word, destruction, floated through my mind. I wasn't sure if he had communicated it or not. If not, where had it come from, and what did it mean?

I stood up and grabbed the backpack from the floor by my feet, then crossed out of the room. As I passed Haden he put his hand at the small of my back and ushered me out protectively. I was astonished. But my wolf seemed content, no longer skeptical or suspicious of his. Or maybe I was too tired to question his motives—too tired to puzzle this out.

8

Haden stayed close beside me and didn't say a word as he guided us out of the Council offices and onto the street outside.

The blood Calliope had given me hadn't been enough, and I could feel my wolf and my lion both pacing just beneath my flesh. I knew it wasn't more blood that I needed—that they needed. I stopped just short of the turn that would lead us to the lycanthrope dining facility. "I need to eat. Can we stop at the dining hall?" I asked.

Haden hesitated, probably recalling the stories he had been told about my last experience at a dining hall—the vampire facility—everyone had heard about it. Finally, he nodded, and we turned down the next street and headed toward the sweet smell of honey.

"Mmmm." My stomach grumbled as I stepped toward the open door.

"That's your friends you're smelling. So, unless you want them for dinner..." Britt's warning played in my head, reminding me that the smell wasn't actually honey, but the smell of sweet blood flowing through the veins of the lycanthropes enjoying their dinner.

I can do this. I can do this. The silent mantra repeated itself in my mind.

"You're not going to go all fanger on me now, are you?" Haden asked, as he put himself between me and the open door, facing me.

That's all it took. He had already called me a "pup" and accused me of "wolfing out." "Fanger" was the final straw. Without warning, I grabbed him by the shirt collar and backed him into the door jamb. "I don't like that word."

He shook me off, but he didn't fight back. I think he was as surprised as I was at my sudden reaction. His face morphed from surprise to chagrin. He tilted his head, and viewed me silently. "I'm sorry. Believe it or not, I was kidding." His hands grasped at the bottom of his shirt, gently straightening it, as if busying himself and his mind before finally looking up. "Something has changed, Zelina. I can't explain..." His voice faded away as he shook his head.

How did I do that? I wondered. Haden was more than twice my size, more like three times my size, and as a new vampire, even a new lycanthrope, I shouldn't have had that much power yet, not outside of the moon cycle.

When I looked into the dining hall, everyone was staring. It could have been the disgusting dried mucus that covered me from head to toe despite the clean clothes, but I was betting they were all staring at the freak vampire-lycanthrope hybrid that had just attacked a security officer.

Great, just what I need.

"Maybe we should just go back to Iris's place," I said, turning to leave.

"No." Haden stopped me before I could escape. "We will eat here. That thing inside you needs to learn discipline. You have to learn to control it."

I wasn't sure which thing he was referring to. It could have been my vampire, my lion, or even my wolf, but I was doubting he meant the last one.

Then, quietly, he added, "I've got you. Trust me."

I looked up at him in disbelief. Was I having another psychotic episode? Was he? He gave me a half grin and then made his way past me and went inside. He got a tray of food and took a seat at an empty table without waiting for me to follow. When I eventually mustered up the courage to get my own tray, I piled it high with steak, potatoes, and bread. I slid into the seat across from his, and pulled both of the blood bottles out of my bag. Within minutes everyone at the surrounding tables had gotten up and left. Only a few people remained, and they stayed as far away as the room would allow. I told myself it wasn't because of me, but I knew better.

"I didn't mean to do that. Throw you up against the wall, I mean." It wasn't an apology, I had been taught that apologies were a sign of weakness, so this was as close as I was going to get.

"You didn't throw me," he said, as if annoyed. "And, I know." At that, I looked up, but his eyes didn't meet mine.

We ate in silence for the next twenty or thirty minutes, and I was thankful for the peace and quiet. It gave me time to think—to plan—if only for a little while.

"Why don't you smell like the rest of them?" I finally asked, after clearing most of my plate and downing the blood.

Haden answered my question with two of his own. "What do you mean? Why don't I smell like the rest of who?"

"The other lycanthropes. They all smell sweet: some like honey, others like fruit, and others I can't really describe, but it still smells sweet somehow. But you don't smell that way."

One corner of his lips quivered for half a second, and I couldn't tell if he was laughing at me or angry with me. "What do I smell like?" he asked.

It's a trap, I thought.

"I don't know. Different," I said.

"Different how?"

"Well, for starters, I don't feel like eating you." His eyebrows lifted as if he was actually considering whether or not I could. I thought about leaning in and taking a sniff, to see if I could describe his smell, but I changed my mind when I realized he was still staring down at me. "You don't really smell like anything, I guess," I quickly added.

He slid his chair back, grabbed his tray, and headed toward the door. "We should go," was all he said.

OK. I grabbed the last of my bread and quickly followed him to the tray rack and out the door.

Once again, Haden stayed close by my side as we walked through the lycanthrope quarters. People were stopping to stare as we walked past. Word of what had happened in the dining hall must have already gotten out, or maybe it was just word of my transformations. Considering that the evidence was still encrusted in my hair, I was a walking reminder of the newly confirmed freak the Council had turned me into. Either way, I didn't let on that it bothered me: I walked with my head held high. I wasn't going to give them the satisfaction of watching me squirm.

"What was that back there?" Haden asked, as we turned down Iris's street.

"I already said I—"

"Not the dining hall," he barked, and I could feel his wolf responding. "I could care less about that."

And I could tell it was true.

"Besides," he continued, "you'd never be able to do it again."

He was probably right. I'd thrown him against the wall, but I had gotten lucky and caught him by surprise. He wouldn't let it happen again; he would be ready next time. Not that I thought there would be a next time.

"Then what do you mean? What was what, then?" I asked, honestly not knowing what he was talking about. For the most part, my mind had been on Ciara since we left the Council offices. What Remy had said, *'I said I wouldn't kill her,'* hadn't been setting well with me. Having gotten some real food in my stomach I was finally able to focus again, and I needed to know if she was all right. I needed to find a way to reach out to her, and to Merick. They needed to know I was looking for them. Besides, Haden hadn't been the chattiest of companions since we left the stuffy little interrogation room.

"Councilman Ash—why did he laugh at you before you left?"

"Laugh at me?" I repeated.

Then it came back to me. Of course: Haden had been there, at the door, during the "private" conversation I had been having with Councilman Ash. He wouldn't have heard it, though. No one would have. I could feel him staring down at me as we walked, waiting for an explanation I couldn't give him.

"Oh, that was nothing."

"It didn't seem like nothing," he said. He wasn't going to let it go.

"Really, it was nothing," I said, stalling while I tried to think of another explanation—any explanation. "It was just a contest of wills. Let's just say he thinks he won."

"Did he?" he asked.

"No."

"Good," he said. I wasn't sure he really believed me, but he let it go anyway, as he turned up the walkway to Iris's building.

I opened my mouth, ready to try to convince him, but he shook his head. "Let's get you home. You've been through enough." He strode off ahead of me.

I followed him inside Iris's building, and down the hall to her door, where he stopped and turned back. "Well, this is you," he said. No one was inside. I would have been able to sense her if she had been inside: hear her heartbeat, even smell her. "I'll stay with you until she gets home," Haden said.

"You don't have to."

"It wasn't really a suggestion," he said, as he reached for the door with an access card out and ready.

"You have an access card to Iris's apartment?" I asked, intrigued that she had actually given him one, and curious about what Remy might have thought about it had he known—and a little surprised that Iris hadn't given me one too. Not that I actually needed one; Iris always seemed to be home when I left and again when I returned. However, it would have been useful at times like this when she happened to be out.

Startled, Haden looked down at the card and shook his head. "No, of course not. This is yours." He held the card out to me, and I thought I saw a hint of pink in his cheeks.

Is he blushing? I wondered. I must have smiled or giggled without realizing it, because his whole body went stiff, and his lips hardened as he glared down at me. I couldn't tell if he was angry or embarrassed.

I swiped the card, and sure enough, it worked. "Hmmm, that's convenient," I said, more to myself than to Haden. I stepped inside and turned back before he could follow me in. "Can I give you a piece of advice?"

Haden's lips softened then, and curled up at the corners, but he didn't laugh. "Sure, what advice do you want to give me?" he asked.

I'm sure he had no intention of actually taking advice from me, but I was going to say it anyway. "It's about Councilman Iris. I don't' think you should be pursuing her. I probably shouldn't be saying anything, but I'm starting to like you, despite the fact that half the time you treat me like you've been assigned to me as a punishment, and the other half you look at me like I'm a snack being dangled on a string in front of you, just out of reach."

He chuckled.

"William likes you," I went on. "He trusts you, and you've given me no reason not to trust you too. Besides, I don't want to see you get hurt. And—"

"What do you mean 'get hurt'?" he asked, cutting me off. "By Iris? Iris isn't going to hurt me." He took a step forward—not in an aggressive way, but as if he was going to come inside—but I blocked him before he was able to get into the apartment.

"She's taken," I said, a little too abruptly.

"She's—?" He actually looked shocked, or maybe it was just surprise. "What are you talking about? Iris isn't—"

"Honestly, it isn't my place to say anything. I don't know the details, and I wouldn't tell you even if I did know. Besides, I'm pretty sure she'd be upset if she found out I told you as much as I have, but like I said—"

"You like me," he finished for me.

"I do."

"Well, don't worry, I'm a big boy. Besides, a little competition is healthy." I opened my mouth to argue, but he stopped me. "I can take care of myself, Zelina."

"As can I," I said, as I reached to close the door. "You don't have to stay with me. I can protect myself." He started to object, but I stopped him. "Besides, you'll be more comfortable at your own place. I'll be fine in here by myself. No one is around, and I promise not to let anyone in." I closed the door between us, clicked both locks into place, and quickly ran upstairs, stopping only to grab a couple of bottles of blood from the refrigerator as I passed through the kitchen. My heart was beating a thousand miles a minute, which for a lycanthrope isn't that unusual, but for a vampire it is unheard of. Just another thing about being a hybrid that makes me different.

I downed the first bottle, and tossed the empty into the trashcan next to the door, then put the second one in the small refrigerated end table next to my bed. I slipped the book Teagan had given me under some clothes in my chest of drawers planning to read it later, took out a clean change of clothes, and hurried to the shower. I could still feel the dried, flaking slime all over me, and now that I finally had the opportunity to wash it off I could think of nothing I wanted more.

I quickly turned the shower on, and as I started to undress I caught a glimpse of my reflection in the mirror. I ran my fingers through my dirty, tangled hair, and realized that I barely recognized myself. It wasn't the crusty goo distorting my image, it was a physical change I couldn't quite explain.

I've always thought of myself as plain, or ordinary. I thought I was more likely to blend into the background than stand out, with my straight brown hair and light brown eyes. I've always been slender, but soft somehow. No matter how much I worked out, how often I ran, or how good I was on the fighting mat, I never looked all that athletic. Maybe that's why so many people underestimated me early on in life.

Now, however, as I studied my reflection I realized that my eyes seemed deeper, more mysterious—more bronze now than brown. The muscles in my arms and shoulders were more pronounced—not quite chiseled, but defined in a way they had never been. I was changing. I wasn't sure if it was due to the vampire or the lycanthrope virus, or an after-effect of my first moon cycle, but not only did I look different, I felt different. I was beautiful and powerful, and more.

It didn't take long for the water to warm up, filling the small bathroom with steam, and it felt amazing to step into the shower. I'm not sure how long I stood there, my eyes closed, enjoying the hot water flowing down my face and body, when suddenly I felt a cool breeze of air brush over my skin.

I quickly opened my eyes, startled, and called out, "Hello?" No one answered, but I knew I wasn't alone.

I was just about to slide the curtain aside when a hand reached in, holding a towel, "Time's up. You need to dry off. The doctor is waiting in your room."

Doctor?

I turned off the water, wrapped the towel around me, and pulled the curtain open.

"Amelia?" I was shocked to find her standing there in her white lab coat, red blouse, and pulled-back hair. "What are you doing here? How did you even get in here?" I could have sworn I had locked the bathroom door and I was positive I had locked the apartment door. "Is Iris home already? Did she let you in? Why are you at our apartment?"

"Your apartment?" she asked, stepping forward and reaching for my arm.

"I..."

A wave of irrational fear washed over me, and I glanced around the bathroom, looking for something I couldn't name, something to use as a weapon. Then it dawned on me that I wasn't in Iris's bathroom anymore. I had astral projected…slipped into a vision…or maybe teleported…I wasn't sure which. There was a silver metal bar that ran the length of the shower and another that surrounded the toilet. The countertop, once strewn with Iris's personal belongings, was completely bare, except for a single washcloth, a small bar of soap, a toothbrush, and a small tube of toothpaste.

"Here, let me help you," she said, still reaching for my arm.

"I'm fine," I said, pulling away and holding the towel tighter around my body. "I just need a few minutes to get dressed." She stood there without answering, watching. "Please, can I just have a little privacy? I'll only be a couple of minutes, I promise. Besides, it's not like I can leave without you knowing. Only one way in or out," I said, nodding at the door behind her. I wasn't sure where we were, but I wasn't about to waste this opportunity. I was going to be focused and get some answers this time.

"Fine, but I'll be right outside." She closed the door as she stepped out of the bathroom. I could feel her out there, waiting. I could hear her breathing, and hear her heartbeat. I could smell the sweet scent of the blood rushing through her veins—no, it wasn't her blood. It was sweet, but not like honey, or berries; it was more like wildflowers.

I dried off, got dressed, and brushed my teeth, wondering who else could be out in the hallway with her.

I felt clean again, ready to face whatever was waiting on the other side of that door. Ready to get the answers I needed. I glanced up at the mirror, as I turned to leave, gasping when I saw the short shoulder length bob haircut. *What the… Where am I? When am I?* It was my face looking back at me, but it wasn't a version of *me* I had ever seen before. *You can do this. You can do this.*

I shook off the fear that had started to bubble in my stomach and took a deep breath in and let it out real slow. I grabbed the door handle, opened the door, and stepped out into the hallway—Iris's hallway. For an instant, I was actually disappointed, but that didn't last long. I could feel the tension leave my body and I quickly reached up, grabbing a handful of long chestnut brown hair. *Oh, thank the stars,* I thought, thankful to be me again. I made my way back to my bedroom, but as soon as I opened the door it all came rushing back.

Inside was the dark, dingy room where I had found Ciara hiding outside the sector walls, only she wasn't there now. Standing in the corner next to the dirty old mattress was a man—a human, I thought at the time. I could hear the steady heartbeat from across the room: too fast to be a vampire and too slow to be a lycanthrope, or so I thought. He smelled like a combination of dirt and sweat. Down at his side, he held an old-fashioned, rusty dagger. He turned and looked over his shoulder just as I opened the door.

He can hear me, I thought.

I could feel his eyes burning holes into mine.

He can see me.

"Where is Ciara?" I asked.

He turned his body square in my direction, and when he opened his mouth to speak, I could see the long fangs that lined his top row of teeth. "Ciara? Is that her name?" he asked, his voice muffled by the grotesque overgrown teeth.

"What have you done with her?" I took a step into the room, ready to fight if I had to, but he stopped me by lifting the dagger and pointing the blade directly at my chest.

"Oh, we haven't found her yet," he said, drool streaming down one side of his mouth. "But we will." He sounded so confident, without even a hint of fear in his voice.

He raised his arm up and back, and just as his arm came forward to release the dagger aimed for my heart, I slammed the door shut between us, and the blade struck the back of the door with a thud. I screamed, I couldn't help myself, and I fell to my knees still gripping the doorknob.

What was that? What is happening to me? I felt like I was going crazy, and hoped I really wasn't.

There was a loud crashing sound from downstairs, and in seconds Haden was at my side pushing me out of the way and rushing into my room. "What is it?" he asked, frantically searching the room, and then pulling the window open and staring out at the ground below, but there was no one there, and there was no sign of the dagger having hit the door. "What was it? Who was here?" he asked, as he turned to help me up off the floor.

"You stayed," I cried. I sank into his chest, overwhelmed, and wrapped my arms around him tightly.

"Of course I stayed," he replied. I could feel his body stiffen under my grasp, and I slowly pulled away. He turned back to the empty room. "Why did you scream? Who was here?" He was clearly ready to do damage to anyone he might find lurking in my room.

"No one. It was no one. I was just…" I was too tired to even come up with a lie. "I thought I saw someone, but it was no one. I'm just tired."

"Zelina." He said it flatly, and it was not a question.

"Yes?" I asked, boldly ready to defend myself if I needed to. Then I gazed up at him, hopeful, defeated, and yes, tired. He reached out and took my hand in his, and gently ushered me to the bed. He pulled back the covers and matter-of-factly gestured for me to get in. I did, and he pulled the covers up, wrapping me in the warm security of my bed, and tucking me in.

"Honestly, you don't have to stay." I said, trying to smile. I didn't acknowledge the questioning look he was giving me, nor was I going to go into detail about what I had seen.

I expected him to argue or demand an explanation, but he didn't. After a few seconds, he turned around and left. I heard him make his way down the stairs and into the living room. I was pretty sure the noise that followed was him fixing the door he had busted off the hinges. When the door finally shut and the locks clicked into place, I wasn't sure if he was inside or out in the hallway. Either way, I was pretty sure he planned to stay, at least until Iris made it back home, and I would be lying if I said I wasn't glad to have him there.

I was too shaken to try and reach out to Ciara on my own. I would have to wait. She had survived the moon cycle: that much Remy had already told me.

I had to believe she would be safe with Isaac and Jabari for a little while longer.

It didn't take long to fall asleep, having been tucked in for the first time in my Sector C memory, and by a wolf that my inner beasts were starting to accept as a friend.

9

"Rise and shine," Iris called from the doorway of my room. "You were already asleep when I got home last night. We thought we'd just let you sleep. I'm glad we didn't wake you." I rolled over, and saw that she was already dressed in her usual bright blue attire, and smiling as if she knew something I didn't.

"We who?" I asked. *Did Haden stay over?* I wondered.

"Oh, just Haden and me. I found him sitting in the hallway when I got home. He said you wouldn't let him in," she said. "I get that you don't like having babysitters, but Haden is a good guy, you should try to be a little nicer to him."

"Nicer like you?" I asked, and the second I did, I regretted it.

Her eyes widened, as her head tilted, slightly to the side, staring me down. "And what exactly does that mean?"

"Nothing."

"Zelina, I'm a grown woman and he is an adult. Besides, neither of us are attached."

Well, I guess that answers the question of her and Councilman Remy. I wonder if Remy knows.

"We can make our own decisions," she continued. "But, if you must know, he came in for a drink, that is it. We're friends. We just ended up staying up most of the night talking," she said, smiling.

I'm sure he liked that. I thought to myself. *So much for heeding my warning, but I guess it doesn't really matter anymore anyway.*

"Nothing else happened," she said, as if trying to convince me. "He left around three this morning. He didn't stay the night," she said, answering my unspoken question.

"I didn't say anything. Besides, it's none of my business anyway."

Her long brown hair flowed in waves around her face, and her hazel eyes glistened in the sunlight from the window. With her porcelain skin, she looked more like a vampire than a tiger, but I knew differently. I had seen the tiger that lies behind those sparkling eyes.

"Right, well, get out of bed," she said, "Haden said you're starting back to work today. That means you've got just under an hour to get there. I've got breakfast ready and on the table downstairs. Make sure you eat before you leave."

"What time is it?"

"Ten after seven, now get up." She turned and headed out the door. Over her shoulder she called back, "And don't forget to take some bottled blood with you when you leave."

"Yes, mom," I mumbled, under my breath.

She stopped, slowly turning back. "What did you say?"

"I…"

Did I just call her mom? Why would I do that? I've never had a...

"I said, yes ma'am."

"No, you didn't."

No, I didn't.

"I'm sorry, it's just an expression. I don't know why I would—"

"No worries," she said with a smile. But her smile didn't reach her eyes this time. "I suppose, growing up, I was the closest thing you had to a mother." She came and sat down next to me on the bed, "Is everything OK, Zelina?"

"Yeah, of course." I didn't tell her about the visions I'd been having, or the fact that Haden had to break down the door to get to me when I screamed last night. I figured that he had probably already told her, and she was just being kind enough not to mention it.

"Are you sure?"

I could feel a lump growing in my throat, but I swallowed it back. I wasn't going to get emotional. "I'm sure, honest." It wasn't Iris I needed or wanted to talk to. There was only one person I trusted completely at this point—even more than I trusted myself, considering the visions that had me questioning my own sanity.

"There's nothing you want to talk about? Tell me about?"

I waited, and the silence between us felt thick and heavy. "No."

"OK, well get dressed, and make sure you eat before you leave."

"I will, thanks." She left, pulling my door closed behind her. I glanced down at the internal monitor on my wrist: twelve after seven. I jumped up. I'd just have enough time to get dressed, eat, and get to the Council offices. "Iris," I called after her, pulling my door open. She was already halfway down the stairs and out of sight.

"Yeah?" she answered back.

"You think I can borrow one of your shirts?" I asked.

She didn't say anything, but I could hear her slowly making her way back up the stairs. "One of my shirts?" she finally asked, as she reached the top of the stairs.

"Yeah, it's just that, living here in the lycanthrope quarters it feels a little odd to be walking down the street in all black. Even though I do have my own personal bodyguard to accompany me everywhere I go."

"Speaking of which, William is downstairs enjoying a bottle. You might want to get down there before he drinks them all," she said, skillfully changing the subject as she turned to leave.

I stopped her. "And the shirt?"

"Right." She turned back. "I'm not sure how Councilman Remy will feel if you—"

"Walk in to work wearing blue?" I smiled. "I've thought about that too, believe me. It's just, I'm a vampire...*and* a lycanthrope. He knows that. I need to be able to be both, even when I'm working for Councilman Remy. Don't you think?"

She took a deep breath. I could tell she was struggling with the decision, but eventually she nodded. "Yes, I do actually. Fine, take whatever you need."

"Thank you," I ran over and gave her a hug, like old times, as if hugging her was second nature, and she was just another person in my life that I could trust—lean on.

I got dressed, and attended to one more matter before heading downstairs: the internal security file and the Sector C maps that I had taken from Merick's and my office at the Council building. I took them out and tucked them into my backpack. I needed to get them back before anyone figured out they were missing, provided they hadn't already. The maps had helped me locate Ciara, and the last thing I needed was the Council finding out I had taken them and used them to figure out where she had been hiding. I knew she wasn't still holed up in the dark little room, but she hadn't moved far when she joined Jabari and Isaac.

"OK," was all William said when I came downstairs wearing black pants, black boots, and a bright blue shirt.

"OK," I echoed, nodding back.

I finished breakfast in under ten minutes: a large glass of bottled blood, two eggs, toast, and a large rare steak. Yes, I still preferred my steak cooked, not raw, and I didn't think that was going to change any time soon. I grabbed a few extra bottles of blood for while I was at work, but since Merick wouldn't be there to tempt me I didn't think I'd need them all.

"So, Haden had the night shift last night. Does that mean you'll be babysitting me tonight?"

"I suppose so," William answered.

"Does it make you uncomfortable? Having to be in the lycanthrope quarters? Late at night, I mean."

He just laughed. "No."

Yeah, I'm sure nothing makes you uncomfortable, I thought to myself.

Most vampires are lean. Don't get me wrong, they are tough, but most of them don't build muscle mass the way William had. Or maybe he had always been a larger guy, and he just never lost his size after the transformation, I'm not really sure.

We walked the rest of the way in silence, which was something I was getting used to. I almost asked if we could stop by the clinic on the way so I could look in on Merick, but I didn't. I knew he would say no, and I knew it wouldn't be appropriate anyway—a vampire visiting a lycanthrope *just because.* Sure, we had been friends as selection students, but somehow all of that is supposed to end after Selection Week. Not for me though—I was a lycanthrope too, and I wasn't willing to alienate myself from any friends I could find in either group. Friends were proving hard to come by. Then I thought about Haden and William. They had stayed friends. *How had they made it work for so many years?* I wondered.

We made it to the Council offices, and I paused on the sidewalk just outside the building. I knew that from here it was only a short three-minute walk to Counselor Teagan's office in the selection student quarters, and I thought about just continuing on down that road.

"What are you looking at?" William asked me.

"I… Nothing, just thinking." I closed my eyes, focusing on the door of Teagan's office in the main hallway: the stained wood, and the polished brass handle. I could see the door in front of me, and I reached out to knock, but then I heard footsteps coming toward me from farther down the hall. I turned to look, and saw three young selection students walking toward me—girls dressed in all grey. I could hear their hearts thumping in their chests, smell the sweet scent of their blood, and suddenly my fangs were exposed, and I was lunging toward them. Their screams filled the air around me and pierced my ears.

"What are you doing?" William shouted, as he grabbed me by the arm and dragged me up the steps of the Council office.

"I…" I didn't have an answer for him. I had no idea what had just happened. I had *been* in the hallway outside of Teagan's office, those students had been real, and yet I had *not* been there. I had been standing on the sidewalk outside the Council offices the whole time. It had felt so real. It was more than a vision. Those girls had screamed. They must have seen me. If it had been a vision, they wouldn't have seen me at all. Yet even though I knew it had been real, I also knew, logically, that it couldn't have been. I hadn't left the sidewalk. "I'm not sure," I finally said.

"Well, you gave a couple of women quite a start, back there. You should be more careful." William scolded, as he pulled open the outside door of the Council offices and led me in.

"Did you say two women?" I didn't remember seeing anyone on the sidewalk with us when I came out of the vision, but I had been a little disoriented.

"The donors," he said, shaking his head. "I'm sure they were headed to the dining hall, but after you lunged at them they ran off in the other direction."

How could it be possible that I was in two places at once? I wondered. We continued past the lobby into the heart of the Council offices.

"Good morning, Zelina," Calliope said, without looking up from her monitor.

"How did you—?"

"I could smell you the second you opened the door," she said. "A foul stench," she muttered under her breath.

"Be nice, Calliope," William scolded, but she didn't acknowledge him. She just busied herself with reading whatever was on her screen, and tapping on her keyboard. William looked at me and smiled. "Don't take her personally. She doesn't like any of the lycanthropes."

"But I'm—"

"It doesn't matter," he said, before I could finish. "Wait here," he said. He walked around Calliope's desk and stood behind her, placing one hand on her shoulder. Her body stiffened instantly at his touch, and I could tell she wasn't happy with him either, but I didn't know why. Then leaning in, he gently kissed her cheek. She didn't look up, but her shoulders relaxed, and the corner of her lips curled ever so slightly into a smile.

William returned to my side, and as we walked away I heard her whisper, "Have a good day,

William." He didn't respond, but out of the corner of my eye I saw him smiling.

We made our way down the long corridor of Council offices, conference rooms, interrogation rooms, and I'm sure some torture chambers, although I had no proof of that last one. When we made it to the large metal door that led into the neutral quarters, I could already sense Haden there on the other side. I knew he sensed me too, because I heard a low rumble coming from his wolf, and mine responded in kind.

"You OK?" William asked, staring down at me like he might need to cage me, or at least muzzle me, before the day was over.

"I'm fine," I said, not sure if I really was. Only the night before, Haden had been unusually protective, and now I couldn't tell if his wolf wanted to eat me or play with me. My heart was racing in my chest, and I could feel my wolf pushing her way closer to the surface as if she was palpable, just sitting and waiting to be let out of her cage—waiting to greet Haden's wolf.

"You sure?"

"Why don't you ask him? He started it," I said, nodding toward the door, hoping to get a glimpse into Haden's intentions.

William turned back and glanced inside through the small barred window in the door. "You good in there, buddy?" William asked.

Haden said, "Yup, all good in here," and I believed him. I could hear the low guttural growl of his wolf getting louder, but he didn't sound aggressive or angry. I couldn't explain it, but I wasn't afraid.

William slid his key into the lock, and I heard the gears slip into place as he turned the key and then the doorknob.

With all the technology we have, I wonder why they still use old-fashioned keys in the Council Hall.

William pushed the heavy door open, and I stepped inside. Haden glanced up from whatever gadget he was playing with, watching closely as I made my way across the small guards room to the door that led into my office. When I didn't acknowledge him, he quickly stood up offered me an uncharacteristic smile. I looked at him questioningly, and his gaze shifted to William, eyes narrowed. "You didn't tell her?" he growled.

William looked confused at first, and then shrugged his shoulders. "What does it matter?" he asked.

Haden growled, "It matters because it will make her happy."

"Happy?" William questioned.

Then I smelled him. I turned to Haden and squealed with childlike delight, and then I flung open the door.

10

As the door slammed behind me I scanned the room excitedly, and sure enough, Merick was standing there behind his desk. My heart was racing, and my palms were suddenly sweaty. I opened my mouth to speak, but nothing came out. The last time I had seen him, he had been bleeding in my lap. My worst fear was that I'd never see him again, but here he was, standing there only a few feet away. Tears filled my eyes, and I slid to the floor with my back against the door and my head in my hands.

"A, are you all right?" he asked, rushing to my side.

I don't know if it was relief because he was there—he was safe—or if it was just the built-up fear and stress that I had been carrying around, but tears just poured from my eyes. It was the first time I had cried in front of anyone in a long time. Had I thought about it, I probably would have been embarrassed, but in that moment it felt like a weight being lifted off my shoulders.

In seconds, he was sitting beside me, wrapping me in his arms. He didn't ask questions or pressure me to talk. We just sat there in silence for a while, the sound of his steady breathing calming me down.

"It broke," I said, pulling away just enough to take the broken vision stone out of my pocket, but not enough that he would feel the need to let me go.

"Your rock?" he asked, taking it from my hand gently, and lifting it to the light so he could see the crack that split it down the middle. "At least the wire held it together. You didn't lose it."

I didn't respond, just held my hand out waiting for him to give it back. Even broken I didn't like other people having it. Somehow it felt too much a part of me.

"Hey, it's ok. It's just a rock."

It isn't just a rock, I thought to myself.

"If it means that much to you," he continued, "I'll find you another one just like it."

At that, I smiled, because I knew he actually meant it. "You can't," I explained, but it didn't really matter anyway, I had still been having visions, even though the stone was broken. "I'll just keep this one."

"OK," he said, content to just sit there and hold me.

I felt safe there in his arms, and I realized I didn't want to hide anything, not anymore, not from Merick. "It isn't a rock," I whispered. I had finally decided I was done with all the secrets. "It's a vision stone."

"A vision stone, what's that?" he asked, sounding clueless but curious.

I slid the small broken stone back into my pocket, and he helped me to my feet. We stood there, face to face, and he looked me steadily in the eye, and then glanced up at the ever-present cameras. He smiled slightly, and I knew what he was thinking: this wasn't the place or the time.

"Do you need a new necklace?" he asked, turning back toward his desk.

"What?"

"I noticed the shoelace was missing. Did you need another—?"

"I'm not going to leave you with only one shoelace again, Merick." I was so grateful for his steadiness. So grateful for his quick understanding and his friendship and his, well... Him.

He chuckled. "You know I'd give it to you, but I actually had something better in mind." He went back to his desk, opened the top drawer, and reached in. When he took his hand back out, he was holding a silver chain.

"Where did you get that?"

A soft smile caressed his lips, "I made it."

"You made it?" I asked.

"Yeah, I mean I never intended for you to wear my shoelace around your neck forever. It took time, but it wasn't that hard to make."

I doubted very much that it wasn't hard.

"Not that hard? Are you kidding?"

"A, it's just wire. Really thin wire is easy to manipulate. I kept it simple, three pieces braided together."

"Seriously?"

"Yeah, the clasp was a bit tricky, only because I didn't want the wire popping out and cutting you, but I—"

"Thank you," I said.

"Can I put it on you?"

I nodded, but before I handed him the stone, I slid one of the broken halves out of the wire that cradled it. Then, handing him the half still wrapped in the twisted wire cage he had made me, I turned my back to him and lifted my hair out of the way. His hands slid around me as he placed the stone on the skin of my chest and moved to clasp the wire necklace. It amazed me how thin and delicate it was. I could feel the heat radiating off his body, and I leaned back against his chest.

"It's beautiful." I said.

I felt his chest rise, as if he was about to say something, but he stopped.

"I was so worried about you," I finally admitted, to him and to myself.

"Hey, I'm right here. I'm fine, I promise," he said.

"I just don't know what I'd do if anything had..." I stopped myself. It wasn't my place. He wasn't mine, even if I felt like he was. "I want you to have this," I said, turning to face him and holding the other half of the vision stone out to him.

He took the broken stone, rolling it around in the palm of his hand. He looked up at me as if he didn't know what question to ask.

"Just keep it with you. I don't know why, but I think you're supposed to have it. I have so much to tell you Merick. So much."

We spent the rest of the morning huddled on the couch. To all appearances we were going through papers and files, but in fact we were silently sharing what we had been through since the last time we were together. I mentally told him everything that had happened since we were locked up in the holding cells. He couldn't remember anything about his own transformations, but he did remember watching in horror as Haden shifted into a lion. He didn't have any memory of the pain he had endured himself, and I was thankful for that.

When I described the clinic that I had seen in my visions, he wasn't sure if it was the same place they had taken him or not.

"Maybe. I guess it could have been another part of the clinic, but I'm really not sure. My room was like a fish tank, A. All four walls were made of glass, and I could see nurses and doctors watching from outside, but Amelia was the only one who came in to check on me." He shook his head. *"No, that's not right, Councilman Ash was there too."*

"*Councilman Ash?*" It wasn't until just then that I remembered William telling me that Councilman Ash had ordered Amelia to keep Merick under observation at the clinic until his wounds were healed.

"What did they do to you?" I asked, not sure I really wanted to know the answer.

"I… I'm not sure. I remember being strapped down on the table. I could turn my head, but that's all. I…" Thoughtfully, he rubbed one of his wrists and then the other, where I'm sure the straps had cut through his skin, but there weren't any marks left behind. One of the advantages of being a lycanthrope is that you can heal almost anything. Almost.

"*Merick?*" An image flashed through my mind of Merick lying asleep, strapped to the exam table during Selection Week. *"Are you OK?"* It had been Nurse Britt who had abducted him that time, but this was different. Amelia had been trying to help, at least that's what I had to believe.

"*I'm all right.*" He shook it off and moved a little closer to me. "*I was sedated most of the time. When I finally woke up, I was all healed. They said I was well enough to be released, and I just wanted out of there. I didn't bother to stick around and check the place out. I wish I had but—*"

"*It's fine, really,*" I reassured him. "*I'm just glad you're OK. No one would tell me anything, let alone let me go see you.*"

"*You tried to see me?*" he asked, sounding more surprised than I expected.

"*Of course.*" At that, he smiled, and cleared his throat as he glanced up at the camera in the corner of the room.

"*Do you trust me?*" I asked.

"*You know I do.*"

"*Then, would you let me try something?*"

"*Try what?*"

"*Close your eyes,*" I said, not sure if what I was about to do would work or just make me seem crazier than I already did. Iris had once guided one of my visions, it was her way of trying to prove to me that Councilman Remy was on my side.

I took his hand in mine, hidden under the files between us on the couch. "*Try and remember what it felt like being strapped on that exam table,*" I said, hoping Merick could guide me into his memory.

His hand tightened around mine. "*A—*"

"*Don't worry,*" I said, "*It will be me on the table this time, not you.*"

I felt him relax, and when I opened my eyes I was staring into a bright light hanging right above me. I turned my head to the left and saw a computer monitor displaying moving charts, and blinking lights, and numbers—none of which made any sense to me. I could feel the cold metal table beneath my back and the pull of cords that had been attached to my chest. When I turned to the right I could see a few people passing by, just outside the room. Then I heard a door open from somewhere at the end of the room beyond my feet, but I couldn't lift my head to look in that direction.

"How is the patient?" It was Councilman Ash. I would have recognized his voice anywhere.

"He's fine. I've never seen a lycanthrope with such severe lacerations heal so quickly."

Quickly? I thought to myself, wondering why he had been kept in the clinic for so long if his wounds were healing.

"Cut him again!"

"Excuse me?" Amelia sounded confused.

"I want you to cut him again," Ash said calmly, as if it were a normal request. "We need to study him. We need to understand how and why he was able to heal at such an exceptional rate."

"I can't do that," Amelia said, sounding as horrified as I felt. "I brought him here to make sure he'd heal. I'm not going to—"

"Cut him again," Ash said again, this time shouting it, and I could feel the table shaking under me as he grabbed it and shoved it forward.

"I…"

"Do it, or I will!"

I heard her moving around the table, and when I looked up she was there, staring down at me. "I'm so sorry," she whispered. Then I felt a sharp pain, as if my insides where being torn out of my stomach. I closed my eyes and clenched my teeth, trying not to cry out in pain. I couldn't move. I couldn't breathe. I couldn't think.

The next thing I heard, only moments later, was Ash's voice. "Incredible. He's healing already."

I slowly opened my eyes, praying it was over, but it wasn't.

"Again," he demanded. This went on five or six more times before he lost interest. "And the blood work? What did it show?"

Amelia turned away from the table, and I could see her gloved hands, covered in blood and trembling at her sides. She pulled off the gloves and tossed them into the wastebasket before grabbing her tablet from the counter. "His bloodwork was normal. Lycanthrope. Wolf."

"That's all?" Ash asked, sounding disappointed, or maybe it was skeptical.

"That's all."

I heard Ash start to walk away, but he stopped before leaving. "Do you smell that?"

"Smell what?" she asked.

He didn't answer. "Just keep looking. I'll be back tomorrow," he said, then the door slammed shut behind him.

Amelia appeared above me again, tears filling her eyes, but she didn't cry. "How did this happen and how am I going to keep him from finding out?" She mumbled under her breath, looking honestly concerned, but I wasn't sure what she had found.

I opened my eyes, and I was sitting there on the couch clenching Merick's hand tightly in mine. I could feel the sweat on my forehead, and my breathing was shallow and labored.

"A, are you OK?" Merick asked out loud. I couldn't speak, not yet, but I managed to nod. He reached over for my backpack and handed me one of the bottles of blood I had brought, and it was gone in seconds. I'm not even sure I tasted it.

Once my nerves had settled down, it was my turn. I wasn't quite ready to tell him what I had just seen in his memory. I didn't know quite what to make of it myself, yet. Instead, I used our mental connection to tell him about the visions I had been having, the man I had seen the night before, and the little girl I had followed down the dusty hallways of the abandoned hospital.

Merick thought the man was probably just a memory from the night the two of us spent searching for Ciara—the night when he kept watch in the cabin while I telepathed out into the wastelands—although he couldn't explain the grotesque overgrown teeth. And he didn't know what to make of the little girl in the yellow dress. *"Where would anyone even get the material to make a yellow dress, A?"*

"I don't know."

He was watching me closely, *"You sure you're OK?"*

"Yeah, I'm fine. I'm sure it's nothing. Maybe it was just a dream, I haven't gotten much sleep lately," I said.

"A?" He said it out loud. One little syllable rolled off his tongue…my name for so many years, and now just a nickname, but that was all it took.

I mental-messaged him. "*No. I'm not ok, or I wasn't, but I think I'm better now. Now that you're here.*" He patted my hand with a quick glance at the cameras.

For some reason that reminded me of the papers in my backpack—the security file and the maps. Keeping my back to the cameras I took them out and slipped them into one of the files we had been going through.

The day flew by, and before I knew it I had drunk all three of the blood bottles I had brought with me, and I needed more.

William and Haden were supposed to be there to help support us, not just guard us, so I didn't think twice about asking them to fetch me more blood. However, when I opened the door, Remy was standing there, reaching to grab the doorknob.

"Councilman Remy, what are you doing here?" I said, startled at first but quickly pulling myself together. "I mean, what can I do for you? Did you need something?"

"It occurred to me," he said, as he made his way into the office, moving me slowly backward step-by-step, "that you may know more than you are letting on."

"Sir?" The burning in my throat was growing stronger. I needed to feed, but I wasn't sure how I was going to manage that with Remy standing between me and the doorway.

"About the young vampire everyone is so eager to find." He cleared his throat. "About your *friend*."

"Ciara," Merick said from across the room at his desk. His eyes were locked on Remy, and by the look on his face he regretted speaking up the minute her name left his lips.

In seconds Remy was standing at Merick's desk, leaning in, face-to-face with him. "Do you know something, wolf?" Remy asked, his head tilted to the side as if he was trying to understand what he was looking at. From across the room it almost looked as if he sniffed him. "You smell..."

Yup, he's smelling him.

"Umm, thanks?" Merick said, leaning back unsuccessfully.

Distracted, Remy was no longer focused on me, or Ciara it seemed, but instead he seemed fascinated by Merick. "What is it?" he asked out loud to no one as he sniffed him again.

Honey and soap, I thought to myself. Merick had always smelled like sweet honey and a new bar of fresh soap.

"He smells like her," Councilman Ash said, interrupting my thoughts, from right behind me. I didn't mean to jump, but he had startled me. I hadn't seen, smelled, or heard him come in.

When I turned he was standing there, holding out a tall glass of blood. "You're thirsty, no?"

How did he know that?

"Go on, take it."

I did as he instructed. The blood was warm on my tongue. It was fresh, not bottled. I paused, not sure if I should continue.

"Don't worry, he was a willing donor," he said, the corners of his lips curling up slightly, and I "remembered" him smiling as he stared down at Merick's quickly-healing stomach wound. The one he had demanded to see inflicted on him, over and over again.

I wasn't sure if I believed him about the willing donor, but I wanted him to stop staring at me in that way, so I downed the rest of the glass and wiped the side of my mouth clean before turning back to Merick. Remy was standing behind him now, with his hands on his shoulders holding him in place. It wasn't an aggressive gesture, but it wasn't friendly either. They were both staring at me. Remy seemed intrigued, and Merick just looked scared.

"Better?" Remy asked, as I placed the empty glass on a shelf next to the door.

"Yes."

"Good, then let us get back to this new mystery," he said. "Why is it that this one," he nodded down at Merick, "smells like you?"

"Like me?" I asked.

"You know it's true. You must have smelled it on him already."

"No, I haven't. I'm not sure what you mean." It wasn't a lie. I hadn't noticed that Merick smelled like me, but I'm not really sure I knew what I smelled like.

Without warning, Ash moved me—transported me—to the seat across from Merick's desk. Teleportation is the only word I can think of to describe how it happened. One second I was standing at the door watching Merick from across the room, and the next second I was sitting in a chair right across from him. Ash, standing behind me, quickly placed his hands on my shoulders, mirroring Remy's on Merick. I tried to look back, to see how far he had moved us, but he held me firmly in place.

Merick's eyes grew wider, if that was even possible. *"How did you do that?"* he asked, using mind-speak.

I tried shrugging my shoulders. *"It wasn't me."* I didn't understand it either, not that I could really have explained it right then even if I did.

"Ash?"

I nodded. *"Teleportation, maybe."*

"Your blood runs through his veins." Remy went on, obviously unaware of our unspoken conversation.

My blood? I thought, and then I remembered. I knew.

"How," Remy asked, a little more aggressively than I had expected.

I don't know, maybe because of the crazy experiments you had Blake's psychotic daughter doing during Selection Week, I screamed in my head.

I watched as he studied me, waiting. *He really doesn't know,* I thought to myself. That night had been weeks ago, but I remembered it like it was yesterday.

"This will only hurt…a little…but don't worry, you won't remember a thing," Britt had said.

It was a lie. I remembered everything. I remembered being carried out of my room and held down on a cold metal table. I remembered seeing Merick strapped down, unconscious. I remembered the needles—three long sharp needles: a sedative, Merick's blood, and Teagan's blood. The sedative hadn't worked, and I remembered it all.

I knew Remy knew what Britt had done to me: she had so much as told me, *"The Council has selected you. You have been chosen,"* she had said. But maybe he didn't know about Merick. Maybe he didn't know that Britt had also experimented on him. Maybe I had been chosen, and Merick had just been a victim of circumstances: a victim of…well…Britt and her personal curiosities.

I had warned her, told her that if he was infected she had to tell him before the release ceremony. She had promised me she would. Maybe I shouldn't have trusted her, but when she didn't say anything I had desperately wanted to believe that his blood tests had come back normal. But now…

"How?" Remy asked, again.

Merick was just staring at me, confused and scared. Ash's grip on my shoulders tightened.

"Because of Nurse Britt's experiments," I said, watching Remy's eyes. But he didn't flinch, and his pupils didn't dilate. There was no sign to indicate that he knew what I was talking about.

"What experiments?" he asked.

"A?" Merick's voice was shaky. I struggled not to look at him, keeping my eyes on Remy's the whole time. I knew that if I looked at Merick I would lose my nerve.

"It was during Selection Week," I continued. "After Merick infected me with the lycanthrope virus during our scheduled fight. You know the one..." I said, pointedly. "I knew the rules, like everyone else. Lycanthropes and vampires aren't supposed to fight each other during Selection Week, but apparently the Council had made an exception for Merick and me." I stared at Remy. I wanted him to admit he had put us against each other on purpose, hoping Merick would infect me, but Remy didn't so much as flinch. "Nurse Britt told me that the Council had ordered her to do more testing. That's when she injected me with more of his blood, exposing me to a higher dose of the wolf virus. She also used Counselor Teagan's blood to expose me to the lion virus. She said she wanted to see if the viruses would cancel each other out, continue to develop, or kill me."

"All this I already know," Remy said, in his usual calm yet commanding voice.

"Did you also know that she injected Merick with my blood? She was trying to see if I could transfer the vampire virus to him, the way he had transferred the lycanthrope virus to me. She wanted to see if our blood combined would kill him or turn him. Did she tell you that? Were you the one who told her to do it? Did the Council?"

No one said anything for a long time. Ash was the one who finally spoke, breaking the silence. "It was not the *Council's* doing," he said, but I had a feeling there was something more he wasn't saying. I wondered if Councilman Ash had ordered it himself. "And he isn't dead. So, no harm done."

"No harm done?" I spat back. "Are you kidding me?"

"A," Merick said, quietly.

Finally, I allowed myself to look at Merick. He was shaking his head, looking from me to Ash and up at Remy. I heard his unspoken questions. *"Wait. What? A, what are you talking about?"* Merick's eyes were locked on mine. *"I'm not a—I mean, I'd know if I was a—"*

"I'm so sorry. I didn't want you to find out like this. I should have told you. I was hoping—" All of a sudden, Ash's hands were no longer on my shoulders holding me down. One was at the base of my scull and the other clamped on the left side of my head, and a familiar sharp stinging pain pierced through the back of my neck. Then a burning sensation started at my temples and moved through my skull like knives.

I tried to fight it. I tried to push him out of my mind, but he was too strong. He had caught me off guard.

"Let go of her." I heard Merick pleading. "What are you doing? What is he doing to her?" His voice was panicked. I could hear him struggling to get to me, but it was no use. He was no match for Remy.

"Restrain yourself, Ash," Remy said, and I could hear the control in his voice.

"This is what I do," Ash snapped. "Let me finish."

If I could have screamed I would have, but my voice wouldn't work. My eyes were open, but I couldn't see. Then, suddenly, I couldn't hear anything either, except for a high-pitched ringing that drowned everything else out. Finally, everything stopped, and I fell forward, my head slamming down on the desk in front of me.

As if from a great distance, I heard Ash's voice. "It is true. He has been infected, just as the girl described." He didn't sound surprised and I wondered again if he had already known. If he had been the one to order it.

"Would that explain how she commanded his shift?" Remy asked.

My heart sank. It was all too much, and this wasn't the way I wanted Merick to find all this out.

"Commanded my—?" Merick started, but Ash didn't let him finish.

"I suppose it is possible," Ash answered.

"And what of the girl?" Remy asked.

"I have her location," Ash replied. "She isn't far. I'll send someone to secure her."

"Secure her, that is all. I want her brought directly to me. Unharmed," Remy instructed.

I knew they were talking about Ciara. I wanted to scream—to stop them—but I couldn't.

"Have this one taken home, but make sure the guards stay with her. I'll have more questions for her later," Remy said.

"And the boy?"

"Leave him. I'll take care of him eventually."

"Are you sure?" Ash questioned, as if he had other plans. I didn't hear Remy's response, if there was one, but Ash was quick to comply. "Of course, you're right."

I was too tired to open my eyes, let alone lift my head. "Please," I whispered, but my voice was so soft I'm sure they didn't hear me. "Please don't hurt her. Don't hurt Ciara." The last thing I remembered was the feeling of warm blood as it rolled down my forehead to pool on the dark wooden desk.

11

"Please wake up. You have to wake up." Her voice was shaky as she called to me, begging between sobs. "Why won't she wake up?"

I wanted to, I really did. I even tried, but I was just too tired. Whatever Councilman Ash had done to me had taken every ounce of energy I had.

Someone covered me with a soft blanket and tucked it in at my sides. It was then that I realized how cold I had been, and a shiver ran through my body.

"You have to give her time."

"Time? I've given her time. We've given her time. All she has is time."

"The medications we have her on are very strong. You know that."

Medications?

"She woke up on her own before. So why do you keep giving them to her?"

"You know why."

"Why not just stop. See if she comes out on her own?"

"We have tried that," Amelia said. "When she wakes up, it never lasts long: a few seconds, a few minutes, a half hour at best. This way is better for her in the long run. If we can gradually wean her off of the medications, then maybe she will stay awake longer next time, maybe even forever. We've gone over this. You said you understood."

I heard the scraping of metal across a hard surface, like a chair being pushed or shoved across the floor, and an exasperated release of breath.

"It's going to be OK," Amelia said softly. "We've seen progress, you know we have. She's a lot more responsive now than she's ever been. She's even had short periods where she's up talking—walking even. Don't lose hope that the medications are working."

Responsive? They can't be talking about me.

"I know. I just... I can't take this. I need air." I heard footsteps, then a door opening and closing somewhere in the distance.

After a few seconds I felt a warm hand wrap around my own. "Just take your time. We'll all be here when you wake up," Amelia said, as she placed her other hand on my forehead. The hand was warm—no, it was hot. "You're freezing," she said, and I recognized the surprise in her voice.

I focused, trying to force my eyes to open. It didn't work. "Amelia?" My throat was burning, and I could barely hear my own voice. *What did Ash do to me?* I wondered again.

"Yes, yes it's me." I could hear the relief in her voice. "Stay still, I'll be right back." Her hand left my forehead, and I heard her rushing to the door. "She's awake. She's awake," she called, as she pulled the door open.

I finally managed to open my eyes, and I was lying on the couch in Merick's and my office. I saw Merick across the room, standing with the door held open. "She's awake," he said to someone outside the door. "I'm taking her back to Iris's apartment."

"Merick?" I whispered.

"Yes, I'm here, A. I'm here," he said, as he crossed back to his desk.

I sat up and slowly swung my legs off the couch, watching as Merick searched through the papers on his desk. What he was looking for I didn't know, but he kept glancing up at the door as if needing to hurry.

William and Haden came in, but Haden hung back, watching me from the doorway.

I looked around, but I didn't see Amelia anywhere. "Where did Amelia go?" I asked.

"What are you talking about?" Haden asked, looking over his shoulder and then back in my direction but not making eye contact. "Amelia hasn't been here." Then to Merick, "How hard did you say she hit her head on that desk?"

"No," Merick answered. "This is all Councilman Ash's doing."

"How is that?" Haden asked.

"I don't know. He was..." Merick's hand nervously grabbed at the side of his head, rubbing at his temples as if to energize his brain. "He was in her head somehow." There was an edge to his voice that I wasn't used to. He was angry, and Merick never got angry. He had always been the selection class clown when we were growing up, yet I realized, suddenly, that I hadn't heard him make a joke in a very long time.

Had his transformation as a lycanthrope changed him? Or was it before that, was it Selection Week? I wondered.

Merick knew firsthand what it felt like to have Ash messing around inside his head. The confusion, the throbbing headache, the stinging pain, as Ash took over Merick's mind, forcing him to do what he wanted him to—when we were out in the woods, at the cabin, when we were looking for Ciara. Merick hadn't known who it was or what was happening then, but now he somehow connected that with what I was going through. I could see it in his eyes.

I watched as Merick quickly took a piece of paper from his desk, folded it, and shoved it into his back pocket.

"You ready?" William asked. He was standing over me, his hand out, ready to help me up.

"Ready for what?"

William reached down, took my hand and helped me up. "Do you think you can walk?" He was watching me closely, ready to catch me if I fell.

I wasn't going to let that happen.

"Yeah, I'm fine." I wasn't fine, but I wasn't going to let them see that.

Merick took my arm and pulled me into his chest. "I got her. I'll get her back to Iris's place."

"You sure?" William asked, as if he and Haden would really allow us to leave on our own.

"Yeah, we'll be fine."

I watched as William and Haden exchanged glances. They clearly weren't comfortable, but Haden nodded his head to a confused William. Something had shifted in my relationship with Haden, and even though I didn't yet understand it, I was grateful.

It didn't really matter if Merick and I left alone; William and Haden wouldn't be far behind. They had a job to do—babysitting me—and there was no way they weren't going to do it. I actually respected them for that, their dedication, even if I didn't like it.

Merick slid his arm around my waist to help me balance, and William and Haden backed out the door, into the small guards room, taking their seats just outside our office door.

"Merick," I said, pulling him close and whispering in his ear. "They've found her, haven't they?"

"They know where she was when you found her, but I don't know if they've gotten to her yet. I just hope she's moved since then."

"Yeah, me too. I need to get to her before they do."

"We will, I promise." I looked up and our eyes met, and I could see his sincerity there in his eyes. He wasn't going to leave me alone to deal with this; he was in this with me. We were in it together, for better or worse.

We left right away. I leaned on Merick for support as he led me through the vampire offices and out the front of the building. He pulled me quickly past Calliope's desk, not stopping to respond to her questioning stares.

When we made it to Iris's building, Counselor Teagan was there waiting.

"We need to talk," she said, quickly taking the key card out of my hand and leading the way into

Iris's apartment without so much as a hello. Iris wasn't there, but I was sure Teagan already knew that. Most likely, Iris was still working. It was still fairly early, and Sector C tends to run on a pretty rigid schedule most of the time.

The lock on the door clicked into place behind us, and Teagan's questions started before I had a chance to sit down.

"Three terrified girls came into my office this morning. Do you know anything about that?"

I wasn't sure how to answer her. What was I supposed to say? When I didn't answer, she continued.

"They said that a vampire had threatened them in the hallway just outside my office—a young female vampire with long brown hair and golden eyes," she said, watching me. "At first they wouldn't tell me who they had seen, but I eventually got it out of them. It wasn't that difficult." She shook her head, and then rested it in her hands. "They recognized you Zelina," she said, with an exasperated sigh. "And even if they hadn't, a vampire dressed in black AND blue, they said. Who else could it have been?"

"Black and—?" Merick said, cutting himself off. "Hmmm, I hadn't even noticed." I couldn't really blame him, boys aren't always that observant. Besides, we had been kind of busy reuniting, and then dealing with Remy and Ash.

It wasn't hard to imagine that the three young selection students would have known who I was. Almost everyone in Sector C had heard of me: the girl infected with both vampirism and lycanthropy. The news spread pretty quickly after Selection Week. The

Council hadn't posted my photograph around the sector as a warning, but then they hadn't really needed to.

"What were you doing in the selection student quarters in the first place?" Teagan finally asked. Then her expression brightened. "Were you coming to see me?" she asked hopefully. "Did you have questions about the other night?"

She took a second to breathe, and I was finally able to answer. "No, I wasn't coming to see you. I was thinking about it, but I wasn't actually in the selection student quarters this morning." It wasn't exactly a lie, but she didn't give me a chance to explain.

"Yes, you were." Teagan stood up abruptly, and walked around behind the couch, where she proceeded to pace back and forth. I imagined the carpet wearing away beneath her feet. "Zelina? Are you even listening to me? This is serious. If the... Zelina!"

"What? I'm sorry I..." I must have been daydreaming, because both she and Merick were staring at me with worried looks on their faces.

"Where did you go?"

"What? I didn't go anywhere. I'm right here."

"That's not what I meant," she said. "Whatever. It doesn't matter. What's important right now is that you're lying to me."

"I'm not—"

"You were in the selection student quarters this morning. I know you were. They described you perfectly, even down to the black pants and blue top you're wearing. Which, by the way, isn't going to help you blend in if that's what you're hoping."

"No, I just—"

"You need to explain yourself, or I'm going to have to go to the Council about this, and I really don't want to do that."

"You would go to the—?" I threw my hands in the air, frustrated, and headed for the kitchen. "I need a drink."

"Zelina!"

I stopped, turning back and calmed myself down with a deep breath before speaking. "I'll explain. Just give me a minute. Right now, I need something to drink," I said, before turning around and heading into the kitchen. I stood there leaning against the wall, trying to figure out how I was going to explain my way out of this one, and then I heard her start in on Merick.

"Did you know about this?" she asked, pointedly.

"No," he answered, sounding genuinely surprised.

"You're telling me that as *close* as you two are, she didn't tell you she was going to the selection student quarters, or that she had been there this morning?"

"I'm not sure what you're implying, but no, she didn't. Besides," he continued, "if she says she wasn't there, then I believe her.

"Thank you." I mental-messaged him.

"You're welcome," he answered out loud, not realizing it had been me, or maybe he knew it was me, but didn't realize it had only been in his head.

"What?" Teagan asked.

Crap, I need to be more careful with my thoughts. "Sorry, Merick."

"Um… Nothing. I just think Zelina has never given you a reason not to trust her. You shouldn't start distrusting her now," he said, covering nicely.

Silence hung in the air between them, and I took the opportunity to grab a drink from the refrigerator. I downed the glass and pulled out two cold bottled waters for Merick and Teagan before heading back to the living room.

"When was it that the girls said they saw her?" I heard Merick ask just as I was coming around the corner.

"This morning, around eight. They were stopping in to ask me about a few things before their first class, and they said—"

"It wasn't Zelina," Merick said, very matter-of-factly.

"What?" Teagan asked, surprised.

"I said it wasn't Zelina."

"I know what you said," Teagan barked. "How do you know it wasn't her?

"Because she was at the Council offices at eight this morning. She couldn't have been outside your office at eight o'clock and gotten to work at eight o'clock too. It's too far, even for someone like Zelina. If you don't believe me, you can ask William. He walked her to work this morning. He's one of the guards who—"

"I know who William is."

I watched as she came back around and sat on the sofa. When she looked up, her features had softened. "You're sure she was there on time this morning?"

"Yes, I was," I answered, not waiting for Merick to respond. "But Merick isn't entirely correct. I think I might have actually been in the selection student quarters this morning too. I'm just not really sure how."

Merick got up and came to stand beside me.

"What are you talking about?" Teagan asked, straightening up in her seat.

"Zelina, it wasn't you. Tell her it wasn't you," Merick said.

"I'm sorry," I whispered. I moved around him to face Teagan head on. The warmth radiating off Merick's body beside me was comforting. But I never took my eyes off Teagan's. She was watching me carefully, too, judging me.

"I didn't attack those girls." *Or at least I didn't mean to,* I thought to myself. "I was standing outside the Council offices, that much is true, you can ask William. He was there. We were about to go in, but before we went up the steps something made me think of you. The way you had hesitated yesterday, when I called out to you—"

"Zelina, I didn't mean to—"

"Don't worry, I get it. I'm sure I'm a lot to take in, especially after the news of my transformations. I just wanted to see you. I needed to talk to you. I needed to make sure we were OK, and I had questions—*have* questions—about being a lion. And now I have even more questions about the book you gave me, about why you had it, why you gave it to me, and about..."

"The book was a gift, but not from me. I should have given it to you a while ago, but I…" She looked down. I could tell she wanted to tell me more, but she didn't say anything.

"A gift from who?"

She swallowed, took a deep breath, then looked back up. Her eyes met mine with such an intensity I almost turned away. "From a friend—from Micah."

"Micah?" My heart stopped when she said his name. Micah had been a castaway. He had been one of Counselor Teagan's students when she was an instructor in Sector M. No one knew why or how she had been transferred to Sector C, and when Sector M was shut down, Micah and so many others were left behind, abandoned and discarded into the wastelands.

But Micah was different. He had made his way all the way to Sector C and communicated with me somehow through my dreams. He was the reason I had been able to find my vision stone. But when he made his way inside the sector walls he was captured by the guards. They locked him up, held him prisoner, and eventually forced him to fight me during Selection Week. I hadn't wanted to fight him. I hadn't wanted to kill him. But he had made it clear that that was exactly what I was meant to do. He had sacrificed his life for mine. I didn't know why at the time. And now to find out that he was the one who had given the book to Teagan, for me. *What am I supposed to do with that information*, I wondered?

"Micah was special," Teagan finally continued. "I believe that, somehow, he knew all that you are capable of. I believe he knew your destiny, whatever that may be," she said. "When I was in Sector M, I was given the book to watch over, as the Leaena, but even then I knew it didn't belong to me. When I was transferred to Sector C, I passed it on to Micah."

"Why Micah? Why not another Leaena?" I asked.

She paused, cleared her throat, and continued. "There were no other lions within Sector M. Micah and I were the only ones. There had been others, but they had all died or defected. I couldn't take the book with me when I left, the sector council transferred me here under orders from the High Council, but they didn't allow me to take any of my belongings with me."

"Wait, you mean you were banish—?"

"No," she snapped. "I was transferred. The High Council saw a need for me here. The sector council wasn't happy so they cut ties, completely."

I could see the pain in her eyes as she struggled to continue.

I trusted Micah. When he said he'd watch after the book until the time it was meant to be passed on again. I knew he would do everything in his power to keep it safe." She stood up, stretching, then paced in front of the couch. "Besides, there was no way I could have known it was meant for you, or that you'd be here in Sector C when I arrived, but somehow he knew. When he was captured by the guards, the book was the only thing he had on him. They took it to Councilman Remy, who had no idea what to do with it. Micah had left me a note in the front cover, that's how Remy knew to bring the book to me."

"Councilman Remy knew that you knew him and he still held him prisoner and had me…" I couldn't say the words. I couldn't admit that I had killed him, not out loud.

"Yes, but he had no choice. The sector residents expect justice when one of the outsiders enter the sector walls. If he had done nothing, there would have been mutiny."

"What did the note say?" I asked, not sure if I really wanted to know.

"My name on the envelope and only two words inside: *for Zelina*. At the time, you were still a selection student. I had no idea who he meant. There wasn't a record of a Zelina in the sector registry. Then, after Selection Week, during the ceremony when your name was announced… I should have given it to you then, but I wasn't ready to accept that it was meant for you, a child, and not for me."

"What do you mean it was meant for me?"

"It's not just a book. It's the history of the lion bloodline. It's our past, our present, and the prophecy of our future."

"You've read it?" I asked. I had only skimmed through it, and I was curious to know more.

"No, but I tried. I've flipped through the pages a thousand times, maybe more," she said, sitting back down and shaking her head. "But, I never could read it. Like I said, it wasn't meant for me, so the words never appeared to me. The prophecy can only be revealed to the chosen. That isn't me."

I took a deep breath. "You're saying that it's me, I'm the chosen?"

She nodded. "That's why it was so important for Micah to deliver the book. Important enough that he would give his own life to ensure that it made it to you. Whatever is in that book… He knew that it was worth the sacrifice of his own life."

It was all more than I could even begin to process at the moment, so I went back to the earlier topic that Teagan had come to confront me with. "This morning, I had questions," I said, trying to sound stronger than I actually felt. "I had questions about why you hesitated when I greeted you, and why you gave me the book, and it had been so long since I had really seen you—talked to you. I realized how much I missed you. And I knew that, even if I asked, William wasn't going to let me go see you. Maybe that would have been for the best, but…"

"What are you trying to say, Zelina?" Teagan asked. I felt Merick take a small step away, but I didn't look. I couldn't look.

"I still don't have my visions under control," I said, and Teagan shifted in her seat, obviously uncomfortable with where the conversation was going. She glanced up at the ceiling. "Don't worry," I said, "Merick already knows, and there aren't any cameras in here."

"When I thought about you, I was standing there on the sidewalk outside the Council offices, and yet I could almost smell you…hear you. Suddenly, I was standing outside your office in the hallway of the building as if I had been there the whole time. I was just about to knock on your door when those three girls came around the corner. I didn't see them at first, but I could hear the beating of their human hearts, smell the blood flowing just beneath their flesh. My fangs came out on their own, and before I knew it I was lunging forward."

"Then you *did*—"

"No. I didn't attack them. That's what I'm trying to explain. William was there, standing on the sidewalk with me outside of the Council offices. He'll tell you, I never left. Apparently, there were two donors passing by. I lunged at them, and they ran off screaming. William grabbed me before I could do anything stupid, and dragged me inside. No one was hurt—maybe scared, but not hurt—not physically. I don't even remember seeing the donors, two women William said, but he swears they were there."

Finally, I looked over at Merick, who was standing there as still as a marble statue, staring at me. Teagan cleared her throat and looked from me to Merick and back. "You're telling me you were in two places at once?"

"No," I answered quickly, without really thinking. "I mean, that isn't even possible. Right? Besides, when you say it like that it sounds insane."

"But that *is* what you're saying. You never left the sidewalk, William will vouch for you, yet you were there in the hallway outside my office. The girls identified you."

I didn't have an answer, so I didn't say anything.

Merick returned to my side. "Zelina?" His voice shook slightly as he pulled me into his arms.

"She needs rest," he finally said. "I'm taking her upstairs. She told you everything she knows. You can talk to William if you feel like you have to go to the

Council, but there isn't anything else she can tell you. Not right now."

He led the way, holding me close, and we made our way through the kitchen and up the stairs. I heard Teagan leave, shutting the door behind her just as we pushed open the door to my room.

12

Merick locked my bedroom door and rushed to look out the window, while I made myself comfortable on the bed.

"She's gone," he said, turning back. "I don't think she's happy about it either."

"No, I doubt she is. I mean, you did pretty much tell her to leave and to go to the Council if she felt like she needed to. I'm sure Teagan isn't used to people talking to her like that."

Merick looked genuinely shocked. "I didn't tell her to—"

"No, you didn't mean it like that, but I'm sure that's what it felt like to her," I said gently. I could see him going over what he had said again and again in his head.

"Don't do that to yourself," I said.

"Do what?" His nonchalant attitude was unconvincing at best.

"Don't beat yourself up over this. It was nice, you defending me like that. Besides, Teagan is a grown woman. She'll be fine."

"What about you?" he asked.

"What about me?"

"Are you OK?"

"Oh Merick," I sighed. "I think you and I need to quit asking each other that question." I gave him a little smile, "I might not be fine, but I'm always better when I'm with you." He gave me a sweet smile in return. I sighed again. "After what I said down there—after what you learned back at the office…" I was sure I had scared him, and I had been waiting for the day when he would turn and start running. But it hadn't happened yet. "Thank you, Merick. I don't know what I'd do…"

"I'm not going anywhere, A. The only thing right about any of this…craziness…is you." He was watching me from across the room, still standing at the window. "Can I ask you something?"

"Always."

"When we were in the woods, that first time you found Ciara—"

"At the cabin," I said.

"Yeah. You never left the cabin when you went to find her, but somehow you were there with her beyond the wall. Do you think what happened this morning could maybe be the same thing?"

"I don't know, but I don't think so. That was more of an astral projection of me. You know what I mean? I wasn't really there: even though she could see me, it wasn't really me. This morning I felt like I could really reach out and touch the doorknob to Teagan's office if I had tried. I think I could have grabbed one of those girls. If William hadn't stopped me, I could have…" I didn't want to say what I was thinking. I didn't want to admit that I probably would have attacked them—fed off them.

"But you didn't. You didn't do any of those things. You didn't grab the doorknob or even knock on the door, so you can't really know, right?"

"I guess not, but it just didn't feel the same. I don't think I can explain it right. I'm sorry."

"Don't be." He came and sat on the bed next to me. "We'll figure it out together. Do you still want to try and reach out to Ciara now?"

"I have to."

"And after everything that's just happened, you think it's still a good idea?" he asked. I could tell by the way he was looking at me that he didn't think it was a good idea, but how could I not? I had to at least try.

"No, but Councilman Ash already knows where to look for her, and if she hasn't moved to a new location it may already be too late. I don't really have a choice."

He took my hand in his. "We always have a choice." Instantly my whole body felt warmer.

"But, she'd do it for me, right?"

He didn't answer at first. When he did, he looked away. "I don't—"

"She would, I know she would," I said, stopping him before he could tell me differently. The burning was starting in my throat. I was hungry again. It seemed I needed to eat more and more frequently. I thought it was supposed to go the other way—get easier. *Maybe with time*, I thought to myself. I reached over and grabbed the last bottled blood from the end-table and popped the top open.

"What does it taste like?" Merick asked.

"I…" No one had ever asked me that. "I don't know, sweet and salty at the same time I guess." He stared at the bottle, but he didn't say anything else.

I took a drink as he watched. I wasn't really comfortable drinking blood in the first place, and having him stare at me while I did it didn't help.

"Can I taste it?"

"What?" I asked, shocked by his question, and also by my quick response.

"I just…" He got up and moved away from the bed. "Never mind," he said.

"Your blood runs through his veins," Remy had said. I knew it was true, but I hadn't really thought about what it actually meant, or how it might be affecting him.

"Merick, are you craving blood?" I asked, but he didn't respond. "It's OK if you are," I said, getting up from the bed and going over to him. "Look, if you want to try it, you can." I held the bottle out, but he didn't take it. "It's really not that different than a Lycanthrope craving raw meat. Besides, like Remy said, my blood runs through your veins. Maybe that means you are part vampire," I said, and I could see Merick's body stiffen at the thought. "But maybe not," I quickly continued. "I mean, probably not. I really doubt you are."

The truth was, I had no way of knowing. I don't think anyone did, except maybe Amelia, and I was just guessing from how she reacted in the vision I had through Merick's memories. And if that was the case, she seemed pretty intent on keeping it a secret. And I was pretty sure that Merick wasn't planning to let anyone get near him with a needle—I know I wouldn't, not willingly, especially after finding out what Britt had done to him, or after spending so much time in the clinic after the moon cycle. Although, I was pretty sure he didn't remember any of the gory details from that experience.

"I just wanted to taste it. I'm not craving it or anything. I just thought that maybe, if I tried it—"

"You thought if you tried it, then you'd know."

"Yeah."

I held the bottle out again, and this time he took it. "You don't have to be scared," I said.

"I'm not scared," he barked, and I could smell his wolf.

"I'm sorry, I didn't mean it like that." Merick was the one person I could be myself around—that I could apologize to without fear that he would judge me— think me weaker for it.

"A, I'm sorry too. I didn't mean to snap at you. I just...I think I just need to know. You get that, right?"

"Yeah, I get it. Honestly." And I did, more than anyone.

I waited while he sniffed at the blood. He was either going to love it or hate it, and I'm still not sure which I was hoping for. When he took his first drink and quickly spit it back out into the trashcan, I almost felt relieved. But a few seconds later, when the taste of the blood settled on his tongue, he licked the remnants from his lips and a low growl escaped his throat. His wolf wanted more, or maybe it wasn't his wolf.

"Merick?" I asked, hesitantly. Not because I was afraid, but because I wasn't sure how he was going to react.

He turned away and finished the bottle before turning back to me, confusion and shock all over his face.

No, I didn't think it was his wolf.

"I'm so sorry," I said, half to him and half to myself. I felt like I had betrayed him somehow, even knowing that there had been no way that I could have prevented what had happened to him. It was still my blood that had turned him. I still felt responsible.

He turned back, wiping his mouth with the sleeve of his shirt before grabbing my arm and pulling me into his chest. "Don't be. I'm fine, I promise."

I could feel him shaking; his whole body was tense and trembling in my arms. "Merick, you're not fine."

"I'm fine," he said again, this time with more force. "If you can handle this, so can I, right?"

Typical, I thought to myself.

"Merick, it's not a competition." I pulled back, reluctantly, and looked up into his eyes, realizing that that wasn't what he needed to hear. "Yes, you can handle this," I said, changing my approach. "You survived the lycanthrope injection, and your first moon cycle, all while secretly infected with vampirism. If you can do all that, you can handle this too." I wanted to reassure him, but deep down I really didn't know what to think.

"There's more blood in the fridge downstairs. You should bring some up," I said.

"A, I'm—" he started.

"I know you are." I smiled, trying to hold back the tears that were threatening to escape. "But can you just bring some up for me?"

"A."

"For me," I said again. "After all, you did just drink my last bottle," I said, before he could argue.

"Yeah, OK." His shoulders sagged as he headed toward the door. We were in this together, and even if he wasn't going to admit it, he knew deep down that it wasn't going to be easy.

"Merick," I said, stopping him as he reached for the doorknob. "If you feel like you need some, drink it. The cravings, they can get bad, trust me."

He just nodded, took the three or four steps back to me, leaned down and kissed me on the forehead. His lips were soft and warm. Instantly, I was back in the girls bathroom before the Sector History prep exam. I had pulled Merick into the bathroom with me, locked the door, and kissed him. It had been our first kiss. At the time, I wasn't sure what, if anything, would come of it. We could both have been banished from the sector, exiled to the wastelands, but that didn't happen. We made it through Selection Week, and somehow, against all odds, we were still together. Me a vampire-wolf-lion hybrid, and Merick a wolf with the vampire virus somewhere in his blood too. I wasn't sure what it meant or where we would end up, but in that moment, I was happy.

His lips left my forehead, and I wanted to pull him back, but I didn't. He brushed the back of his hand across my cheek. I gave him a playful little push, and he went to fetch the blood. There were just no words right now.

I made myself comfortable in the middle of the bed and waited for Merick to return. It didn't take long, but when he came back he had an armful of blood bottles—and a tag-along. Haden.

I looked at Merick quizzically, and he answered in my mind, *"Your guess is as good as mine."*

Haden took a breath, and then shook his head. I could see he was struggling with something, but what it could be I had no idea. "Zelina," he finally said, "I think we need to talk."

"You mean tonight? Like, right now?" All I could think was, *I don't have time for this, whatever this is.* But I couldn't tell Haden about Ciara, so there was no easy way around it.

"Yes." He was staring at his feet. He turned toward the stairs, expecting us to follow. We did.

In the living room, he gestured for us to sit. We did.

"This is not easy," he said. His fists were clenched at his sides, and his words came slowly. "But it's not going to go away. So you might as well get comfortable. It won't take long to tell, but it might take a while to sink in."

"What are you talking about?" I asked, more confused than I had been in a long time, and that was saying a lot considering everything I had been through.

"Zelina, you are my Alpha," he said. His voice was trembling, not from fear but from what seemed to be shame.

What? No! Wait, what?

"Haden, you're wrong. You're an Alpha. Iris told me. So, I *can't* be your Alpha. Besides, the Alpha in a wolf pack is always a male. Everybody knows that. It's like Lycanthrope 101."

"Historically, yes, but not in this case. I don't know how or why, but every bone in my body knows it to be true. You are my Alpha. That would make me—"

"My Luna?" I asked.

He must have thought a lot about this, because he answered almost before I spoke the question. "NO!" He had expected it, but he still sounded shocked to hear the word spoken. "The Luna is a female. She is the mate of the Alpha. As a female Alpha, I'm not sure what your mate would be called. But I am not him," he said, glancing quickly toward Merick then back at me, as if embarrassed. "Nor could I be. I am your Beta, your advisor. That is why I smell different to you, different from the other lycanthropes. We are tied together, as a unit. I serve you. I think I've known it for a while, but I only fully realized it when you…the other night at the dining hall."

I sat there in stunned silence, wondering if this was really happening, or if it was some bizarre dream.

"What happened at the dining hall?" Merick asked.

"I threw him against the wall," I told him using mind-speak. Haden didn't need the embarrassment of hearing it aloud.

"We can announce it now to my pack—your pack if you so desire. It is your decision. I live to honor you and uphold the pack." I could tell he meant what he was saying, but even as he said it I knew it was hard on him. "But I wonder if it might be in your best interests to wait—to conceal your power until we can unravel what is going on here in Sector C and with you personally." He unclenched his hands and held them out to me, palms up, in a classic gesture of goodwill. The tension fell away from him, and he squared his shoulders proudly. "Your welfare is of the utmost importance to me, and to the pack, even if they don't know it yet."

"How can you be sure that I'm your Alpha? How can you know? I'm not even—"

Haden cut me off. "I know. And if you are honest, you know it too. And you, Merick," he said, turning to Merick who was still sitting in silence. "She commanded your change during the moon cycle—and you went mad trying to protect her—you know it too."

Merick didn't pause, he just nodded once.

I was stunned. How could this even be possible. "How can I be the Alpha? I barely know the laws of the pack. I only know what we learned in school, which wasn't much, by the way. I haven't even been initiated as a lycanthrope!"

"I'll help you. I can continue to pose as Alpha, for now. I don't think any of the others have felt the shift just yet. Then, when you're ready, when the time is right, we can tell them together."

"How will I know when that is?" I asked.

"You'll know, trust me."

I nodded. I didn't want him to be right, but deep down I knew he was. What was more, I had a feeling it wasn't only my wolf who was going to be making changes within the sector, but I didn't say that out loud.

"When it's time, how will it happen?"

"That will be up to you. You'll have to do something to prove yourself as the Alpha. Although I already know it, no one else will accept it unless…"

I waited, but he didn't continue, and he didn't meet my eyes. "What?" I asked.

"Typically, a new Alpha takes their title by force. By…"

"Killing the old Alpha," I said. It wasn't a question: that much I had learned in my classes. He answered anyway.

"Yes."

"That isn't going to happen. We'll find another way," I said.

He nodded, and changed the subject. "There's more, Zelina."

Oh-my-stars, now what? What more can you dump on me? I thought to myself.

"There are prophecies as old as the lycanthropes themselves: prophecies that span the depths of time. I believe they can give you the answers you're seeking."

"Prophecies?" I asked. It was all too much. First, the responsibilities of the lioness bloodline, and now this. "Haden, I'm not—"

"I know that Teagan gave you a book on the lioness. I saw it. Honestly, I'm not surprised it would have been handed down to you. The lions and the wolves are the strongest bloodlines within all the lycanthrope breeds. We were the first, and the only two breeds whose bloodlines have never been synthesized."

That got my attention.

"Synthesized?"

"You didn't know?"

"Know what?" Merick asked, speaking up for the first time since Haden announced I was his Alpha.

"That the lycanthrope injections for the wolf and the lion—the ones they give at Selection Week—they both come directly from the first generation of lycanthropes. All the other breeds were developed by the High Council when the Sectors were created. Or by scientists working for the High Council that governs all the sectors. But, because true-blood werewolves and werelions were among the Founders, their blood is used throughout the Sectors to create each new generation that follows."

"You're telling me…" I started, trying to process it as I went, "that every wolf in Sector C carries the same bloodline, as does every lion?"

"I'm telling you, every wolf, throughout all the sectors, shares the same blood line. As do the lions, yes."

I sat down on the sofa, trying to imagine how many infected that might mean.

"There is another book—one that chronicles the histories of the wolves, and foresees what is yet to come." As he said this, he pulled a black leather-bound book out of a bag he had slung over his shoulder. It was almost identical to the one Teagan had given me. The only difference I noticed as he handed the book to me, was that this one bore a title on the cover: *We Are Wolf*.

"This book has been kept safely hidden, watched over by the elders for centuries. When I became the leader of my pack, it was handed down to me, as its new keeper. I had no idea what it was. I was told only to protect it, but not why. I was told I would know what to do with it when the time was right. It wasn't until the moon cycle, when you shifted, that I realized—"

"The prophecies are real," Merick said in a whisper. It wasn't a question, but Haden answered him anyway.

"They are."

"My stone...my visions...the astral traveling." Everything made sense, and yet I understood nothing.

Haden raised an eyebrow, and I knew it was my turn to talk. I took a breath, and began.

13

I had only ever known Haden as a guard, as someone who seemed to resent me, and why shouldn't he? He had been assigned to be my babysitter, after all. It was only just recently that I had started to see him as more than a dutiful guard, and even as a possible ally—and maybe a friend. I knew he was an Alpha, but I had never thought of him that way. I had never seen him with his pack. I had never given any thought to the power he must possess.

Suddenly, sitting there in Iris's living room, I felt stronger with him at my side. I started at the beginning. I told him about the nightmares I had had as a selection student, how I found the vision stone, and what the Council had done to me throughout Selection Week. I told him about the astral projections and visions I had been having since even before being infected with either virus. Everything came out in a rush—I told him about Ciara, and what she had told me about how our classmate Wyatt had died. I even hinted at my hopes, shyly looking at Merick, that he and I could one day be together, which of course came as no surprise to Haden, my ever-present shadow. Merick though, grinned widely, and I had my first glimpse of the boy I knew before selection week.

Haden didn't ask questions. He just listened, and I could almost see the pieces click together in his mind. He stood with his arms folded across his chest, and from time to time he nodded. When I stopped, he remained motionless, thinking, and I knew that he was ten moves ahead, already planning our next step. I could see why he had been the leader of his pack for so many years. It was reassuring. I felt like answers were on the way, and I was so done with being a clueless victim.

Merick was about to leave, and I found myself in his head, whispering, *"Stay."* It was easier to use mind-speak—saying the word aloud felt awkward and, well, embarrassing.

He didn't say anything, just gave me that grin again and followed me up the stairs, and before long I was snuggled into his chest, falling asleep to the steady drumming of his heart.

I awoke to find myself alone, which I completely expected. It wouldn't have been appropriate, much less permitted, for Merick to be seen leaving with me in the morning. I smiled. His scent was still in the air around me. Besides, I knew I'd be seeing him again soon enough. Then I saw the note on his pillow.

The outside of the folded paper said:

I found this on the floor. It's a note from U. Try to get in touch with her. Haden and I will look into the prophecies. See you soon with answers. —M.

As soon as I unfolded it, I recognized Uma's handwriting. She had always embellished her writing with swirls and curly endings. It was undeniably girly in a society where girls and boys are trained to dress, act, think, and even fight alike. Yet somehow Uma had stayed irrefutably feminine. I envied her for that.

The small folded paper was the note she had sent me during the moon cycle.

> *A ~ You'll never believe what I've discovered. We need to talk. This is huge.*
> *~ U*
> *P.S. Good luck with the moon cycle. You've got a lot of people rooting for you out here.*

I still didn't know what it meant, but thinking about it even for only a second was all it took. I opened my eyes, and I was standing in what had to be the clinic's delivery ward, holding a newborn baby swaddled in a tiny white blanket. For once I had actually directed my travel. *Go me!* I thought, silently congratulating myself. I remembered Merick's advice to try to get in touch with U.

"Shhh, you're OK," I said, but it wasn't my voice. Looking around the room—the nursery—I saw that I was in the middle of several rows of cribs. Most of the cribs were empty, but there were swaddled, sleeping babies in quite a few of them.

Oh no—! All these tiny babies, and me still not completely able to control my thirst. I was regretting not having had breakfast, or at least a quick bottle of blood, before picking up the note.

"Who said that?" Uma said, as she spun us around, clutching the baby even more tightly to her chest.

What do I do? What do I do? What do I do? Think Zelina, think! A dozen tiny heartbeats clouded my thinking.

"Zelina?" she asked, whipping us around again. I could feel the baby squirming in her—our—arms. "Where are you?" Uma asked.

That's when I realized I was sharing U's body, just as I'd done with Ciara. A rush of relief swept through me as I realized the babies weren't in danger, at least not from me. Now to convince U not to freak out.

I wasn't sure what to say—think—do. *"I'm...go to a mirror,"* I said in her mind, trying to sound calm, and hoping she could do the same.

"What?"

"Just put the baby down and find a mirror," I said, hoping she would just do what I told her to do without me having to physically cause her to do it.

She did what I asked. She/we placed the now-sleeping baby in its crib, to my great relief, and weaved our way through the rows of cribs.

"They seem so peaceful," I thought.

"Who?" Uma asked, still looking left and right as she walked, trying to figure out where I was hiding.

"The babies. Not a care in the world, no fear, no pain."

"They're babies, Zelina. What could they possibly have to fear?"

Me! I thought to myself, but what I communicated to Uma was a little less scary. *"You! You're a vampire!"*

"But, I would never hurt them!" she said, sounding shocked, as if I had just offended her.

"Of course you wouldn't."

"Zelina, are you OK?"

"Yes," I said, as we stepped up to the sink at the far end of the room. There was a mirror just above the sink. Uma's flowing brown hair reminded me of my own, but her glowing complexion and her gentle smile were all her. Her face was slightly rounder than mine, with soft plump cheeks and perfectly arched eyebrows.

"What is happening?" I heard her ask, and suddenly I realized I had been fixated on her reflection in the mirror, and was smoothing her eyebrows with the tips of my/her fingers. I quickly centered myself, looking away from the mirror and down at her hands instead.

"We're here," I said.

"We?"

"OK, I need you not to freak out. Can you do that?"

"Seriously, A. Stop playing games. This is silly, where are you?" she asked, turning away from the mirror. "Because it's starting to feel a lot like you're—"

"In your head," I said at the exact time she said, "In my mind."

"That's because I am. I'm here," I said, in her mind as I spun her back to the mirror.

"You're—?" She grabbed the counter as I spun her, "Woo, what was that? A, did you just—?"

"Shhh, it's OK. You're not crazy. I'm not there in the room with you, not physically anyway. I'm just here… in your head."

"Yeah, no. That's not crazy." She leaned forward, turned on the water and splashed us in the face. "How? How are you in my head?"

"I don't know, I can't really explain it. Even if I could, you probably wouldn't want to know."

"Then just tell me why you're in my head."

"I actually thought that part was obvious." I said.

"No, no not obvious," she said.

"Your note. You said you had something to tell me. Something huge."

"My—?" I could feel her searching her memories. It's a strange feeling being in someone else's head when they have total control.

"Oh right, my note." She took us into a small office just off the nursery. "Hey," she said, I could feel her lips curling into a smile. "Mind watching the little ones while I run to the restroom?"

"What? No, Uma…I can't…that's not how this—"

"Not you," she answered, without actually speaking. She was handling the whole situation a lot better than I expected. Better than Ciara had the first time. Better than I probably would have.

"Sure thing." A tall, thin woman got up from a desk in the corner and made her way toward the nursery. "Take your time, I haven't had a chance to cuddle those cuties all day." The door swung closed behind her, and Uma and I were left alone.

"Who was that?" I asked.

"Just one of the nurses."

"OK, now what?" I asked.

"Just give me a second." Uma made her way to the desk, grabbed a tablet, logged in, and started scrolling through screen after screen. "Now that I work in the clinic I have access to all the medical archives." Since we were alone, she said it out loud. Maybe that was easier for her, or at least maybe it seemed more normal.

"So?" I couldn't figure out where she was going with this. Why would the medical archives be so important that she had risked getting caught sending me a note through Amelia?

"So, this," she said, proudly holding the tablet in front of us.

I focused on what she was looking at. It was a birth record. *My* birth record.

Sector: C
Year: 2365
Birth Rank: A
Date: 53
Sex: Female
Weight: 6.8 lbs.
Length: 19.61 inches
Status: Healthy
Breeder: C20M103 (Mary)

"OK, it's my birth record. What about it?"

"Don't you see?" She pointed to the last line, tapping the screen with her index finger. "The breeder, C20M103—Mary. When we were selection students, we never had access to information about the breeders. Heck, no one does, just the nurses and doctors in the infant ward in case there is something wrong with one of the babies. I only have access because I work in the nursery and I've started my training. I'm sure they never expected me to be curious about the breeders. It's not like they are ever a part of our lives after birth, so what does it matter who they are? Besides, they aren't even considered residents. Not really." She was rambling, something U had done since we were kids.

"Uma, slow down."

"Look!" she said, swiping the screen, to the next record.

Sector: C
Year: 2365
Birth Rank: B
Date: 53
Sex: Male
Weight: 4.3 lbs.
Length: 14.15 inches
Status: Stillborn
Breeder: C20M103 (Mary)

"You had a brother."

"A brother? Wait, what?" Then I saw it, his breeder. *"Mary? Is that even possible? Couldn't there just be two breeders with the same name?"*

"I haven't met all the breeders yet, but it's doubtful. Even if it was possible though, they have the same indicator, C20M103. It's impossible for two sector residents to be given the same indicator. So that tells me—"

"He would have been my brother."

"Would have, but he died. It's not surprising. Most of the babies don't survive," she said, matter-of-factly.

"Is that what you wanted to show me?"

"Nope. This is," she said, swiping the screen again, and when it stopped I was looking at Ciara's birth record.

Sector: C
Year: 2365
Birth Rank: C
Date: 53
Sex: Female
Weight: 7.63 lbs.
Length: 20.16 inches
Status: Healthy
Breeder: C20M103 (Mary)

"Hmm, she was bigger than me." I had never really paid attention to the birth records before. Then I saw it. *"Oh my stars. Mary? Is that even possible? Uma, what are the chances that a breeder would have not two but three babies at the same time?"*

"No clue, but the records don't lie. The Council is crazy strict about us recording everything, and I mean everything."

"We're really sisters. Ciara and I are really sisters?" I spun us around and started running toward the door. "We're really sisters." I was no longer thinking of Uma, and I could feel myself pulling away...pulling out of her mind just as I reached the door.

Then she was gone, and the door was no longer there.

14

I was still running, but now I was running down a long empty hallway. There were flickering lights every ten or fifteen feet. Doors along the way were either standing open or hanging off their hinges. It wasn't the abandoned hospital, I knew that much, but I didn't have a clue yet as to what or where it was.

What happened here? I wondered, as I slowed down to take a closer look. There was a familiar smell in the air, but I couldn't identify it. I couldn't put a name to what it was.

"Ciara?" I called out. I needed to find her, and I hoped that maybe—somehow—I had managed to direct my vision travel again. "Ciara, are you there?"

Out of nowhere, someone grabbed me from behind. A man's hushed voice whispered, "Shhh," and he clasped a heavy hand over my mouth and pulled me into a dark room and shut the door behind us. His breath was warm against my neck.

I couldn't move. His arm was wrapped tightly around me pinning me back against his chest. I couldn't speak or breathe past his other hand. My eyes hadn't adjusted to the darkness yet, but I could see a thin sliver of light shining through the space beneath the door. I struggled in the man's grip, but he was too strong. I couldn't get away.

"Calm down." He was still whispering, his lips almost touching my ear. I sensed an urgency—an eagerness—in his voice, and a low rumble came from deep within his chest.

Lycanthrope, I thought to myself. I sniffed the air around me. *Lion.*

My lion reacted instantly. I could feel her pacing just below the surface of my flesh, like a caged animal just waiting to be let out. Ready to meet my captor's lion face-to-face, even excited at the idea.

"Calm down," the man said, and both I and my lion reluctantly obeyed. "You can't run around these halls screaming like that. They'll hear you." He took his hand off my mouth, but still kept a tight grip around my torso. "Ciara is fine," he said, and it was then that I finally recognized his voice.

"Jabari?" He loosened his grip, and I was able to turn around. Jabari had wavy jet-black hair that hung just below his shoulders. His eyes were so dark you couldn't tell where the pupils ended and the irises began. His skin was naturally sun-kissed, a light golden brown. His arms, still holding me loosely, were strong but gentle.

"Jabari? Where is she? Where are Isaac and the others?"

"They aren't far. Don't worry, they're safe, for now. But the sector security team has been through here multiple times in the last two days. It's like they know she's here somehow."

"They do," I said, swallowing back the guilt I felt for letting Ash take that information from me. "Where is she now?"

"We've moved her to another building just up the road."

"Then why are you here? Why aren't you with them, protecting her?"

"I came for you," he said, as if he had known I'd be here.

"Were you—?"

"Waiting?"

I nodded, but he shook his head. "No." His answer was abrupt, and harsher than I had expected. "It's complicated."

"How did—?"

"I knew you'd come. I can explain later, but right now we have to go. They'll be back soon, and I don't want you here when they get here." He grabbed my hand and started toward the door, pulling me behind him.

"No." I pulled back, planting my feet firmly in place. "You're not dragging me out of this room without more of an explanation than that. I'm so tired of everyone walking on eggshells around me. Either treating me like a freak—a monster—or treating me like I can't handle the truth. I'm not a little girl, and I won't be treated like one any longer."

He stood there, mouth slightly agape, waiting to see if I was finished.

"I..." I wasn't about to apologize for standing up for myself, but I did recognize that he didn't deserve to be lashed out at. "I didn't mean to—"

"No, you're right. You do deserve to hear the truth. It's not my place to keep it from you, nor was I trying to. I only wanted to get you to safety before the guards returned. And they will return, Zelina, and it won't be long. Isaac and the others are close. When we get to them, we will explain everything."

I nodded. I knew he was right. Besides, the sooner we left, the sooner I would get to see Ciara again, and make sure she really was OK.

15

"Oh my stars, A!" Ciara rushed me, throwing her arms around me the second I came through the door. Jabari barely had time to move out of the way to avoid being trampled. "You came back," she said as she spun me around. "And you're you! I mean, you don't seem different at all."

"What are you talking about? Of course, I came back. I told you I would."

"What happened? Where did you go? How are you feeling? Tell me about the moon cycle." She was still spinning me around, and I was starting to get dizzy. "You shifted. You really shifted. What was that like? Did it hurt? I bet it hurt. Oh wait, you don't know do you? Wow, yeah, I remember that from class. Weird. You don't remember anything do you?"

"Actually," I said, stopping her. "I do remember, and yeah, it hurt. A lot." I could feel the other lycanthropes in the room shifting uncomfortably in their seats. They all knew it wasn't normal to remember anything about your first few transformations, but nothing about me was normal. I was coming to grips with that.

"Will it happen again?" She continued her litany of questions. "What does it mean? What did the

Council say? Were they surprised? Angry? Excited? What about you? How are you feeling? What does this mean for your job with the Council?"

"Give her room," Isaac said, and his hand on Ciara's shoulder calmed her almost instantly. With a gentle touch, he guided her to the side. She moved as if willed, but not far. The others were watching quietly, from couches and chairs that were arranged in groups around the large room. Still smiling, Ciara slid her hand into mine, like a child waiting her turn to play with a new toy.

Isaac moved around me, ignoring Ciara as he studied me. He didn't tell her to move aside. He didn't have to. She countered his every movement as if anticipating what he would do next, and moving out of his way instinctively. It was like a beautifully choreographed dance.

Isaac had light blonde hair, almost white. It was short at the sides and slicked back on top. He was tall and slender with a firm jaw, high cheekbones, and a chiseled profile that could have rivaled any marble sculpture. His features were perfectly symmetrical, handsomely so.

"Is she hurt?" Isaac asked, looking past me to Jabari, who I just then realized was still standing less than two feet behind me. I could have reached back and touched him, and something inside of me wanted to, but I didn't.

"No," Jabari answered.

"Was she being followed?"

I'm right here, why don't you ask me? I thought to myself, but for some reason didn't ask.

"No."

"You're sure?"

They both looked at me, then exchanged an awkward silence.

"I'm sure," Jabari finally answered.

"How are you feeling?" Isaac asked, addressing me directly for the first time since I walked in the room. "Are you thirsty? Do you need to feed?"

I swallowed, taking a mental assessment of myself and how I was feeling at that moment. My throat had begun to burn. *When was the last time I fed?* I wondered. I had lost all sense of time, all sense of what was real and what were merely visions.

The bottled blood, back in my bedroom with Merick? No, he drank that. Back at the Council office? I couldn't remember what day it was, let alone when I had fed.

Wait, that would mean this is just a vision, I realized. *If this is a vision, or I'm just an astral projection, then I won't be able to drink anyway.*

"Zelina," Jabari said my name as his hand landed heavily on my shoulder. "Do you need to feed?"

"I can feel you," I said out loud, much to my dismay.

"I can feel you too," he said, confused.

"No, I mean… Never mind, it doesn't matter," I said into the silence Jabari, Isaac, and the others were staring at me as if I had two heads. In reality, I was wondering if maybe I really did have two heads— and two bodies—one there with all of them, and the other lying on my bed back in Iris's apartment.

"Do you need to feed?" Isaac asked again.

"Yes, please."

"Bring one of the survivors," Isaac said, motioning to someone near the door, who quickly made his way out of the room.

I opened my mouth to object. I didn't want to feed on anyone, but then I thought better of it. I knew that they probably didn't have bottled blood in the wastelands, or at least not a large supply, and especially now that they had moved from their usual living quarters to what seemed to be a poorly furnished basement in yet another abandoned building. If I was going to survive even for a short period of time out here, I'd have to feed the way they did.

"After you've fed," he continued, "we should get you caught up. A lot has changed in the few days you've been gone."

Of that I have no doubt.

Jabari told me the details of how they had locked down during the moon cycle. Even the oldest lycanthropes in their group had refrained from hunting. "It was a sacrifice we were willing to make." A low murmur spread through the others in the room.

"When the moon cycle was over, we sent scouts out to search the area, but it wasn't long before the sector guards picked up Ciara's scent. Although she had kept mostly to the abandoned building next to ours, once she left, word spread of a young rogue vampire."

I couldn't help but wonder if that was my fault. I had made her leave that dirty little room. I hadn't meant to put her in danger, but I had. I had intended to help her get back home, but I hadn't been able to do it.

"I'm sure the locals were more than willing to share that information with the guards. Trading information for their lives is often the only way to survive out here. You can't blame them. Survival of the fittest often leads to what should be unnecessary sacrifices."

Isaac joined us, taking a seat across from mine. "We left our shelter, using the tunnels to relocate here."

I could already see that it wasn't as nice as the place I had first found them in. There was no electricity, only candles, and there probably was no running water. If this room was all there was, then there was very little privacy either.

"How do you know they won't just track you through the tunnels?" I asked.

"We don't, but they haven't found us yet. Besides, we won't be here long. Now that you've arrived, we'll be moving again this evening. We're going to make our way deeper into the wastelands."

"Deeper into the wastelands, but why?" I asked.

"Because we have more allies out there," he explained.

"But isn't it more dangerous?" I asked.

"Not exactly. The Governing Council designed all of the sectors with the same basic structure. Family Unit arrangements and other rudimentary lifestyle changes were made over time, but the laws remain the same. All sector guards are trained according to the Governing Council's plan. Their mission is to protect the sector at all costs, while ensuring that the residents within the walls are subject only to minimal danger."

"Minimal?"

"Minor," Isaac clarified.

"No, I know what minimal means. I'm just surprised."

"The members of the sector guard are trained to stay within a twenty-mile radius of the sector at all times," Jabari explained. "The next sector is hundreds of miles from here. So anyone who manages to get safely outside the guards' reach has a better chance of survival out here."

"A better chance?"

"Yes."

"But not guaranteed survival, right? I mean, you still have the castaways to worry about,"

"Yes, as well as other rogue vampires and lycanthropes who have made their way beyond the walls. Everyone out here is struggling to survive. We all fight for food. We fight for blood. We fight for territory. Living beyond the wall isn't safe, nor is it pretty, but we have survived, and we will continue to survive together. If we get beyond the reach of the sector guard, we won't have to worry about them coming after us anymore. That much I can promise you. Besides, the farther you get from the sector, the less you'll find outcasts that kill first and ask questions second. Here, they are used to fighting first—relying on their primitive weapons or brute force—trying to protect themselves and their families from the sector guards."

"But twenty miles? You have to be crazy to think that's even possible. No one knows what's out there, or even if you can survive that far out." I scanned the faces of the others sitting around the room, but it seemed I was the only one who was concerned about this. "Where will you go? What will you do when you get there? How will you find food?"

"We have traveled much farther than that," Isaac answered. "Most of us come from sectors that have long since closed down. Cumulatively, those seated around you have traveled hundreds, if not thousands, of miles on foot. We will survive the same way we always have. Together. The question you need to be asking, or rather answering, is whether you will be coming with us and joining the Resistance, or staying behind."

"The resistance?"

"We're a faction made up of lycanthropes, vampires, and humans," Isaac explained. "We seek only one thing—peace."

"A, come with us," Ciara pleaded.

"I—"

I can't. Can I?

"I don't know," was all I could think to say.

"You have to come with us," Ciara said, sounding even more desperate. When I turned, her eyes were begging, threatening to overflow. "I can't do this without you, A."

"Then don't," I said. "Come back with me. I've already talked to Remy, and he said that if you turn yourself in he won't let them hurt you. They won't lock you up. I've made a deal to protect you. You can come back to the sector with me." Without realizing it, I had started to cry, again. I felt the tears streaming down my face. "Remy said he would call off the hunt if you came back on your own." Ok, maybe that wasn't all true, but he had said he wouldn't kill her, and I had to believe he was a man of his word.

"Of course they'd call off the hunt—they'd have her," someone said from a seat along the back wall. "What are they going to do, take your word that she didn't do it?"

"C, please…ignore them and come back with me. We can make this right. *I* can make this right."

She let go of my hand, her gaze falling to the floor in front of her. "You know I can't, not after Wyatt's death."

Wyatt had been another one of our classmates when we were still selection students. He had selected the vampirism injection, and after Selection Week he and Ciara had gotten close. One night, after having been stuck in the vampire community center for weeks, they decided to sneak out. They just wanted to take a walk, get some fresh air, feel normal for a little while. They were walking along the bank of a small creek that runs through the sector when a water moccasin bit Ciara's leg. Her leg instantly went numb and she collapsed. Before she passed out, she remembered watching as Wyatt bit into his own arm then pressed his bloody wrist against her lips. When she woke up, she was covered in blood, and Wyatt was dead. We all knew the venom of a water moccasin is poisonous to vampires: without feeding she would have been dead within the hour, probably less. Wyatt had tried to save her life the only way he knew how, but in the end, she had drained him, unable to stop feeding once his blood touched her lips. At least that's what she had believed.

"The Council would never believe the truth of what happened, that it was an accident," she continued. "They'll want someone to blame—someone to punish. They will never let me live. I was foolish to even think they might."

"They will. I can make them believe. I can show them."

She wrapped me in a tight embrace, and I hugged her back, focusing as hard as I could—trying to see what had happened that night. I had done it with Merick, and I wasn't going to give up on Ciara.

Suddenly, I was there. The cool water splashed my ankles as I walked along the edge of the stream.

"Careful, you'll slip," Wyatt said, and I turned to him, just as he grabbed my hand. "Careful, I said."

"I am being careful. It just feels so nice to be—Ouch!" A sharp pain in my calf crippled me, my leg went numb and I fell to my knees.

"Ciara, what happened? Are you all right?"

I couldn't talk. I couldn't move. I felt Wyatt ease me down onto the ground, and I knew he was lifting the leg of my pants, even though I couldn't actually feel it.

"It was a water moccasin," he said, sounding frantic. "You need to feed. Ciara, you need to feed."

Then I smelled it—fresh blood, as Wyatt put his wrist to my lips. I could feel the warm, sweet blood as it ran down my throat. I could feel my leg healing even as I drank, but I still felt woozy. Then his arm pulled away and I heard a scream, but I was still too weak to move.

When I finally opened my eyes, I was covered in blood. Wyatt was lying on the ground next to me, his wrist still bleeding, but there was also another set of teeth marks on the side of his throat. Not fangs, but teeth, as if a whole row of teeth had torn into him.

I was jolted out of the vision, pulling away from Ciara and gasping for breath. "It wasn't you, Ciara, it wasn't you!" I was yelling, lifting her up off the ground before I realized that the whole room had gone silent, and everyone was staring at us.

"You can't know that," she said, almost whispering.

"But I do! I saw it! It wasn't you!" I spun her around, oblivious to the silence in the room. "Ciara, I can make them see. I can show them what happened. Don't you understand? You don't have to leave."

"But I do. It's not just Wyatt and what happened. I can't go back, A. I can't go back to living within those walls. There is so much more in this world than just Sector C and what is trapped inside those walls. I'm part of *this* now, part of the Resistance. Maybe one person can't make a difference, but I know that if I'm with them..." she paused, glancing around at the others in the room, "...then I can at least be a part of the change."

"You can't leave me," I whispered. "We're sisters."

"And we always will be. Sisters by choice are sisters for life, remember?" she whispered back.

"No." I gently pushed her away just a little, and held her face between my hands. "No, you don't understand." I swallowed back the pain that was threatening to take me over. "We. Are. Sisters. Friends by chance, but sisters by blood."

"What?"

"I've been to the birthing center. I've seen our birth records. Mine and yours. I've seen our breeder's name, Mary, C20M103. I memorized it. My breeder and yours, she's the same."

She just looked at me, shaking her head.

"Don't you get it? That connection we've always felt—it's real. We're sisters, C. Twins. Actually triplets, but our brother…he didn't survive. You have to believe me, I'd never let them hurt you. You can't leave me. You have to stay and fight."

"I can't. I don't have that fight in me anymore, A." Her arms fell to her side, and her shoulders drooped. I was losing her.

"You look like her. Your fair skin and fiery red hair, you get that from her," I said, through silent tears. "I've seen her. She's beautiful, just like you." The tears were streaming down my face now, but I didn't care.

I had had a vision of our mother more than once. *"I'm your mom,"* she had told me, but I hadn't believed her. I hadn't known what to believe at the time, but I believed her now.

"I've seen her, Ciara. I've met her. You can't just leave, not now. You have to come—" I stopped myself. *What am I saying? I know it isn't safe for her. I* was being selfish, and I knew it. "I'm sorry. I just don't want to lose you," I admitted.

"I don't want to lose you either," she said.

"Then what do we do? Because, honestly, I'm out of ideas."

Jabari looked at Isaac, and got a nod. Jabari's steady gaze met mine, and his eyes began to glow with an amber light—his lion. When he spoke, his voice had deepened, and his words held power. "Zelina. The wastelands is not the desolate, treacherous place you have been led to believe. It is not overrun with monsters and misfits and outlaws. Yes, they are there but the truth is that they are only a small portion of the population out here. Indeed, it is the opposite. We have maintained this illusion for our own benefit and protection. The truth of the wastelands is so much more. Yes, it can be dangerous, but the true monsters—those in control— reside inside the sector walls, and not outside them. Or, at least those living out here are found only in small pockets, just outside the sector. That is why it is safer for us to get further away."

"But those men, the ones who tried to kill Ciara when I first found her. They—"

"They were scared, and why wouldn't they be? Most sector residents who venture out beyond the wall are security guards with two objectives: to kill anyone who gets too close to the wall or to capture anyone they find illegally within the sector limits. Our people—the outcasts of the sectors and the humans who have abandoned the alleged safety of the sectors—are not aggressive unless we have to be. Unless we are threatened. Yes, there are still dangers in the wastelands; I won't lie and tell you there aren't. There are many savages who do still live in the abandoned buildings around the sectors, not willing to join the Resistance or leave the places they were born into. But those of us who believe in the

Resistance, and the change we can bring, we live together in harmony, because we have discovered a secret." He paused, and another murmur spread through the large room.

"What kind of secret?" I asked.

Jabari looked to Isaac again, and again Isaac nodded. "It is the secret of our True Divine Potential, our birthright. We have finally become humble enough to reclaim our roots."

"I don't understand. Humble enough? Roots? What do you mean by divine potential?"

"It's a lot to take in, I know, and we probably don't have enough time to explain it all right now, but I will try to explain as much as I can." He studied my face, and I knew he was waiting for some indication that I would be willing to accept—or at least listen to—what he was about to tell me.

I nodded.

"Zelina, thousands of years ago, humans were powerful cosmic beings who thrived on this planet. The imbalance between life and nature that we know today didn't exist. There was a harmony—a unity—of mind, body, and nature. This accord existed throughout everything we did, and all that we were. Everyone, every man and every woman, was born with the powers of both lycanthropy and vampirism. We were one with nature, waiting only to awaken those powers within us."

I was mesmerized by his words, and felt currents of electricity flashing through my body as he spoke. It was as if he was telling me a story that I had always known, but had forgotten.

"What happened?" I asked. "Why did it change?"

"Slowly, the humans began to separate and explore outside of their communities. As they separated in physical distance, they lost their cohesion—their solidarity, their identity as a society. They began leaning on their individual uniqueness. Over centuries, they began to evolve differently. And although it isn't wrong to have distinct singular identities, the more people began to concentrate on their differences instead of what made them the same, the more conflict arose. This conflict resulted in a lowering of their overall lifeline vibration, and as they lowered their vibration, the earth became vulnerable. That vulnerability opened us up to becoming a host to other cosmic beings—beings that thrive on conflict, societal divergence, separateness, and chaos."

"The monsters," I said. I knew this. All that he was saying was like a song I'd forgotten I knew how to sing. I had composed this song.

"Yes," answered Isaac.

"And now we are back at the beginning, or at least closer than we have been in thousands of years. Humans have come full circle, and we are on the brink of regaining our lost unity, that cohesion that we once had. We are taking back our birthright. You've heard the rumors of the other sectors failing. Being brought down. That has been us." I glanced around the room, seeing those around me for what felt like the first time. Vampires, lycanthropes, and even humans—together—united.

"But, why? To what end?" I asked.

"The sectors were created with good intention, to help protect the population and limit the conflict across regions. But, they had no way of knowing that the *monsters*, as you called them, were already among those living in—even running—many of the sectors. The Resistance was born naturally, maybe out of fear, but also out of unity for a greater good. So many of us have united in what you know as the wastelands, but what we know as Dohiyi."

"Peace," I breathed.

He smiled. "Yes, Dohiyi means peace, which is what we are trying to bring. And we are so close to regaining what has been lost. We've been looking for the final element. The one who embodies all that we are, without the lust for division. The one who embodies every gift, and desires only peace."

"How will you know when you've found that person?" I asked.

They all stared at me in silence, as if they knew something that I didn't.

"Don't you see, Zelina? It's you."

"No."

"Yes," said Isaac. "You are the Bridge—you are the one foretold in the prophecies—"

"The prophecies," I echoed. It wasn't a question, but an understanding.

"But knowing it doesn't bring about the end of the monsters."

"The end of the monsters?" I asked.

"That is your destiny. To do it, you must live out the prophecy. Experience, life, and bad choices led us to our fallen state, and we must experience every instant that will bring us back to our highest vibration and return us to that powerful cosmic state that is our birthright."

This was a little too much for me. They were looking at me like I was some great answer, a cosmic solution. The same way Teagan had looked at me when she told me about the prophecies of the lioness's bloodline. The same way Haden had looked at me when he gave me the ancient book protecting the past, the present, and the future of the werewolves. But I didn't feel like the answer to anything. I felt like a living, breathing question. I was nervous, no, downright scared, and I could feel my heart racing in my chest. I needed to move. I needed space. I needed air.

Without warning, I pushed away from them and ran out of the room and down the hall. I found myself in a cold, dark corner, curled in a ball. It was quiet, perfectly quiet. After a few minutes I could feel the fear slowly fading away. I finally had an idea of what had been going on with me. The prophecies of the lycanthropes and now this, the Resistance sent to reveal the prophecies of the human race. Relief washed over me and I found myself once again face-to-face with Isaac. I hadn't left at all. "What do I do?" I asked with more confidence than I felt. *Do I want to hear this?*

Isaac faltered. "Zelina. You are the answer. We can't tell you what to do."

"What?" *Back to square one.* "You don't have a plan? What about the prophecy? Aren't there instructions?"

"Zelina…" Jabari took over from Isaac. "That's sector thinking. Rules, formulas, maps, prejudices—

small thinking. That isn't the way of the ancestors. That isn't our way any longer."

My mouth fell open. I snapped it shut. *Just great. I'm the Answer, and all I have are questions.*

Ciara came and put a hand on my shoulder. "Just be You, A. Wherever you are, whatever you do, Be You."

"That's not an answer! What does that even mean? Who else could I even be?" Beyond frustrated, I lashed out at my sister. "Why don't *you* do it? You're my twin—*you* be the Answer—*you* be the Bridge. I don't want to!"

She pulled away. "I'm going to Dohiyi. And I'll be doing my part there," she snapped, obviously irritated. Not at all a representation of the harmony and balance they were describing. Ciara sighed in frustration. "You always think too much, A. Just live."

"What? Where is that coming from, C?" It was a relief of sorts to snap back at her.

"Oh please. What about Merick? You kept him at arm's length for years, just because of the rules. You don't even know how to live!"

"Me? I don't know how to live? You lived in my shadow for years. Then, after Selection Week you abandoned the sector and took to the shadows out here in the wasteland. I barely got you to leave that disgusting little room without a fight."

"That's enough," Jabari said, stepping between us.

He looked back at me, holding my gaze. "Just be your best self in every situation. That's how you be You. You have to live with all of your gifts and abilities, and be You, not what they tell you to be. Simple."

Simple, right.

He turned away, and I felt the room begin to swirl. I was leaving my people, and feeling more alone than ever before. *This doesn't feel like unity,* I thought, as I moved on to another reality.

16

I awakened with a start, lying in a bed in another clinic room. My heart was racing, and I couldn't seem to get enough air. Even though I knew that logically, as a vampire, I didn't need it, suddenly breathing seemed like the most important thing in the world.

I heard muffled voices just outside the door. "What if she asks for them again? Ciara and the other one, the boy?"

"Merick." It was Amelia. Not Doctor Amelia— this one insists that she is a nurse. They look alike, and at first I couldn't tell the difference, aside from the way they dressed. But now I can hear it in their voices. Doctor Amelia is assertive and confident, whereas Nurse Amelia is soft-spoken, and almost seems timid at times.

"You play along, just like you have been," said Nurse Amelia.

Play along?

"But, he's not real. She made him up when she was three years old. He was just an imaginary friend. Before the accident he was all but gone. She had grown out of that phase, but now she's… Why is he back? I can't keep lying to her."

What is she talking about? Merick is real. I didn't make him up! I wanted to yell it, but I kept quiet and kept listening.

"He is real enough, and Ciara is there with her," Amelia said, echoing my thoughts.

Thank you. Wait, real enough? What does that—?

"He is real to her," she clarified. "She has lived with them in her head for years, and that's all that matters. What you need to focus on is that she is here. The fact that she has been experiencing periods of lucidity doesn't make them any less real to her. You just need to keep her talking, keep her focused in this world. Ask her about her friends if it will get her talking. The longer she talks to us, the longer she stays here and remains lucid, the more real *this* world will become to her. That's what's important right now. We can worry about all the other stuff later, after we know she's back for good."

Back for good? Back where?

"It's so hard. I thought it would be easier. I thought that if she ever woke up—snapped out of it long enough to see me—I thought she'd recognize me, that she'd remember. I just..."

"It's OK, Mary. We'll get her back."

Mary? Oh my stars.

"It's just... It's harder than I expected. Having her look at me but not recognize me. Not remember that I'm her mother. That empty stare she gives me, as if she wants to remember but just can't. I never would have thought *that* would be harder than watching her lie here day after day, unresponsive."

Unresponsive?

"Mary!" The shock in Amelia's voice even surprised me.

"I'm sorry, I'm so sorry. I didn't mean that. It's just so hard." Mary was crying now, and soon she was sobbing.

"It's OK, Mary. This is never easy. Just try to calm down. Mary. Mary? Mary!"

"Mary, Mary quite contrary..." I turned my head, and there she was, just beyond the end of my bed— the little girl in the yellow dress. And she wasn't alone. She was holding hands with a girl with chestnut brown hair and dark brown eyes. They were skipping in a circle, singing.

"...How does your garden grow?" Their happy, childish voices filled the room. "With silver bells, and cockleshells, and pretty maids all in a row."

"Follow me," called the little girl in yellow, and the two friends ran to a closet door and disappeared inside.

I got up and followed them, determined to get some answers.

I opened the door, but it wasn't a closet. *Of course not.* It was a long corridor, and the girls were already about twenty feet away, holding hands and giggling as they skipped away from me.

I closed the door behind me and followed.

"Wait, please," I called after them, but they didn't seem to hear me. "Stop! Where are you going? Let me come with you."

They stopped! They turned around and waited for me to catch up to them, and when I did it was the little girl in yellow who spoke. But first she smiled.

"Are you finally ready to talk?"

"Me?" I asked in surprise. "I'm the one who's been trying to find you."

"But you haven't been ready, not really. Not until now." She giggled, then turned to her companion. "This is going to be fun!"

"It's time?" the young brunette asked.

"It's time!" The little redhead turned back to me. "If you're really ready to talk, it means the change has already occurred."

"The change?" I wanted to ask if they were talking about my first moon cycle transformation, but how could they have known about that?

"Of course," she said, still giggling. "And now your beasts are awake," she said, not looking at me but at her friend.

"And our fangs have grown," they said simultaneously. They continued to giggle, as they turned back to me.

Taking my hand in hers, the little redhead in the yellow dress whispered, "And it also means you are ready for your present! Are you ready?"

"I… I don't know. I guess so."

The two little girls jumped up and down in excitement. They began humming a tune—it was a melody I had never heard, but it seemed so familiar I felt like I could sing along. Like the words were on the tip of my tongue just waiting to be sung. I could imagine a thousand voices singing this song, causing the very air to vibrate to its perfection.

Everything was happening so fast. My brain was scrambling to process it all, trying to make sense of everything. The next thing I knew, there was a noiseless explosion of light, and I was holding what seemed to be a sphere of light. It shimmered with a medley of colors that I cannot describe. There were colors of all shades and hues—colors that don't exist, at least not in my world!

The two little girls now stood motionless, silent, and…radiant. Their eyes reflected the same colors I held in my hands. I didn't know if I was mirroring them or if they were reacting to me—to the sphere—but in that moment I knew that we were somehow connected.

I'm not sure what I would have thought if I had been a witness to what was transpiring. Perhaps I would have run away in fear. But as I stood there watching the colors twist and twirl and glisten in my hands, all I could think was how utterly amazing it all was. I could feel my mind trying to make sense of it, of course, but even more than that I was surprised to find that I wasn't at all afraid. I wanted to know what it was and where it had come from, but at that point I couldn't form a question, much less ask one. I had been struggling so hard and for so long to understand what was happening to me, and why I kept shifting in and out of realities, that now I just let it go and focused on enjoying this incredible present. And a wondrous peace flowed over me and through me, and permeated every part of me. Tears of joy filled my eyes.

The little girls resumed their happy jumping up and down. They clapped their hands in delight. I realized that I had been in some kind of a daze

"What is this?" I whispered, still not wanting to take my eyes off the swirling lights.

"It is your activation. Can't you feel it?" the little redhead asked.

"What do you mean, my activation?"

"With this you hold the record of all human life: the beginning and the end. You are the seer, the traveler," she explained.

"Seer..." I repeated. "I've heard that word before."

"Of course you have. Your guide already introduced it to you. You've known what you are, even if you didn't fully understand it. Now you've been granted access to all the power you hold."

"My guide? Who is that?"

"Your guide has come to you in many forms. One of the lost...a castaway from the wastelands...a mentor...a trusted teacher...even a sibling, though your conscious self might not recognize him as such."

Him? I wondered. They smiled, sharing a quick glance, and I wondered if they had heard my thought.

"Let's pretend I believe you, and I really am a seer... Is that why I was able to recognize the vision stone? Is that why I found it."

"You didn't find it. It found you."

I thought about that for a minute. I had probably passed by it a hundred times over the years. Why had I noticed it that day, what had changed? Maybe she was right; maybe it had found me. Maybe it had been waiting for me to be ready.

"Then what is a traveler?"

They both looked at me, heads tilted to the side is if they were studying me. "You already know," said the little redhead.

"I…" *Do I already know?* I wondered. "Is that how I'm here? You mean my visions?"

The quieter little brunette put her hands around mine, and the orb faded away. "You are the Bridge across time. You connect the past, the present, and the future. Not only do you exist here in this hospital, you are also there, in Sector C far into the future."

This sounds a lot like what Jabari was trying to explain. Yet now, somehow, it feels…right, like they were filling in the empty spaces of a puzzle.

In that moment, I believed what she was saying. I believed I was the Bridge between what we were, what we are, and what we could be again.

"You, and others like you, exist in an extra-dimensional plane of existence," she continued.

"Wait," I said, stopping her. "An extra-dimensional…what?"

"An extra-dimensional plane of existence. Think of it like layered maps, one on top of the other. Only the maps are layers of time. As a traveler, you have the power—the gift—of traveling from one map to another, one timeline to another. Right now, by sleeping here in the timeline you were born to, but living there in the future, you are able to influence the future, essentially providing humanity with a better option. If you can bring the powerful vampires and lycanthropes together with the humans and reach harmony, the humans here will never have to experience the great war that divided them in the first place. The war that created the chaos and separation that led to the existence of Sector C—of all the sectors. If you can unite the future beings, there will never be a need for the division in the past!"

"But, how can changing the future change the past?" I asked.

"Think of time like a circle. The past affects the present. the present affects the future, AND the future affects the past. It isn't a beginning a middle and an end. They say that history is doomed to repeat itself, but in reality, history is constantly changing." She let go of my hands and stepped back. "Reach into your heart, and you'll know it's true."

"I…" She was right, I did know it was true. What I didn't know was how to make sense of it all.

"Wait… You said me and 'others like me'— what others?"

"I think you know that too," she said. "Micah, for one. He had the gift of travel. Micah saw your future and your past."

"Are there others?"

"There are, but you won't meet them all. There are others in your world, spread across the sectors. There are others still, in different timelines, trying to bring about a change in their own worlds, in their own times. Their changes can affect your past, even your future, just as yours can affect theirs."

The idea that there could be people spread across space and time, all working toward a common future, seemed impossible.

The little girls each took one of my hands, and we formed a circle. The orb reappeared, floating in front of us. Basking in its transcendent glow, I felt the truth in what the girls had said. I still didn't know what it meant, exactly, or even what I would do next or where I would *be* next, but as I gazed at the swirling lights of this present I had been given, I knew that it was the key to my life's purpose, my mission. And I knew I was capable of accomplishing that mission. It is what I was made for. This I knew, with every ounce of my being.

We lowered our hands, and the orb slowly drifted closer to me. I reached out my palms, and it floated into them and settled there for a few moments before it slowly melted away. I felt its warmth—first in my palms, and then slowly moving up my arms and intensifying as it spread through the rest of my body. It didn't take long, and when the feeling faded I missed it. I looked down at the girls, who smiled up at me.

"So, who are you two?" I asked. "Are you angels?"

They smiled. "No, we're not angels, silly," said the cute brunette. "I am you. I'm your present, your past, and," she smiled, "your future."

"My future?"

Nodding, her smile grew. "Your future in Dohiyi, years into the future and a lifetime away."

"And you?" I asked the redhead I had been pursuing through so many visions.

"I am your heart. Your sister. I am Ciara. The Ciara you knew and loved and lost in your past, the soul of the Ciara you long to save in your present, and the Ciara you will once again be reunited with in your future."

"Lost?"

"That is for another time. You're not ready yet."

I didn't know what to say. I just stood there, speechless, as the weight of her words sank in. *'You're not ready yet'* told me there was more to her existence, but I was afraid to ask. Afraid to know the truth.

The brunette—the little mini-me—piped up again. "We are holding a space in time so that you can learn to bridge the divide between the past, the present, and the future. We will stay as long as you need. Until you are fully aware and comfortable in maneuvering through all of the planes of your existence."

"All of them?" I asked.

They giggled, together. "There is no limit to where—or when—you can go. The only limit is you."

"But how—?"

"Instinct. It will take time. It will take practice. But you can control your travels—your visions, as you call them."

It *had* seemed that I had guided my last two visions, but wasn't sure I believed that.

As if reading my mind, she said, "Don't focus on what seems impossible. Believe you can and you will."

I had so many questions I wasn't sure where to start. *How? Why? Who?* "And the others? Mary—my mother? Amelia?" I asked. "What about the two of them? Why are they both here, and there in Sector C?"

The girls looked at each other meaningfully. Young Ciara spoke first. "They are in both worlds, as are many others you have yet to discover. They play their roles, but unlike you they are asleep to the truth, as if they have amnesia, but they aren't meant to wake up. Not like you."

"Why are they asleep?"

"Because that is how the universe works. Past lives stay in the past, and our future existences remain a mystery. They exist in both worlds, having gotten from one life to the next the way most do, through life and death. Through reincarnation."

"We learned a little about that in our classes," I said.

"Their energy signatures remain constant from one life to the next. They will never know how important they are to your journey. Only you can know that, now that you contain the knowledge of the record of life."

"I don't feel like I know anything more than I did before, except maybe…"

"What?" they asked, simultaneously.

"Except that, somehow, this feels right."

"Zelina, most people don't even believe in past lives, let alone get to experience both past and future lives all at the same time. Only a tiny percentage of the population is granted the gift of seeing into the past or into the future, and society usually scoffs at their abilities, calling them imposters—fakes—scam artists—frauds," said young Zelina.

I was amazed at how profound and insightful they were. They didn't seem like children, and yet they were.

"Very few are given the gift of living without the boundaries of time," young Zelina continued.

"But how—?"

"Close your eyes."

I did.

"Now picture a time when you were happy. The happiest you've ever been."

"That's easy, I was—"

"Don't tell me," she said, cutting me off. "Just think about it. What did you hear? What did you smell? Who was with you? Was it warm? Was it cold? What were you wearing?"

I did as she instructed, and when I opened my eyes I was there, on the selection course, sitting at the top of the warp wall with Merick. He smelled like soap, as if he had just gotten out of the shower. I could hear the rustling of leaves in the wind, and the chirping of birds in the treetops. I felt his hand gently brush against mine.

Then young Zelina's voice came again. "Now think of a time when you were nervous."

I was standing face-to-face with Merick, though at the time I knew him as M126, and we were in the girls bathroom just down the hall from Professor Kade's class where we were about to take our Sector History class prep exam.

"Um, you know I can't be in here, right?" he said.

"Yeah, I know." We stood there, just staring at each other.

"So, what am I doing here? I mean, clearly I don't mean anything to you, so—"

I kissed him, and when I opened my eyes I was back in the hall with the two little girls. "Oh," I said.

"Think bigger, dig deeper," said young Zelina.

"Deeper?"

"You're focusing only on your recent experiences. You need to pull from deeper in your memories, deeper in your soul. I want you to pull from this life, the life you had before you ended up in the hospital. Pull from your past lives," she urged.

"I can't."

"You can."

"I don't know how."

"TRY!" young Ciara snapped. She was suddenly fiery, just like the Ciara I had grown up with in Sector C. Other than the red hair, it was the first real resemblance I had seen.

I closed my eyes, pushing away the memories of Sector C, pushing away the visions I had had in the hospital, trying to empty my mind. I opened my eyes, gasping for breath. I was holding on to one of the posts of a large four-poster bed.

"Stand still, Zelina," someone said from somewhere behind me. "Now exhale." Suddenly my body felt like it was in a vice. When I looked down there was a garment—a corset—cinched tightly around my torso.

"I... can't... breathe."

"You're fine," she said, sounding slightly annoyed. She finished tying the laces and patted my back. "Now finish getting dressed and come downstairs to greet our guests." I turned around just in time to see Mary before she turned and left, closing the door behind her.

On the bed was a gown like nothing I had ever seen. It was pale blue with white flower accents, and layers and layers of lace. I struggled into it, and after I clasped the last hook-and-eye of the front opening, I stood in front of the full-length mirror, staring in awe. Never in my wildest dreams had I imagined such a garment. Then I noticed it, the light glistened off a small silver cross hanging from a chain around my neck.

"It's beautiful," I said, as I reached for the charm.

"Zelina?"

"What?" I asked, spinning toward the door, but the room was gone, and the dress and necklace with it. I was back in the hallway, with young Ciara and young Zelina. They were smiling up at me.

"You see!" said young Ciara. "It worked. You have the power to control your travels. It only takes practice."

I wasn't so sure it was me, and not their assistance, that had made it happen, but she was right, it had worked.

It was a lot of information to take in all at once, and I was starting to feel lightheaded. I reached for the wall, and they moved to catch me, helping me ease slowly to the ground. "What happens next?" I asked.

"You will continue to travel the worlds, and experience life as it changes around you. Your guide in the past, the 21st century, will help to keep your connection open and strong. We will be here too, always around, watching, ready to help if needed."

"And the others?" I asked.

"They will remain asleep, aware of only the world they are residing in. Their timeline exists only on the dimensional plane in which you meet them."

"That doesn't seem fair. I can't do all this on my own."

"You're not alone. We are with you, and there are others. Others who also believe in the prophecy."

The prophecy, I thought to myself. "Jabari and Isaac?"

"Yes. And the others who follow the Resistance."

"How do they fit into all of this?"

"They believe. Because they believe, their actions will help to slowly change the way others think. They will help, but in a different way. Their place is in the wastelands, bringing together those who are seeking something more than just to exist. Your place is within the sector, uniting the vampires and the lycanthropes, and working to expel the monsters, those who would threaten your way of life and the rebirth of humanity."

I watched as their figures began to fade in and out, like a light flickering during a storm. "And Ciara? She seems to know something," I said. Her comment about Merick had left a bitter taste in my mouth.

"She knows in theory, which is good. That will help you…" they faded in and out again.

"Wait, I have more questions. How are you so young? If you're my future, does that mean—"

"Goodbye, Zelina," they said, smiling. I heard their giggles in the distance as they faded away.

"Does that mean I die?" I asked the empty space around me.

I leaned back, resting my head against the wall. The silence was deafening, and yet comforting at the same time. I couldn't recall a time when I had ever felt so alone, so scared, and so content all at once. That was when I realized I had been clutching a small crumpled piece of paper in the palm of my hand.

*You'll never believe what's been going
on. I can't wait to tell you all about it.*
	*P.S. We love you. You've got a lot of
people praying for you out here.*

It was written in Uma's swirly handwriting. I re-read it multiple times, even though I knew what it said—what it should have said. But it was wrong. Somehow, it was wrong. I couldn't pinpoint the inconsistency—the inaccuracy. And then I did.
	Praying for me? I thought, and I found myself travelling back to my other life.

17

When I opened my eyes, I was sitting on my bed in Iris's apartment, and the first thing I noticed was a tingling sensation on my upper arm. I looked and saw a tattoo—a sphere of swirling colors just under the surface of my skin.

My first order of business was to find Merick and Haden. When we parted, we were all on fact-finding missions—I to find Uma, and Merick promising that he and Haden would find more information about the prophecy. With what I knew now about my relationship to Ciara, and my multi-dimensional existences, I was even more curious and excited to see what they had discovered. However, I found that the strength and confidence I had felt while talking with the two young girls had dissolved. Traveling across time? Unifying the races? A bleak feeling of hopelessness hit me full force.

I have Merick, Haden and his pack; I have an assorted group of lycanthropes, vampires, and humans living just beyond the wall in the wastelands, I mean Dohiyi; and I have a group of friends who existed in both times, yet have no memory of it. It's not nothing. But unification? I was doubtful, to say the least.

It seemed like ages had passed since I had found Uma's note where Merick had left it on my pillow, but I was still clutching it in my fist. I opened it again slowly...

> *A ~ You'll never believe what I've discovered. We need to talk. This is huge.*
> *~ U*
> *P.S. Good luck with the moon cycle. You've got a lot of people rooting for you out here.*

What? It had said 'praying' the last time I had read it, not 'rooting.' Well, either way, I would take all the help I could get at this point. In all honesty, I think I was a little relieved to see Uma's original note. So much had happened—changed—in a short period of time, I was thankful for a small piece of consistency.

"Merick?" I whispered, "Haden?" When there was no response, I tried mind-speak. Still nothing.

It was dark outside, and I wasn't sure what time it was or even what day, but it was after curfew, I knew that much. I could hear the distant screams that had so often filled me with fear during my life as a selection student.

But, I'm not a selection student any more, I reminded myself, *I am the Bridge between time. A powerful traveler with a cool tattoo,* I added with a smile. Besides, I knew now that the screams were rarely from attacks, although they did happen. More often than not though, the vampires would play games with willing donors. The donors would be set loose in the woods and given a head start before the vampires would hunt them down. The object wasn't to kill them. It wasn't even to scare them, although that happened more often than not. It was more an exercise designed to keep the vampires' hunting skills sharp. I'm sure the donors got something out of it too, although I can't for the life of me imagine what that would be. Maybe a sense of excitement or adventure, maybe the thrill of the chase was just as fun for them as it was for the hunters. Suddenly I saw it for what it was: chaos disguised as normal behavior, designed to keep us small and divided.

The fact of the matter was, I didn't need to be scared anymore. Sure, Remy, William, and even Haden would tell me differently, but I wasn't a child and this was the world I lived in. If I was going to try and make change, I couldn't be afraid to get out there in the thick of it.

I changed my clothes and called to Iris. "Iris, are you here?"

"In the kitchen. Are you hungry?" she called back. I headed toward the stairs. "You've been up there a long time. I didn't want to bother..." she stopped when I stepped into the kitchen. "You're back in all black," she said, with a hint of disappointment in her voice.

"Yup." I was wearing the black jogging pants, black running shoes, and the black hoodie that I had worn the night I left Sector C to find Ciara, although Iris didn't know that.

"You look like you're going out. You know it's already 9:30. Were you planning—?"

"I know, curfew. But that doesn't really apply to me anymore, right?"

Reluctantly, she answered, "No. No, of course not. It's just—"

"It's just a walk, or maybe a short run. I won't be gone long, I promise. I'm just feeling a little antsy in here."

She turned back to the stove and flipped the steak she had been cooking. "It's rare, just how you like it. Don't you want to eat before you go?"

I didn't. I *really* didn't. I just needed to be outside. I needed to clear my head. I needed to find Merick and Haden and tell them what had happened—what I had seen and learned.

"You think I can just warm it up when I get back?" I asked. "I'm really not hungry right now," I added, to reassure her.

She was already plating the steak, along with a large baked potato and two dinner rolls. "Sure, no problem," she said, her shoulders slouching slightly forward as she grabbed another plate and flipped it over, covering the neatly prepared dinner. She slid them into the microwave. "It will be here when you're ready." She was smiling hopefully when she turned around. "Did you want company? For your walk, I mean."

No.

"I'm good. Besides, I'm assuming when I go in the living room either Haden or William will be waiting, right?"

Please be Haden. Please be Haden.

"William."

"Yeah, I thought so."

Just my luck, I thought to myself. *Why couldn't it have been Haden?* But I already knew the answer; it was William's turn to babysit me.

"Can you do me a favor?" I asked. "Nothing big, just ask him to give me a little space? I get that he has to follow me. It's his job. I just need a little alone time, to think."

She leaned across the counter and whispered, "How about you eat the steak and then I give you a five-minute head start?"

"Seriously?" I asked, wondering if it was just a ploy to make me stay. Then I realized it sounded an awful lot like the vampire-donor game, but I'd take the head start anyway.

"Seriously," she answered.

"Deal."

She snatched the plate out of the microwave and set it on the counter in front of me along with a fork, a knife, and a tall bottle of blood.

I ate the steak, the potato, and the rolls, and drank two bottles of blood. Turns out I was hungrier than I had thought. When I finished, and my plate was cleaned and put away, Iris pulled me aside. "You've got five minutes. William is an excellent tracker. It won't take him long to find you." She winked, and nudged me toward the living room, and I realized it was exactly like the vampire-donor game. And I had a sneaking suspicion that she was enjoying it almost as much as if she were playing the game herself. I heard her turn to William and ask, "William? Can you come in here for a minute, please?"

He glanced my way, and I casually took a seat in the chair closest to the door as he followed Iris into the kitchen. "Is everything OK?" he asked.

"Yeah, I just needed to ask you something. Do you know if Remy…?" I didn't hear the rest of what she had said, because I had slipped out the front door. I was going to take full advantage of my five-minute lead.

Instead of heading out to the street through the front door, I turned the other way and headed out the back door. I knew exactly where I was going. Merick hadn't been there when I had woken up, and I needed to talk to him. His place wasn't far, but I had to make sure William wasn't able to follow me, so I stayed off the main streets as much as I could. When I got to Merick's place, the door was unlocked, but Merick was gone.

I couldn't wait around. I knew William wouldn't be far behind, so I left a note under Merick's pillow, hoping he'd find it before going to bed.

M ~ Meet me at our place, 23:00.

I didn't know when Merick would be back, but meeting at 23:00 gave him a little more than an hour. I didn't sign my name, or even my initial. He would know it was from me, and I didn't need to give William any extra help.

In the meantime, I helped myself to a few of the *toys* he kept in a crate at the end of his bed. I strapped a silver dagger to my thigh, wrapped a silver garret bracelet around my wrist, and put a wooden stake up each of the sleeves of my jacket. You just never know what you might need. He had a couple of guns in the crate too, but I skipped over those. I had never liked guns. They seem like cheating.

"Professor Gunner made you the vampire in that scenario and H the lycanthrope! Why did you take a stake onto the mat?" Ciara had once asked me, while in training.

At the time, I hadn't really known why I had grabbed the stake. She was right, If H was a lycanthrope a stake wouldn't have killed him. It might have slowed him down, but not for long. To be fair, I had also grabbed a knife. However, in my current situation things were different. Being both a vampire and a lycanthrope, I wasn't sure which weapons could kill me. Maybe none of them, but I had to assume they all could. I also had to assume there were people on both sides of the line who didn't care too much about what I was, which meant I could find myself fighting both vampires and lycanthropes.

"Maybe practicing with multiple weapons wasn't such a bad idea, huh C?" I asked out loud to the empty apartment.

Just before I closed the crate, I noticed a small white envelope near the bottom. Curious, I picked it up. Inscribed on the front, in my own handwriting, was my name, but I didn't remember writing it. The envelope had already been torn open, so I looked inside, where I found a small silver cross. I knew the cross as a historical religious symbol. In Sector C, and as far as I know throughout all of the sectors, religion isn't practiced or recognized. The Council abolished all religious practices after the war of 2082. Because the Council doesn't approve of organized religions, all I know about them is what I've read in books. Crosses were supposedly holy objects: sacred items blessed by *God* himself. We had been taught that all holy objects had been destroyed after the war. *How had Merick gotten hold of a silver cross?* I wondered. Even more importantly, *why was my name written on the envelope in my own handwriting?*

If the folklore was right, I knew that I shouldn't even be able to touch a cross. I was a vampire, after all, and unholy in the eyes of God. *If there even ever was a God,* I thought to myself. I stared at the shiny silver cross there in the envelope. It seemed so delicate.

It is pretty, I thought. Then a memory flashed through my mind. A tight corset, a beautiful gown, and a shiny silver cross. "It was mine," I said aloud, before I could stop myself.

I tipped the envelope over, hesitantly, allowing the cross to fall gently into the palm of my hand. If I'm honest, I was a little scared, half thinking that it actually might burn me. But nothing happened.

Just folklore, I thought, thankful. *Where in the world could Merick have possibly gotten this?*

I unclasped the silver necklace Merick had given me and slid the cross onto it, next to my vision stone. It was long enough for the cross and the stone to fall just below the collar of my shirt. I folded the envelope and shoved it in my pocket. I'd ask Merick about it when I saw him. If he wanted it back, I would certainly give it to him, but it did have my name on the envelope and a tingling sensation radiated through my tattoo reassuring me that I needed the cross.

I didn't want to leave the same way I had come in, because William might already be waiting in the hall, so I slid out the back window. The park was only thirty yards from the back of Merick's apartment complex, and I made it there in no time, taking shelter under the trees.

With almost an hour left before I was supposed to meet Merick, waiting outside his apartment and staring up at his window wasn't going to work. I needed to stay active—distracted. I headed into the woods beyond the park—still part of the lycanthrope quarters. I didn't start out with that intention, but something was drawing me off the path and away from the lights that were scattered throughout the park. Maybe it was instinct telling me William would have a harder time finding me if I was in the woods, or maybe it was something else. Either way, I soon found myself standing outside the deserted cabin near the wall.

"Stay at least twenty yards out at all times," Merick had instructed me the last time we were there. But it hadn't really been Merick. It had been Councilman Ash. I knew that now.

I made my way around to the back of the cabin. I couldn't hear or smell anyone inside. There was no heartbeat, no movement. The windows were boarded up. *That's new,* I thought. I tried the door, but it was locked. Someone had been there since Merick and me—probably Ash, covering his tracks.

I grasped the doorknob and tried to focus my energy—tried to see who had been here—but it didn't work. As much as I wanted it, I couldn't force a vision. They either came or they didn't. Why they would happen sometimes and not others I still didn't understand.

"What are you doing here?" said a deep and commanding voice from behind me. I knew it wasn't William.

I whipped around, pushing my back against the door to see who it was. It was one of the internal security guards, which meant he worked for Serenity.

Despite her name, Serenity was one of the meanest, most conniving vampires in Sector C. She was pure evil, and she had had it out for me since before Selection Week. She had even gone so far as to have one of my classmates, Nash, spy on me.

The guard was standing about fifteen feet away, just watching me. Waiting.

Damn it.

He was dressed in all black. Vampire. *Maybe I could use that to my advantage.* The hood of my sweatshirt cast a dark shadow across my face. *Maybe he hasn't recognized me.*

"I said, what are you doing here?" he asked again.

"I... Nothing. I was just taking a walk and found this old place. I was just curious." I played the naive young vampire, hoping he wouldn't figure out who I really was. If he didn't get too close, he might not smell my wolf...my lion.

"In the woods?"

"Yes."

"This late at night?" He took a step forward with each question, slowly closing the gap between us.

"Yes."

"All by yourself?"

OK, maybe coming out here wasn't the smartest decision.

"No," I said, even surprising myself.

He looked around, scanning the trees behind him. "I don't know, it sure does seem like you're all alone out here," he said. He raised his head, sniffing the air around him, and a smile crept across his face.

What is he doing? We're both vampires. We're on the same side, I screamed in my head.

"Little girl like you, all alone in the woods—"

"I'm *not* a little girl," I said.

"No, you are not. I know exactly who, or should I say *what,* you are," he said, stressing the word *what.* "Lost out here in lycanthrope territory... well... anything could happen, and who do you think they'd blame? Not me. I'm internal security, here for your protection." He laughed. Not a guttural laugh that comes after a funny joke, but a laugh that stems from a place of pure evil. Yup, Serenity had taught him well.

I straightened my back, stood a little taller, and took a deep breath. "This isn't a game. I get it, you're a big, strong vampire. I'm not willing prey," I said.

"I sure hope not," he said, smiling.

OK, so not just like the vampire/donor game.

I placed my hands against the door behind my back, and pushed off toward him, sliding the wooden stakes out of my sleeves and into my hands as I went. I stopped only a couple of feet in front of him. "Did she send you?"

"She?" he asked, genuinely confused.

"Councilman Serenity." I knew Councilman Serenity didn't like me; she had never even tried to hide it. But I hadn't seen or heard from her or Nash in weeks. I had almost thought she had dropped her vendetta. Maybe I was wrong.

He laughed again. "No. No, she didn't send me. But you can trust me when I say that she won't be disappointed when she hears about how I found you—mutilated by the savage lycanthropes who couldn't stand to have you living among them any longer."

"You'd frame them? Why?"

He cocked his head to the side, studying me. "You're so naive. I remember being young like you. You've been *awake* all of a minute, and you think you know how the world works, don't you? Well, I'm sorry to tell you, but you're wrong. Everything you think, everything you believe—it's wrong." He took another step forward.

"Why don't you educate me then?" I said, straight-arming him in the chest. "I might be new to the game, but like you said, I am *awake* now. What am I missing?"

"You are missing the fact that some factions *like* the chaos, and even thrive because of it. Some monsters need the animosity among the races—they feed off the hatred and the hostility in order to exist. And…" He drew himself up, and his face darkened and contorted into a monstrous mask of human and animal and evilness. He wasn't a lycanthrope, but he wasn't like any other vampire I had ever known. "I am one of those monsters!"

He lunged for me, clawing at me. I managed to turn away, falling to the ground just in time, as he ripped the sleeve of my sweatshirt off. I scrambled to my feet and was about to run when I saw the color drain from his face. He was paralyzed. His eyes filled with panic and disbelief as he saw the tattoo on my arm pulse to life.

"No. Impossible," he growled. "You can't possibly have the Knowledge of Existence."

"Until others have accepted you, you're in danger," Sector Leader Remy had warned me. *"You don't know the monsters of our world."* I hadn't understood at the time, but in that moment, I realized that he had been right. Although I didn't like the idea of William shadowing me everywhere, right then I'd have given anything to have him at my side.

"Well then, I guess we should get on with it," I said. I was trying for humor to disguise the fact that I was freaking out to be standing in front of one of the monsters Remy had warned me about, the monsters Jabari had told me about, the monsters I had heard nightmarish tales about all my life. They weren't just in the wastelands, which is what we had been taught as students. Maybe there weren't any monsters in the wastelands at all. The more I learned, the more it seemed that everything we had been taught about the wastelands was a lie, a deception to keep the chaos within the sector walls, where the monsters roamed free.

He smiled again, and this time he let his fangs down: a row of jagged fangs all across the top row of his teeth. Not normal vampire fangs, but fangs just like the grotesque overgrown fangs of the man I had seen in a vision not long ago. That man had been looking for Ciara, but this man—this monster—was happy enough to have found me. I could have screamed, but no one would have heard me that far out in the woods. No, I only had one choice. I had to fight.

He came at me straight from the front, the way most people fight, but I'm not most people. I spun left, swinging the stake out at my side and just barely missed his lungs. He stood up and laughed.

"My, my, my, you are a feisty one. This should be fun."

I didn't wait for him to attack again. I made my move, bouncing back to my feet and hurling myself forward, spinning in the air and striking him in the jaw with my right foot. He was thrown back, off balance, and probably a little shocked, but it didn't knock him over. He turned back to me, wiped the blood off the side of his mouth with the back of his hand and licked it clean. The smell drifted through the air, and my fangs came down instinctively.

"Oh, look at you with your big girl teeth. You ready to really fight now, or are you still warming up?"

Looking back, I could have said so many things. Bring it on, show me what you've got, do your worst. But no, I'm just not that witty. Those are things Ciara would have said, or even Merick. Me? I said, "Sure."

He went low, which actually surprised me. He grabbed hold of my legs and pulled me to the ground. I lost one of the stakes as I fell, but I still had the other one in my left hand. He was nearly on top of me, pinning my legs to the cold ground and reaching for my arm, as I swung out with the stake. This time I made contact. The wooden tip pushed through the thick cloth of his security gear, and I heard it tear through his skin. He pulled back, letting go of my legs.

He stood hunched over, one hand on his knee and the other on his chest where the stake had almost pierced his heart.

His eyes narrowed as he glared down at me. "You think you're smart?"

I didn't answer.

"That was a stupid move, little girl."

I had gotten to him. I scrambled backward and got to my feet, grabbing the fallen stake as I stood up. Fully armed again, I stood there face-to-face with a monster who could probably easily have killed any other vampire he wanted, but it wasn't them he wanted. He wanted me.

I channeled Ciara—the bravery she had always shown on the mat, the way she would stand up to anyone without fear. "I don't want to hurt you," I said. I was being honest. I didn't *want* to hurt him. I didn't want to hurt anyone. But that didn't mean I wouldn't hurt him if he came after me.

"Well, I can't say the same."

He came.

After that, everything happened so quickly that I'm not exactly sure how it transpired. I dived right and rolled to my knees just as he hit the ground and rolled onto his back. I turned and stabbed the stakes directly into his chest and stomach. I hadn't hit his heart, but he was down, and in a lot of pain. My fangs were already out, and I leaned in, pushing the stakes deeper, and I sank my fangs into the soft skin of his throat. His hands gripped my sides as he tried to push me off of him, writhing under the weight of me now that I was fully on top of him.

Then the struggling stopped, his arms fell to his sides, and I backed away from his lifeless body, watching, waiting for him to move again. I tried to speak, but nothing would come. My throat burned, but it wasn't hunger. When I looked down at my hands, they were gone. In their place, were paws covered in thick golden fur. I didn't remember shifting. I shouldn't have been able to shift at all outside of the moon cycle.

The smell of blood was all over him, and when I looked more closely I realized that his throat was completely torn out...mutilated. There were large gashes in the clothing across his chest and abdomen and blood had already started to seep through, soaking his shirt.

What have I done?

18

Breathe. Just breathe, I told myself. I was pacing, circling his body and trying to figure out what to do. I didn't even know his name. I couldn't tell anyone even if I wanted to. Besides, if the Council found out I had murdered one of their guards, banishment as a punishment wouldn't even be an option.

I had shifted back, but my clothes were ruined, and I was covered in that clear, sticky goo, not to mention blood. I couldn't go back to Iris's. Her place was too exposed. I could try Merick's place, but the chances of getting in again without anyone noticing me were pretty slim. Especially since I was naked.

Just then, my alert senses picked up movement. *Not William, not now.* I groaned inwardly. I may have just killed my first (and please, only!) monster, but I was still me, and incapable of hurting anyone innocent. If William found me here I would simply have to face the music and go where he led.

Then I smelled them: Haden and Merick. *Finally,* I thought. *Merick must have gotten my note, but why would he come here,* I wondered. *I told him to meet me at the selection course.*

The two men came into view, and I quickly put myself between them and the body. I opened my mouth to explain, only to get a quick shake of the head from Haden.

"How did you find me?" I asked Merick, using mind-speak.

"When you weren't at the course, Haden and I got worried. We stopped by Iris's, but she said you were out for a walk. This was the only other place I knew to check."

"Well, I'm glad you did," I said, as I slowly stepped away from the body.

"Oh, my stars. A, what is that...thing?" Merick asked in shock, gesturing toward the bloody form on the ground.

"Monster, I think. I thought he was a vampire, at first. Maybe he is, but I'm not sure."

Haden was circling the body, trying to make sense of the mess. Then he gave a start, and looked up. His eyes widened, and I knew he had picked up on our mind-speak. He eyed Merick curiously.

"Well this will help things," he mind-spoke drily. He looked at me, *"Alphas and Betas can often mind-speak, but only with each other. I'm not sure what that means about Merick..."*

"I..." What I wanted to say was that it made perfect sense to me. Merick was my equivalent of a Luna. But I stopped myself. I wasn't sure how Haden would react. I had thought that was clear to him already, but maybe not.

"Merick, you see what I see?" Haden asked.

"Yeah. I'm guessing he's not the only one that's made it inside the walls, unless..."

"Unless he was already here." They exchanged a look I couldn't read.

I intercepted their thoughts. *"I'm not too concerned with how many of these guys there are in here right now. I think we have more immediate problems at the moment,"*

"Right," Haden responded.

I had gotten myself into a mess, and now with both of them there, they were involved as well. I knew I needed to protect them, but I wasn't sure how to do that. The only place I knew of where none of the sector residents would be up or out so late at night was the selection student quarters. Even the guards weren't allowed in there after curfew. It was against sector regulations for any resident to go into the student quarters during curfew hours unless there was an emergency, and a caregiver or member of the medical staff was needed, so I knew it would be safe there. Safer than anywhere else, at least.

I closed my eyes, trying to visualize the fastest, most shielded route to the selection student quarters. This wasn't a super power I had gained as a vampire or a lycanthrope, I had just memorized the sector maps. A good memory was something I'd had since I was young.

I knew that we could either go the long way, around the edge of the sector following the wall and staying hidden by the cover of the trees, or we could go the short way through the selection course. However, in order to get to the selection course, we would have to cross through the lycanthrope quarters. I could try teleportation, but I hadn't mastered controlling my visions or my astral projections: I wasn't confident I could teleport myself there, let alone get Merick and Haden there with me. Nope, the wall was the safest route.

"Any ideas on what to do with…" Merick paused, *"the body?"*

"We leave it. Right now, we need to get to the selection student quarters," I said, taking Haden and Merick by surprise.

"What? No!" Haden protested.

"It's the safest place to go. No one would think to look for us there and I need to clean up before I can go back to Iris's apartment."

I could see him thinking, trying to process the situation. *"Your scent is all over the body. Someone needs to stay behind to clean this up, make it look like he had been ambushed. It can't look like a single lycanthrope took him down,"* he argued.

"I'll do it," Merick offered.

"No, you go with Zelina. I'll take care of the body." Then he grabbed Merick's arm and pulled him so close their faces were only inches apart. "You keep her safe," he whispered, and beneath his words was a warning, a deep growl coming from his wolf.

I could feel mine responding, stirring just beneath the surface. *"Let him go,"* I said to Haden alone, and he did.

I gathered up my ruined clothing—I couldn't leave anything behind that might incriminate me—and Merick took off his sweatshirt and handed it to me. He had a tight blue t-shirt on that hugged the muscles of his arms and chest. *Has he grown?* I wondered.

"A, you are coming, right?" he asked, and I quickly pulled his sweatshirt over my head and we took off into the woods toward the wall, while Haden shouldered the body and headed off in the opposite direction. I didn't know what he planned to do with the body, but I trusted him.

I took Merick's hand in mine, not wanting to let him go, but knowing I had to. "You know where we are, right?" I asked, after Haden was far enough away that I was sure he couldn't hear us.

"Yeah. That's the old cabin where we—"

"Right. So, I need you to do me a favor," I said, cutting him off.

"Anything."

"You know where we are, so I need you to find your way back to your apartment, get inside, and lock the door. You can't be caught out here with me."

"Zelina, I'm not leaving you," he said, pulling me closer. He leaned down, his lips only inches away from mine, and I could feel the warmth of his breath on mine. "I—"

"M," I said, stopping him, but he didn't give me a chance to finish my thought.

He kissed me. It was soft at first. I dropped the ruined clothes and wrapped my arms around him. His hair was soft in my hands, and he tasted like sweet honey. I could have gotten lost in his arms, but the reality of where we were—what was happening— finally came back to me.

"M, please stop," I said.

He looked down at me, eyes wide. "Did I hurt you?"

"No. No, you didn't hurt me." I could feel myself blushing as a rush of heat ran to my face. He must have noticed it too. He took it as a sign to continue, leaning in and pulling me tight against his body. I could feel the slime that covered me wiping off onto the inside of his sweatshirt. "M..."

"I love you, A."

"M, I..." *No,* I scolded myself. *This isn't the time for this.* "M, I can't lose you. Right now, there is nothing to incriminate you, but if they find you with me..." I pleaded.

He pulled away, "I'm not leaving. You haven't even given me a chance to tell you what Haden and I found."

"What do you mean, what Haden and you found?" I asked, successfully distracted.

"It's about the prophecy."

"What?"

"No, I'm not telling you. Not unless you let me come with you. I'll make sure you get to the student quarters safely, tell you what I know, and if you still want me to leave, I will."

It wasn't a hard decision, I knew I wanted him with me even though it wasn't safe for him. I nodded. "Fine, but you're not staying."

"We'll see," he said.

I knew taking the route through the woods meant we'd be out there longer, with more risk that someone would notice we were missing and come searching for us, if they weren't already. But we had to chance it.

I glanced at my internal monitor: 23:53. I was pretty sure we were making good time. We hadn't come across any more of the sector guards, but I wasn't sure how far we were from the student quarters.

Snap.

I heard the crunch of dried leaves and twigs coming from up ahead. When I looked back at Merick, I could tell he had heard it too. I pulled him back, and we pressed our backs tightly against the wall. I could only hope the shadows would shield us. *"Try not to breathe,"* I told him, and I slowed my breath and focused on my heart rate until I had become no more than a statue. It's a vampire trick, usually learned after hundreds of years of practice, but I didn't have that kind of time to learn.

Three guards turned the corner up ahead, making their way in our direction. Suddenly, as if instinctively, they all stopped and scanned the trees around them, looking directly at…and then beyond where we were hiding.

They can't see us, I thought. Hoped.

Cautiously, and in unison, they began moving in our direction. Their weapons were out and ready. Merick let out the tiniest of breaths, but it was enough.

"Did you hear that?" one of the guards asked.

"I smell it," another hissed.

"Wolf," the third said.

"And lion," the first guard added.

Well, it is lycanthrope quarters, I thought, sarcastically. I knew they were smelling Merick's wolf, maybe mine too, but definitely my lion. She was the one who attacked the guard. Why she had come out and not my wolf I wasn't sure.

They continued past us, stopping briefly just in front of me. I could have reached out and grabbed them by the collar, but I held back. Merick and I couldn't take on three grown vampires all on our own. It would have been suicide.

I waited until they were gone, then waited a little longer just to be sure. I took Merick's hand and moved away from the wall, unsure of how we had escaped detection, and we slowly moved on. When I thought we had gotten far enough away that they wouldn't hear or smell us, I gave Merick the heads-up. "Let's go!" And I took off running, with Merick close behind me.

We didn't stop until we were deep inside the student quarters. The streets were empty, I knew they would be, but the cameras would be watching, so we stuck to the walls. The only place I could think to go was back to the comfort of our old barracks. We slipped in using the vent that opened into the girls bathroom. The screws were still loose. Apparently, no one had noticed them since Teagan had loosened them for me. The Council hadn't installed cameras in the bathroom; it was the one place they allowed us to have some privacy, so I knew we could slip in without being discovered.

A new selection class hadn't been moved in yet, and wouldn't be for a few more months. That meant we had the whole place to ourselves.

"Are you sure this is safe?" Merick asked, once we were inside, and the vent was closed behind us.

"No, but it's safer than staying out there."

"Yeah," he said, nodding. He walked to the sink, ran the cold water, and splashed it on his face. I'm not sure if he was tired and trying to wake up, or just nervous.

I buried my destroyed black clothes in a half-filled trash bin, knowing the cleaning crew would come in before the next class moved in and toss it out without thinking twice about what was inside. Then, I pulled his sweatshirt off over my head.

"Hey, what is that?" he asked.

"What?" I asked, quickly turned to look behind me, but there was nothing there.

"On your arm," he said.

When I looked down, there was just a faint shadow of the tattoo left behind from the glowing orb—my activation.

"Right, that. That is a long story, and I promise to tell you, but first I need to shower, and you should probably clean off your sweatshirt. Sorry about the goo," I added, handing it to him so he could run it under the water, and scrub at the goo before it had a chance to harden. "I need to clean up. When I'm done, you're going to tell me what you know and I'll explain this," I said, rubbing my hand across the tattoo.

"Right."

"You think you can you find me some clothes?" I asked. "Try my old footlocker: if they haven't moved anyone in yet maybe they haven't cleaned those out either. But make sure you stay out of view from the cameras." Then I grabbed a towel from a shelf, stepped into one of the shower stalls and turned on the water.

I heard him turn off the water, wring out his sweatshirt, and leave, as the warm water washed over me. I still didn't understand how I had shifted outside of the moon cycle. It isn't unheard of—shifters do it—but usually it takes years to get that much control over your beast, or, in my case, beasts. Not that control had anything to do with it—it was more a lack of control.

I grudgingly turned off the water, dried off, and got dressed in the selection student gray clothing that Merick had found for me. I was a little surprised they hadn't cleared everything out already, but I was glad to have the clean clothes.

"Where did you get that?" Merick asked.

"Get what?"

He slid his hand under the necklace that I had thoughtlessly forgotten to tuck inside my shirt. "The cross."

"Oh, right. I found it at your place. I was going to ask you about it, I just…" I pulled back a little, sliding the necklace beneath the shirt. "With everything that's happened I didn't have a chance to tell you. Is it ok?"

He hesitated. "Of course." There was an uncertainty in his voice, a reservation I hadn't heard before, and I quickly pulled the cross back out.

"If you want it back, you can—"

"Are you kidding? No, it's yours. Besides, it looks good on you. Really."

"You're sure?"

"I'm sure."

I followed him into the main room, quickly ducking into the bottom bunk of the nearest bed to avoid being seen by the ever-present cameras above.

"What are you doing?" Merick asked.

I grabbed his arm, pulling him onto the bed with me. "The cameras."

"They're off. I checked when I came in to find you some clothes, and none of the lights are active. I guess since no one's living here the Council didn't see a need to keep them running."

Well, that's convenient.

I climbed back out, and we picked one of the bottom bunks back in the corner away from the windows and farthest from the door. Just because the monitors weren't watching didn't mean we needed to be careless.

I sat there, remembering the last time I had been there, surrounded by my classmates. It felt like just yesterday. I could hear Darius and Forrest arguing about who was stronger, vampires or lycanthropes. I could see Quinn and Riker egging Forrest on until the teasing became physical. I pictured Opal and Tamsin primping in front of the bathroom mirror, and I could hear them giggling. I could see Uma, sitting in her bunk near the front of the room, quietly studying by herself. I could see them all—except Ciara. I knew she had been there. She had given me her lip gloss, and we had shared a hug that told me that maybe everything would work out. But no matter how hard I tried, I couldn't picture her here right now. Everybody else, but not Ciara.

"You OK?" Merick asked, pulling me out of the daze I had fallen into.

"Yeah, I'm good. I was just remembering the last time we were here."

"A lot has changed since then," he said, leaning back against the wall and staring out across the room.

"So, what did you and Haden find out?" I asked. I knew it wasn't safe for us to be here, but I couldn't go back to Iris's place wearing only Merick's sweatshirt and covered in blood and sticky secretions from my transformation. But that didn't mean I want to keep him here any longer than necessary. If we got caught... I didn't want to think would could happen if we got caught.

"Wow, nothing like getting straight to the point," he said, sounding almost disappointed.

"M—"

"No, it's fine, I get it," he said, shifting in his seat. "Haden and I, we followed Councilman Ash. Haden said he didn't trust him, not that I blame him, especially after what I saw him do to you in the office."

Or what I saw him do to you in the clinic, I thought to myself.

"Anyway, he went beyond the wall, so we followed him. There's an old gate that isn't even on the maps, and it seems the guard doesn't patrol it. About a mile or two out, Ash disappeared into an old warehouse. We couldn't get in, but we managed to see inside through one of the windows on the back side. Ash was meeting with a large group of men and women. We thought they were vampires, or castaways, but after seeing the guy you..."

"Killed," I said, finishing for him.

"Yeah. After seeing him, I'm pretty sure Ash was meeting with more like him."

"More monsters, you mean."

He just nodded. "They all had that same torn fabric tied around their upper arm. Just like the guy you killed."

Torn fabric? I thought to myself. I hadn't noticed anything tied around his arm, not that I was paying much attention to how he was dressed.

"If he got into the sector, I'm just wondering how many others got in. There had to be over a hundred of them in that warehouse, A. With Ash leading them, who knows how many more there are."

Merick was right: Ash could be very persuasive when he wanted to be. If he was in charge, there's no telling how many people he had recruited. If they were all as strong as the guy in the woods, we were going to need a lot more than just Haden, Merick, and me to fight them.

"Did Haden know what they had to do with the Prophecy?" I asked, trying to piece together everything I had already learned with this new information.

"No, he was hoping there might be something in one of your books."

"Maybe, but we aren't going to find out tonight. The books are back at Iris's place. I'll have to check them in the morning. Besides, I'm exhausted. You must be pretty tired too. It sounds like I'm not the only one who had a long day."

"I'm not that tired," he said, sliding closer to my side of the bed. I felt the heat radiating from his body, and my heartbeat raced in return.

"I..."

He didn't let me finish. He leaned in, his lips met mine, and everything else slipped away. I'm not sure how long it lasted: it could have been two minutes or two hours, and I could have stayed there in his arms forever. But reality sank in, and I remembered where we were, what had happened, and the danger we were both in if we got caught.

"Merick," I said, pulling away slightly, but not out of his arms. "Merick, you can't stay. It isn't safe."

"A, I can't leave you."

"Yes, you can. You promised me, remember. You said you'd make sure I got here safely, you'd tell me what you know, and then you'd leave." I hated the idea of sending him away, but I knew it was the right thing to do. "It's time."

"I'm not leaving," he insisted.

"Yes, you are." I swallowed back the fear that was building. "I'm your Alpha, and I'm ordering you to go." My voice was shaking. I didn't want him to leave, but I didn't want to lose him. If my actions caused him to be hurt, or worse, I'd never forgive myself. I slid out of bed and stood there, staring down at him.

"I—" He stopped himself. He stood up and headed off toward the bathroom. I heard him pulling the vent grate out and then wiggling it back into place as he left. I could only hope he was doing what I asked. I could only hope he'd be safe.

Looking back, I wish I had let him stay. I'd give anything to take back the words I said to send him away, but I thought I was protecting him. I didn't know it would be the last time I would see him for a very long time. I watched him go believing I'd see him again the next morning. Believing I was sending him to the safety of his apartment. Believing it was the right decision, the only possible decision. I was wrong.

I leaned back against the pillow, curling up on the thin mattress and closing my eyes. His scent filled the air all around me, calming me. I knew that if I could get just a couple hours of sleep, I could wake up early enough to slip out unnoticed and make it back to Iris's place.

Wrong.

I had been sleeping for maybe an hour, two at the most, when I was abruptly pulled out of the bed and thrown over someone's shoulder. I hadn't seen who it was, and they didn't smell sweet like a lycanthrope, so it was either a vampire, a human, or worse. I was betting on the former. The situation was way too familiar. I was just glad I hadn't been bound and gagged again this time.

"Don't say anything." It was William's voice, and he sounded angry.

I heard him pull the door open and felt the cool breeze of the night air wash over my skin.

"Let me explain—"

"I said don't say anything." This time his voice was hushed.

We had made it out of the barracks without setting off the alarm somehow.

Maybe the alarm wasn't set for the same reason the cameras weren't on; because that particular building was supposed to be empty, I thought.

We were off the streets and into the woods that surrounded the selection course before he finally put me down.

"Do you have any idea how stupid that was?" he asked. "Well? Do you?"

"I..." I had no idea what to say or how to answer him. I wasn't sure if he was referring to my killing the guard, my breaking into the selection student quarters, or just my running off without him. At the moment, I was pretty sure just about every decision I had made that night had been stupid.

"You could have gotten yourself killed."

Yup, that applied to just about every decision too.

"You're lucky no one saw you out there tonight."

Oh, my stars, does he know about the guard?

"I know you want to be seen as an adult, but it still isn't safe out past curfew, especially for you. There are things out here you can't even imagine, nor would you want to," he said, and all I could think about was the vampire and how his face had mutated—changed into something I could only describe as a monster.

"I don't know how many times I have to tell you that," he continued. "What is it going to take for you to realize you aren't safe? Is someone going to actually have to try and kill you for it to sink in?"

Nope, he doesn't know. And yeah, that's what it took, but I think I've learned my lesson. I remembered the guard's mutilated face after I had killed him. *All that blood... What did I do?*

"Not to mention the fact that you're in the student quarters after dark. If the Council were to find out, you could be banished from the—"

"Then why did you come get me? I'm sure you wouldn't care if they banished me. It would mean the end of your babysitting duties. Besides, couldn't you get banished too?"

He stood there, staring down at me. "You're my responsibility, whether I like it or not."

He didn't.

"How did you find me?" I asked, hoping he hadn't followed my trail through the woods.

"I'm a vampire, and you're young and stupid. It wasn't hard to track you. Besides, you're not the first fledgling who's escaped back to the student quarters."

That last part surprised me. I wondered if he was referring to any of my classmates, or maybe he had done it too, long ago. "You?" I asked, but he didn't answer.

"I'm taking you back to Iris's place, and this won't happen again. Do you understand?"

"Yes, sir."

He took my hand in his and started running. "Keep up."

He was faster than I expected.

When we got back to Iris's place she was pacing in the living room, and her eyes were red and swollen from crying.

"Oh, my stars, Zelina, where have you been?" She grabbed me as William shut the door behind us. I wasn't sure if she was going to hug me or shake me.

She hugged me.

"Don't act like you weren't part of this," William said, staring at Iris like he was targeting her through the sights of a rifle.

"She wasn't," I lied. "She had no idea I was leaving. I just needed some time to myself, I swear. Please don't blame her." How could I get her in trouble, when she had only been trying to help me? I couldn't, so I lied.

Iris loosened her grip and pulled back just enough to question me with her eyes, but she didn't try to correct me.

"And you decided that the selection student quarters were the best place to have a little *me time*?" William asked.

"Zelina!" Iris was more surprised than I expected.

I couldn't tell them what had happened, why I had gone there. What I had done.

"Wait, what are you wearing?" Iris asked, finally noticing I was out of my blacks and back into the light gray pants and shirt of a student. She spun me around. "Zelina?"

"They're mine, or they were. I just…" I closed my eyes, focused, and tried to think of another lie— one that wouldn't come back to bite me later. "I needed to feel like me again. That's all. Everything has changed so quickly. I just needed to—"

Iris pulled me close again, wrapped her arms around my shoulders, and pulled me down to the couch with her. She believed me. "It's OK," she said. "I get it. It's hard going from being a selection student to a vampire or even a lycanthrope. I hadn't thought about how much harder that must be on you, trying to fit into both worlds. It's OK that you needed some time, but you still have to follow the rules. You're a sector resident now. You cannot be in the selection student quarters during curfew. You know that." Looking up at William, she nodded toward the kitchen, and he left without a word.

"It's been hours. You must be starving," she said.

Honestly, I wasn't. I *really* wasn't. I had drained the guard and torn through his neck like he was the last steak on earth. I didn't think I'd be hungry for a long time. It was actually the first time I had felt full since Selection Week, but I nodded anyway. It's what she expected. She couldn't have known about what I had done, and I wasn't about to be the one to tell her. In fact, I hoped she'd never find out.

When William came back he was carrying three bottles of blood: he put two on the table for me, and the other he tipped back and finished off in seconds. "Drink up," he said, slamming his empty bottle down on the table in front of him.

I did as I was told, and even though I didn't need the blood, my fangs came out as soon as the sweet taste hit my tongue. It wasn't as good as the fresh blood I had already had, but instinct takes over whenever blood is involved.

Iris and William sent me off to bed, promising we'd keep this between just the three of us. I think Iris honestly wanted to protect me, but I was pretty sure William wanted to protect himself. If Remy found out William had *lost* me, my bodyguard would probably be out of a job, if not worse.

I didn't bother to change; my old selection clothes were worn in and comfortable…calming even. I was out within seconds of my head hitting the pillow.

19

The next morning came way too early. The alarm started to buzz, and as I rubbed my eyes open I saw that it was only five-o'clock. "Why did I set an ala—?"

Then it hit me. The digital clock wasn't mine. The white side table, the fluffy blue and green comforter, the white dresser with matching mirror, the blue fuzzy chair in the corner—none of it was mine.

I froze. *Where am I? When am I?* I wondered, remembering the conversation with the two little girls: mini-me and young Ciara.

"You, and others like you, exist in an extra-dimensional plane of existence," said the younger version of myself. *"…You have the power—the gift— of traveling from one map to another, one timeline to another."*

I wondered what timeline I was in, and I forced myself to sit up to look more closely at my surroundings, but I closed my eyes for a few seconds first.

Please be alone. Please be alone. Please be alone.

Nope.

There were two matching beds in the room, and young Ciara was sitting cross-legged on the other one. Smiling.

"Ciara?" I asked.

"You're awake," she said, jumping off the bed excitedly. "Come on." I moved to follow her, noticing a second white dresser with matching mirror on this side of the room, and another fluffy chair—this one yellow and pink. I swung my legs over the edge of the bed and hopped down.

"Wow." The bed was higher than I had expected. I glanced in the dresser mirror as I hurried toward the door, and I instantly realized two things: first, the bed wasn't high, I was short; and second, I wasn't me. I was five or six years old, and I was wearing a blue nightgown. My hair was dark brown and reached below my waist. Tiny little freckles spattered across the bridge of my nose like specks of paint flung from the end of a paintbrush. My eyes, still light brown, like coffee with lots of cream, were the only things I recognized. "Oh my." I was the younger version of myself. How, or why, I had woken up in her timeline I wasn't sure, but I planned to find out.

I reached out to touch my reflection, but Ciara poked her head back through the door.

"What are you doing, silly? Hurry up and come with me." Then she disappeared again.

I followed. I always follow her.

The house was quiet.

House? Where am I? What is this place?

"Where are we?" I whispered.

She tiptoed down a flight of stairs, giving me a quick look back over her shoulder.

"Is this my past?" I asked.

She stopped and turned to look at me, confused. "You're so weird," she said. Then she giggled. Clearly, she had no idea what I was talking about. "Now be quiet. We can't make any noise or they'll wake up."

"Who?" I asked, whispering because she was.

"Mom and Nash, silly."

"Nash?" I said, a little too loudly with my new squeaky voice. "Why is he here? You can't trust him. He's a snitch." She reached up to cover my mouth, giggling.

"Of course he is. All boys are." She took her hand off my mouth. "Now stop yelling or they'll hear us."

She took my hand and we continued down the stairs and into the kitchen. She took a container of milk from the fridge and two spoons from a drawer, and put all these on the counter. Then she pulled a chair up to the counter, climbed up on it, and took two bowls out of a cabinet and a box of something I didn't recognize from another cabinet.

"What are you doing?" I asked.

"Making breakfast," she said, smiling, and in a few minutes she handed me a filled bowl and a spoon. She climbed down from the chair and took her own bowl, spilling half the milk on the counter, to the kitchen table and sat down, so I took my bowl and followed her.

I looked at the small floating pieces in the bowl, and pushed them around with the spoon. Finally, I took a bite. "Mmmm." The cold milk mixed with the sweet, sugary pieces of food was so good. "What is it?"

"Ummm, cereal?" she said. "Why are you acting so weird this morning?"

From our places at the table we could see out a big front window, and I watched as a group of young men, all dressed alike, trotted by in a single file line.

"Where are they going?" I asked, surprised again by my youthful, childlike voice.

"I don't know," she said, then shoved a large spoonful of the cereal into her mouth. "What is wrong with you?" she asked, with a full mouth.

"What?"

"I said, what's wrong?" I spun around in my chair, and Iris was standing in the kitchen doorway. "Zelina? What's wrong?

I looked down, and I was no longer that little six-year-old version of myself. Young Ciara was gone, and I was a grown woman sitting at the table in Iris's apartment, staring down at a plate of steak, eggs, and toast that I didn't remember making.

"Nothing, I'm good." I could still taste the cereal, and I pushed the plate of food aside. When I looked up at Iris, I could see that she was concerned. She didn't believe me. "Really, I'm good. Just not hungry right now."

I tried to remember my morning. I didn't remember getting out of bed, taking a shower, or even getting dressed, let alone making breakfast. I felt Iris watching me, so I grabbed a couple bottles of blood from the refrigerator, tossed them in my bag, and headed toward the living room—trying to act as casual as possible.

"So, who's walking me to work today?" I asked, as I turned the corner into the living room. "Oh, wow, both of you. What's the occasion?" I asked, as William and Haden stood up to greet me—looking somber.

"Friday," Haden said, as he turned and headed for the door. His light brown hair had gotten long since the moon cycle, touching just below his collarbone, and I hadn't realized how wavy it was. I wondered if his transformation had anything to do with it, or if I just hadn't noticed it before. It wasn't long in a feminine way. Nothing about Haden was feminine.

"Did you hear the sirens last night?" Haden asked, as we made our way down the main road to the Council offices.

"No," I said, glancing back at William. It wasn't a lie. I hadn't heard them, but I wasn't surprised they had gone off. "Why were they going off? What happened?"

"A member of the guard was killed," Haden said, not going into detail. But he didn't have to. I already knew the details better than anyone.

"External?"

"No," he answered.

"Oh." I swallowed back the lump that was forming in my throat. "How?"

"Mutilated."

"Mutilated?"

"That's what I said."

"Right." I kept walking, my eyes straight ahead. "Do they know who—?"

"Not yet."

"So," I cleared my throat, "they haven't caught the—?"

"No," William said, at my side. "They haven't caught them."

"Them?" I asked, honestly curious now.

"Yeah, by the way his body was torn apart, there had to be at least two or three, maybe more lycanthropes that attacked him."

Torn apart? I wondered. I had torn through his neck and scratched up his chest, but I hadn't touched the rest of him. When I glanced up at Haden, he quickly looked aside.

"Haden?"

"I told you I'd handle it," he answered, using mind-speak. *"I did what I had to do to protect you. They won't be able to connect the body to you."*

"And what about connecting it to you?"

He didn't answer.

"Haden!"

"It will be fine, they won't connect it to me either, I have an alibi."

"We suspect it was a group of the lions, but the faint scent of wolf was also present." William continued. "Don't worry, we'll catch them soon enough."

Does he suspect Haden? Or Merick? I wondered. A jolt of fear ran through me. *Why had I let them help me? What have I done?*

Haden was keeping pace on my other side. I was sandwiched in between the two of them, and right then I really didn't mind. William seemed to think I might be afraid because there were killers on the loose. He had no way to know that what I was afraid of was being caught.

"Don't worry, Zelina," William said. "The attack happened deep in the woods behind the lycanthrope quarters—nowhere near Iris's apartment.

I took a deep breath, and a sigh of relief escaped as I replied. "Oh. OK, good. That's good."

Not really what I was worried about. At least I knew he wasn't considering me as a suspect.

"Actually, I'm surprised anyone found the body." Haden said, "The guards don't usually patrol the riverbed, and the body was found floating in the river near the sector wall, at least that's what I heard."

"Was he a friend of yours?" I asked. "I mean, being internal security and all, I'm just curious if either of you knew him."

They exchanged an awkward glance. "We knew him," was all William said.

When we finally made it to the Council office, Merick wasn't there. Nor did he make it in that day, or the next, or the next day after that.

"Where is he?" I asked, like a broken record. It had been a week, and Haden had just walked me to work and ushered me into the once-again empty office.

"I told you, I don't know," he replied.

"Well, that's not good enough." My wolf was pacing just beneath the surface. She wanted out. She wanted answers. A low growl started from somewhere deep, and I could feel myself starting to change.

"Give us a minute," Haden said to William, who was also there in the small guards room. Haden shoved me into the office and closed the door behind us. "Get yourself together or you'll—"

I shifted. Out of cycle.

"Damn it," he whispered.

He knelt on all fours in front of me, but his eyes never left mine. "Zelina, you have to calm down. Take deep breaths and focus on relaxing. If the Council sees you like this…"

He was right. They still hadn't caught the lycanthrope who killed the security guard. If they find out I'm capable of shifting outside of the moon cycle, I'll become their number one suspect. As quickly as my wolf had appeared, she was gone, and I was left crouching on the floor, naked and sticky, with tears streaming down my face.

"You can't *do* that," Haden said sternly. "You'll get caught."

"I know, I'm sorry." I wiped away the tears with the back of my hand, but it was the first time I had allowed myself to cry since Merick had disappeared, and I couldn't stop.

"Zelina. Breathe." Haden's voice was calmer now, less demanding. "We will find him."

I swallowed back the tears, nodded, and looked up. He was staring down at me as if he wanted to fix me but didn't know how. "I'm fine," I said. It was becoming too easy to lie.

"There's a change of clothes in the bottom drawer of your desk. I'll get rid of the security recording and keep William out. Get yourself…and this room…cleaned up," he said as he left.

20

The next couple of weeks went by slowly and uneventfully, except for Merick's continued mysterious absence. The sector guard never found anyone to blame for the murder of the guard member, but it wasn't for lack of trying. They interrogated all of the werelions and werewolves in Sector C, or at least the ones they believed could have made the transformation outside of the moon cycle. Thankfully, I was not on that list. Aside from Haden, who was going out of his way to protect me, they all still doubted my abilities, and I was grateful for that.

My visions had subsided to only one or two a week, usually in the middle of the night, and on those occasions, I'd wake up uncertain as to whether I had had a vision or just a bizarre dream. I was starting to feel like I had imagined having visions in the first place. If it wasn't for the tattoo on my arm, I might actually believe that I had made everything up: the conversation with Jabari and Isaac, the two young girls, waking up in the clinic—everything. No matter how hard I tried to find Merick, both by physically searching the sector and mentally reaching out to him, he wasn't there.

I managed to establish something of a routine: I even started running the selection course again each morning, secretly hoping Merick would show up. I went to the office every day, longing to see him there. But every day I was disappointed. I attended Council meetings and half-listened to discussions on everything from security reports to selection class updates, hoping someone would mention the disappearance of the lycanthrope liaison. No one ever did, and when I brought it up they ignored my inquiries.

After work each day, I'd make my way through the lycanthrope quarters and stop by Merick's apartment—my personal bodyguards only a few steps behind me at all times.

We knew that we were suspiciously observed by the residents, and this gave Haden an idea for a plan to enlist help locating Merick. It was time for me to come out as the pack leader and that meant a show of force.

"Are you ready?" Haden mind-messaged me as we approached Merick's building.

"Yes."

"You have to make it believable!" he cautioned. *"We can't hold back, either of us, or William will suspect something."*

"I know."

"He isn't home," Haden said, almost shouting, and stepping in front of me just as I was reaching out to open the front door of Merick's building.

"Yeah, I get it." My voice was strained, almost shrill. "He's not home. Just like he wasn't home yesterday, the day before yesterday, or the day before that," I said, pushing him aside and pulling the door open. I started stomping up the stairs. "He hasn't been home for weeks. He hasn't been to work for weeks. He wasn't in the holding cells during the last moon cycle with the rest of us, either. So, where is he?" By the end of my speech I was yelling. A few of Merick's neighbors cracked open their doors, peeking out. "He isn't in the clinic or at the hospital," I shouted, as I made my way down his hallway to the door to his small one-bedroom apartment. I knocked, like I always knocked. "Merick? Merick, are you home?" Making it seem believable was turning out to be easier than I had expected. I was desperate to find Merick, and had been for a long time. I wanted answers, and if this was how I was going to get them, then I was going to put everything I had into it.

"He isn't home," Haden said again, from just behind me. He spoke in an annoyed monotone voice. He didn't have to shout. We had enough eavesdroppers. "You are so stubborn. Stop for a minute and listen. You're a vampire, use your abilities and listen for him. Listen for the blood rushing through his veins, the pounding of his heart. Listen to what is behind that door and you'll know he isn't there."

"I can't," I screamed back. "All I hear is your yammering, the blood in your veins and the pounding of your heart. I hear the beating of hearts all around me, neighbors cowering in their rooms. I can't focus right now. I can't focus enough to only hear Merick."

I turned back to the door, taking a deep breath in a useless attempt to calm myself down, and continued to knock, trying again to ignore Haden and the peeping neighbors up and down the hallway.

"Merick, if you're there, please open up. I just need to know you're OK, then I'll leave you alone if that's what you want."

"Zelina, he isn't home."

I felt Haden's hand on my shoulder and I turned on him, yelling, finding it a relief to let go of these feelings, even though it was planned. "So, where is he? Where is he if he isn't here?" No longer able to limit my emotions to mere yelling, I screamed, and shoved him into the wall. He hit hard, harder than I had intended, and he shifted as he did. His wolf was dark brown, almost black, with white eyes. He was crouched by the wall, growling up at me. I hadn't expected him to shift, and I probably should have been scared, but I wasn't—and he didn't make a move toward me.

William grabbed me by the shoulders and held me back against the wall next to Merick's door. "Don't," he warned. He glanced over his shoulder to Haden, "You OK man?"

I guess he believed it, I thought.

Haden answered with a low growl that formed deep in his chest, a warning—but I knew it wasn't directed at me.

William shifted his weight, leaning into me and away from Haden. "Haden, stop!" William ordered.

I watched as Haden deliberately slowed his breathing. He shook his head then his body, as if trying to shake the wolf out of him. When he stopped, he was Haden again, crouched on the floor against the wall, naked, and covered in sticky goo. His clothing lay on the floor in shreds.

"You OK man?" William asked again.

"Yeah, I'm great," Haden mumbled under his breath. He stood up, turning and heading down the hall. "I'll be back," he said. He banged on the first door he came to. It opened quickly, and he headed inside without waiting for an invitation.

Suddenly, there outside Merick's door, the reality of his disappearance hit me. Uncontrollable tears filled my eyes, and threatened to spill over. *I'm not going to cry. I'm not going to cry. I'm not going to cry.* My breathing became erratic, and I struggled to take a deep breath that I didn't really need.

"You need to calm down," William said. "You're a vampire. We don't need to breathe, much less hyperventilate. Focus on being still." When I pushed back he held me even tighter. "Trust me, it helps."

He was right. I got my breathing under control just as Haden stepped back into the hallway. His hair was wet, but clean, and he was wearing a dark blue sweat-suit that was at least two sizes too small, but I wasn't about to tell him that.

"You good now?" William asked me, looking down as if trying to decide if it was OK to let me go.

"I'm fine," I answered. *"Are you OK?"* I asked Haden, in mind-speak. He just stared at me, I could tell he wasn't happy. This hadn't gone exactly the way we had planned. I was only supposed to overpower him. The plan hadn't been for me to force his transformation, essentially emasculating him in front of William, in addition to the eavesdroppers we had planned on. *"I didn't mean for it to—"*

He cut into my thought. *"It worked. That's all that matters. Don't stop now,"* he said, prompting me to continue.

As soon as William released me, I spun around and started banging on Merick's door again. I grabbed the doorknob, expecting it to be locked like it always was, but this time it wasn't. The door opened on the first try. Thrown off balance, I fell forward into the apartment.

I jumped to my feet and ran from room to room, calling his name. For the first time in weeks, I was hopeful that he might have come back. The search didn't take long. The apartment was empty, save for the standard sector-issue furniture. There was no sign that Merick, or anyone, had ever lived there. Even the refrigerator had been emptied out and cleaned.

I spun on William and Haden, who stood in the living room looking just as shocked as I was.

"Where are all of his things?" To my amazement, I wasn't yelling. In fact, I actually sounded calm. Looking back, I think it may have been shock, but at the moment I was thankful for the momentary stillness.

"I honestly don't know," Haden finally said, his eyes never fully meeting mine. "But I'll find him for you."

"You'll what?" I knew what he had said. I had expected it. But his sincerity still surprised me.

He reached out and put his hand on my arm. Gently. "Zelina, I know this isn't going to make sense to you. It doesn't really make sense to me either, not yet. But you can trust me. I mean, *trust me*, trust me." I already knew where his speech was going, but I hadn't expected a pledge of loyalty. "You've been through a lot, and I haven't given you any reason to see me as an ally, but just..." He blew out a breath.

"I'll prove it to you, as is our way. But know that from this point on I've got your back." I didn't doubt a single word he was saying, and though I knew this speech was for our listeners, and that he had indeed given me reason to trust him, it felt so good to hear the words out loud. He turned and left without waiting for me to respond.

"Thank you," I whispered. "Haden..." I started to call him back, but I couldn't finish. I was choking on my emotions, something I hadn't expected.

William went after his friend, and stopped him before he got to the front door of the building. I wasn't far behind.

"Haden, what are you doing?" asked William.

Haden didn't turn around, or lift his eyes. "I have to..."

"You have to what?" William demanded. "Where are you going?"

"She's my Alpha," Haden said flatly, almost grudgingly, and I wondered if it was just an act or if he really was upset. If the reality of what we had agreed to do was finally hitting him too. "I am going to find the boy. It is my duty," he said, and then he was gone.

William turned back to me, his eyes filled with confusion. "What did you do?"

"I...don't know. I didn't do anything," I said, but that was a lie. I had forced Haden's transformation. I had asserted myself as his Alpha. An Alpha takes control of a pack in only one of two ways: by killing the current Alpha, or by overshadowing and diminishing the power of the current Alpha. I hadn't been willing to kill Haden, so I had done the latter, and even though William was the only public witness, that building had been filled with people listening behind closed doors or peeking out through slightly opened ones. Word would spread, was probably spreading already. Haden had stepped down as Alpha of his pack and relinquished his position to me. It had been our plan all along, but at that moment I wondered if Haden was regretting it.

I hadn't wanted to be pack leader, nor was I ready, but that time had come, so what I wanted didn't really matter anymore.

21

That evening, I found myself standing in the park, just beyond where Merick and I had had our first dinner together after Selection Week. Our picnic. Only this time it was no picnic. Haden stood at my side, and close to forty men and women—all wolves in Haden's pack, my pack—stood waiting to hear what we had to say. What he had to say. He had been their Alpha after all.

Even I was curious to hear what he would tell them.

I had been dragged here—not kicking and screaming, but not completely willingly either. Haden said he couldn't tell me where we were going or what would happen when we got there. He said he wanted his pack to see the truth in what he would be telling them, and that this was the only way. William hadn't come along, and Haden had distinctly told Iris that this was pack business, and that she wasn't to follow.

Haden stepped forward and spoke. "Many of you have already heard." His voice was deep and commanding. "Maybe you came here tonight to see if the rumors were true. Maybe you came to challenge my decision, or her power. Whatever your reason, it does not matter." He looked down at me, as if to make sure I was paying attention. "Zelina's presence here among us has not been a secret. The fact that she was infected with both vampirism and lycanthropy may have come as a surprise to everyone, but no one here could honestly say they were surprised at her transformations."

Grumbles of disapproval filled the air as the crowd started to become restless. Like a true leader, Haden raised his hand to silence them, and it worked.

"I have been your Alpha for over ten years now, and I have been proud to serve as your leader—your voice." The previously restless crowd grew calm, and here and there a cheer rang out. "I think that is what makes this so difficult." There were no cheers for this. "There has never in my life been a pack leader in Sector C who didn't *take* his place—*demand* it—physically, and with blood. And yet, tonight I stand here knowing full well that I am no longer your Alpha." At first the crowd was silent. Then came a shouted protest, and another, and several more. But Haden didn't allow it to continue for long. He shouted over the hostility, proving why he had led his pack so successfully for so long. "Silence! Whether you like it or not, she is our leader now. Is she young? Yes. Is she inexperienced? Yes. Does that mean she can't learn our ways, learn to lead us? NO!"

I was drawn in, entranced, by his speech, as if I could actually start to believe what he was saying.

He continued. "And I will stand by her side: guide her, teach her, and give her counsel as her Beta, if she will accept it."

There was a long pause before I realized he was staring down at me, waiting for a response, making eye contact with me for the first time since I had forced his transformation in the hallway of Merick's apartment complex.

"Yes," I blurted out. "Of course." He had already known my answer—we had discussed it weeks ago—but his pack needed to hear it aloud.

"Good," he said. He placed his hand on my shoulder, and we both took a step forward. "There are close to twenty wolf packs in Sector C. None is as large as ours, or as strong, but you can choose to defect, join another pack if they will accept you. We will not object. However, if Zelina is half as powerful as I believe her to be, half as strong, then it will not be long before she has taken over those packs as well."

What?

I looked up at him, and he was looking down at me again, but I wasn't sure what, if anything, I was supposed to say. I turned back to the crowd, and they stood silently, looking almost as shocked as I felt.

"As her pack, it is our duty to bring home our lost wolf. The one they call Merick," Haden announced, and a wave of relief washed through me. I had almost forgotten why Haden and I had started all this, but with a pack behind me I had a real chance of finding Merick.

"He hasn't chosen a pack yet," a man from the crowd called out.

"How are we supposed to track him?" a woman's voice called. "He wasn't one of us."

"He was mine, and that makes him one of us," I said without thinking, and before I could stop myself. Everyone's questioning eyes turned to me.

"It is true." Haden stepped in before they could argue. "The Council didn't want you to know, but under the circumstances, I think it's only right that you do. During her first moon cycle, Zelina forced Merick's transformation..." Then, reluctantly, he added, "just as she did mine. She was his Alpha before he had a chance to choose, and she is ours now."

A few people pushed their way out of the crowd, grumbling, and made their way back toward the lycanthrope living quarters.

"Don't worry," Haden said, leaning in so close I could feel his breath against my ear. "They will come around. They will see."

What? What will they see? I wondered, but I didn't ask. Haden had gone from seeing me as a mere child only a couple of months ago, to what had felt like despising me, to treating me now with a level of respect I never could have imagined, nor that I was sure I deserved.

I wasn't so sure I agreed that the pack would come around, but I didn't really have another choice. I could only hope he was right.

Looking out over the crowd, I scanned the faces of those who had chosen to stay, "Thank you, for not walking away," I said.

Haden tapped my arm. "Do not thank them," he scolded me. "They are your pack. They stay because you are now family, because it is the correct option. They stay because that is what packs do."

"I..." I began again. *I have a lot to learn,* I thought to myself.

"Show them you are a leader," he said. "Tell them what you want from them."

I took a deep breath. I didn't need it, of course, but being the only vampire among a pack of lycanthropes, I was pretty sure it would make them more comfortable. It actually did make me feel calmer and centered. The crowd seemed to be waiting for something.

"Merick is important to me, and I want him found, by any means necessary," I said. There were a few gasps and some hushed whispering, but no one objected. "There is something else," I said. I paused and waited for silence. "I know you are all surprised to find me standing before you today. You've been loyal to Haden for so long, and asking you to afford me that same respect may seem premature, but I need a volunteer: one of you who truly feels you can be loyal to me. Know that I will not hold it against you if you don't volunteer, but Haden and I have another task that needs discreet attention." I felt Haden's eyes on me. I could almost hear the thoughts running through his mind, questioning what this task might be. I could have peeked into his mind and stolen a glance, but I didn't need to.

"Ash?" he asked, through mind-speak. I nodded.

After a few moments, a young man stepped out of the crowd, from near the back. I couldn't see his face. It was shaded by the hood of his jacket, but there was still something oddly familiar about him.

"I will help," he said, moving forward through the crowd.

At first the crowd began to part, making a path for him, but suddenly the energy of the pack changed into restless agitation.

"Lion!" one man called out, and the others, as if it had been rehearsed, moved in and formed a circle around the man in the hooded jacket.

I could hear the low rumbling of the wolves threatening to attack, but no one did. They waited, glancing back at me—their leader—waiting for guidance.

"Let him through," I instructed. Reluctantly, my pack followed my order, making a space to let him pass through.

The man came forward, and when no one else stood between us, he knelt before me. His face was still hidden in shadows.

"What...What are you doing? What is he doing?" I asked, turning to Haden, who stood there shaking his head, unsure himself what was happening. No lion had ever bowed to a wolf before.

"We have come to represent the lions of your pride," he said.

"We?" I looked up, quickly scanning the crowd. Then I saw them, standing off near the distant tree line. They were almost hidden in the shadows of the trees, and if it hadn't been for the glints of light reflected from their golden eyes, I never would have seen them.

"You are our Leaena," said the man.

"Your—?"

"The leader of our pride. Your blood runs through us. I felt it—the shift—during your first moon cycle. We all felt it. I knew it the first time I met you. I am not your enemy. We...are not your enemies."

"Stand up. I want to see your face."

The mystery man stood, slowly, and pulled back his hood.

"Jabari?" I said, rushing toward him and grabbing hold of his arms. I couldn't believe he was actually there. "What are you doing here? How? How are you here?"

He quickly but gently pulled away, and turned to study the crowd.

They needed my guidance. "He is a friend," I said, turning to Haden for assistance, and he was right there with it.

"You know what you must do," Haden said to the pack. "If there is any word of the boy you will come directly to me." He cleared his throat and quickly added, "or Zelina."

The crowd dispersed, heading back toward the lycanthrope living quarters, whispering as they went, and they soon disappeared from sight. I looked out to the tree line, searching for the lions, but I no longer saw the golden sparkle of their eyes. Only Haden, Jabari, and I were left there in the clearing.

I was hopeful that someone would bring news of Merick's whereabouts, but I wasn't holding my breath, so to speak.

22

We couldn't go back to Iris's apartment. Jabari didn't live in Sector C, and since I didn't have my own place, that left Haden's. He was hesitant to invite Jabari in, not knowing him or where he had come from, not to mention the fact that he was a lion. But I assured him everything would be fine. I was still young and naïve in Haden's eyes, but I was his Alpha, and no matter how much it displeased him, he was loyal. He had already proven that much.

"I'm not much of a host," Haden barked, as he shut the door behind us. "You want something, feel free to get it yourself. The refrigerator is in the kitchen, through there." He nodded in the direction of the kitchen and plopped himself down on the couch, as if the weight of the world was on him. "The bathroom's through the bedroom back there," he said pointing behind him. The layout of his apartment was identical to Merick's, and I felt a wave of sadness as I realized this.

Haden leaned back on the couch. He closed his eyes and took in a deep breath and let it out, before looking up at me and speaking through clenched teeth. "I don't like this, Zelina."

"I know," I said, taking a seat next to him. The couch was firmer than it had looked, and I bounced a little as I landed. After finding the most comfortable position I could, I glanced up at Jabari, who was still standing by the door looking as uncomfortable as I probably should have been. "Please, sit down," I said.

He did as I asked, taking a seat across from me. I could tell it was going to take time for the two of them to trust each other, if that was even possible. However, I needed for them to try. As Haden's Alpha and Jabari's Leaena, it was my responsibility to get them to try. After all, I had been charged with bringing the vampires and lycanthropes together. If I couldn't get these two to work together, how much hope did I really have?

The tension in the room was thick as Haden and Jabari sized each other up.

"You trust him?" Haden asked me, not taking his eyes off of Jabari.

"I do."

"How do you know him?"

I wasn't sure how to respond, but luckily I didn't have to.

Jabari answered before I had a chance. "She doesn't, not really."

Well, that's not exactly true, I thought. *Also, probably not the answer that will instill trust in Haden either.*

"We've only met a few times," Jabari continued.

Two, I said, correcting him in my head and he turned his smoldering brown eyes on me. I wondered if he had heard my thoughts.

"Just a few times?" Haden asked, sounding suspicious. He wasn't going to let it go.

"Yes," Jabari and I said in unison.

"But when you saw him in the crowd…? When she saw you…" Haden started, but stopped himself.

"Her lion recognized me, just as your wolf recognizes hers," he explained. He looked at me, and our eyes met. I shifted in my seat, leaning forward toward him. It was an unconscious decision, but when I realized it I didn't stop myself.

Did my lion really recognize him? I wondered.

"But she called you a friend."

"Her blood is strong, and our connection is stronger. As my Leaena, we are more than friends," he said. "We are family." Then he turned back to Haden. I tried to will him to look at me again, to answer all the unasked questions I had, but he didn't.

Haden stood up without another word and went to the kitchen. Jabari and I sat in the silence waiting for him to return. After a few minutes, I knew from the rustling sounds that it was going to be a while.

"Why did you come into the sector?" I asked, leaning in and trying to be quiet so Haden wouldn't hear us. "How did you even get in? Why would you risk being caught? Has something happened? Is Ciara all right?" I could feel the panic bubbling up inside of me like a teapot about to sing. I hadn't given myself time to wonder why he was there until just that moment, and now I could only think of the worst-case scenario. "What has happened? Is she hurt? Where is she? Where is Isaac?"

"She is fine. They are together."

"Then what? Why did you come?" When he didn't answer, I knew. "Please tell me they haven't left for Dohiyi, not yet."

"I'm so sorry. But yes, they are gone." His voice was soft, gentle even, but his words cut like a knife into my heart.

They had gone, leaving the sector boundaries to get away from the sector guard.

"The sector guard is trained to stay within a twenty-mile radius of the sector walls at all times. If we can get safely outside their reach, we won't have to worry about them coming after us anymore," Jabari had explained.

I had thought they were crazy at the time. The idea of leaving was crazy. I hadn't actually expected them to do it.

How am I supposed to unite the vampires and lycanthropes within the sector, let alone those outside in the wastelands—in Dohiyi—especially now that my only connections to the wastelands are gone? I wondered.

Jabari reached out and took my hand, as if he could feel my anxiety building. The warmth of his hand around mine was almost too much, but I held on tight to the comfort it provided.

"I'm so sorry," he said again. "She wanted to say goodbye, but they couldn't wait any longer. It had been weeks since we heard from you, and the sector guard was getting closer and closer every night. Besides, they had stayed far longer than we ever intended to in the first place."

"I...

"She loves you, you know that, right?"

I had tried to reach out to her, but my visions weren't coming as regularly, and I was still having a hard time controlling them. When I did have them, they were always of young Ciara, and, when I was lucky, young Zelina. I had gotten used to the idea that they were my guides, that they were there to help me understand and maneuver through what was happening to me. But even they weren't all-knowing. They couldn't tell me what I had to do or say to fix the divide that separated the races.

"I understand why they had to go." I didn't, not really, but it was the right thing to say. I swallowed back tears. Ciara was gone, and there was nothing I could do about it. She had made her choice, and I had to respect it. Even though it wouldn't be easy, I knew I had to let her go.

I looked up, and Jabari was still watching me, waiting.

"What?" I asked. He said nothing. I could tell there was something else he wanted to say, but he just stared at me. "Tell me."

"The wolf you're looking for—"

"Merick?" I asked, my voice louder than I intended.

"He is with the Resistance."

Wait. What?

My brain went blank, and for a moment I forgot how to speak. I stood up, sat back down, stood up again, then sat down and stared at him. I was trying to make sense of what he had just said.

"Where? You mean he's out there... He's with Ciara and the others?" Jabari nodded. "When? How?"

"It was a few weeks ago. He was brought to us in the middle of the night. We thought you knew."

"How? How could I have known? He's been missing. I've been...We've been searching. Why didn't he...?" I couldn't catch my breath, and in that moment breathing seemed more important than I knew it was.

"I'm sorry. When we didn't hear from you and it was time for them to leave, I made him go on with the others."

"You what?" I was shaking, clenching my teeth trying not to scream. I could feel the anger building. My hands gripped the armrest of the couch.

"Had I known how important he is to you, I would have tried... I'm not sure what. We were told that it was the only way to keep him safe."

"Safe from what? From who? From the Council? From Remy, or from Ash? Who brought him to you?"

"Your leader, the one you call Remy. He is not who you think he is. He has been working with the Resistance, from within the sec—"

"That's not possible," I said, cutting him off.

"It is and he has. I didn't know his sector identity until now, and I don't know why he didn't tell you about Merick. I'm sure he had a reason, but you can trust him."

I swallowed back the pain I was feeling. Forced the tears not to come. I had to be strong. "And Merick, he really is safe?"

"He is. He isn't happy that we made him leave, but he is safe."

At least there is a silver lining.

"Will I ever see them again?"

He smiled, "You can, yes. It would take time to get there on foot, but there is no need for that. Not for you. You already have the ability to travel there, you just need to use the key."

"What key?" I asked, my interest afire.

"Your vision stone is the first half of the key."

"It's broken," I said, disappointed. I'm not sure it works any more.

"The fact that it is broken doesn't matter, but I know you gave the other half to Merick. He wouldn't stop staring at it the last few weeks. You do know that you can use your half to communicate with him, right?"

My jaw must have dropped to the floor, because he smiled, almost laughed.

"You'll never truly be without him. Not anymore, but you've got to learn how to use your gifts."

"What is the second half of the key?" I asked, eager to know exactly what I needed to do to get to Dohiyi.

"The cross. The one that has followed you from one lifetime to the next for centuries. That piece of your past has kept you grounded. It keeps you connected to your true self, no matter what lifetime you're in."

I pulled my necklace out from beneath my shirt to reveal the cross I had found at Merick's apartment. "You mean this cross?"

He just stared at it. "How did you—?"

"I'm not sure. Apparently, I sent it—the cross— to Merick to hold for me. I'm guessing it wasn't really me who sent it, but maybe my future self. But Merick didn't give it to me. I found it by chance, in an envelope in his apartment."

He shook his head. "Not by chance. It was fate."

"Fate?" I wasn't sure I believed in fate, but whatever it was, if it helped me find Merick then I'd believe. "How do I use them?" I asked.

"I'm not sure, but I know that together, with the power of your visions, they can help guide your travels and get you safely to Dohiyi."

"Have you been there?" I asked.

"I have not, but Isaac has, and he has told me of its beauty."

Excitement and relief washed over me all at once. Then, remembering that Haden was right there in the kitchen, I was brought back to reality. I still had more questions.

"How did you find me?" I asked. "Tonight, at the meeting," I clarified.

"Like I said, your blood is strong. I can feel you, even when you're not close. That connection is what allowed the members of your pride to find you. It is how lions remain connected even when we are far apart."

I remembered the day he had found me in the hallways of the abandoned building, the last time I saw Ciara. "Is that how you knew I was coming to find Ciara? That night you—"

"Yes."

The idea that we are all connected in such a way, through blood, was amazing. It seemed impossible to think that this man, who I had only met a couple of times, had such a strong connection to me.

"Why are you still here?" It came out harsher than I had intended, and Jabari pulled back. "No," I said, squeezing his hand that still held mine gently. "I didn't mean it like that. I'm glad you're here. I just mean, why didn't you go with them? They were your family. Why did you stay?"

"You are my Leaena. I could not leave, even if I wanted to. I have known since your first transformation, since before that really. I stayed with Isaac and the others as long as I could, but I could not leave with them."

What does that even mean? The weight of his words, the responsibility that came with being his Leaena, *and* being the Alpha of the wolf pack, was overwhelming. Not to mention the charge I had been given to bridge the past, the present, and the future. To unite the races so that past generations would not have suffered in vain in the war that nearly destroyed their world—my world. I was just beginning to stand up as Haden came back into the room carrying a tray of food and drinks. Had I felt better I would have given him a hard time for being such a *good host*, but he stopped me before I could.

"Eat," he said, sliding the tray across the table. There was an assortment of breads along with several platters of raw meat. Jabari quickly helped himself to the meat, and started eating, I declined. I still liked my meat cooked, which was an unpopular choice among the lycanthropes, but I didn't think I'd be changing any time soon.

I lifted one of the glasses from the table and sniffed it hesitantly. It was blood. "You keep blood on hand?" I asked.

"William needs something to drink when he's here hanging out, and I don't care how good a friend he is, I'm not opening a vein for him."

"Right, I should have known." I downed the glass in seconds, my fangs coming out instinctively the moment the blood hit my tongue. I was hungrier than I had thought. I put the empty glass back on the table, and took a piece of bread to gain a few seconds to think. I wasn't sure how to tell Haden about Merick without saying too much about Isaac, Ciara, and the others—and the truth about how Jabari and I actually met. I decided uncensored honesty was the best choice. Besides, he needed to know about Councilman Remy.

It took about two hours to update Haden on everything we knew, and to answer all of his questions. When we were done he didn't freak out, like I thought he might. He simply nodded, and said, "I guess we can let the pack know the hunt is off."

He was right, I had the whole pack out there, ready to do whatever it took to find Merick, but he was already safe, far outside the sector walls, and I hadn't even thought about letting the pack know. *This is why Haden has been such a great leader,* I thought to myself, wondering if I would ever live up to that standard.

"But first, there is another matter we need to discuss," Haden said, interrupting my thoughts.

I waited.

"Ash."

"Right." A shiver ran through me at the thought of Ash and his monsters. I picked at my bread for a few minutes, then cleared my throat, and began. "Before Merick disappeared, he told me how you and he followed Ash beyond the sector walls. How you saw him holding a secret meeting, a gathering of some sort, with a group of men and women you suspect may be somehow connected to that thing I—" I couldn't say the words. I couldn't admit to having killed the security guard, even if he was a monster.

Haden just nodded, but Jabari gave me a quick look, as if he had just put two and two together.

"Tonight…when you spoke to the pack. When you asked for a volunteer, you said there was a task that needed to be done. Does the task involve this Ash person?"

I nodded.

"And what do you want to happen to him?" he asked.

That's a good question, I thought to myself. I wanted him killed, but I wasn't going to say that. Besides, keeping him alive could prove more useful, at least for a little while, until we knew for sure what he really is.

"We just need to keep an eye on him. For now," I said. "I'm less worried about Merick's safety, now that I know that he has gone with Isaac and the others, but I still don't know what Ash is capable of, or what his intentions are."

"It is your safety I am concerned with," Jabari said.

Haden nodded in agreement. "And right now, you look tired. Why don't you go lie down for a while?

Let us talk," he said, glancing at Jabari. "We can come up with a plan, and run it by you after you've rested."

"I don't know," I said, about to argue, but they didn't let me finish.

Jabari and Haden stood up in unison, as if it had been choreographed. "Trust us," Haden said.

I swallowed, cleared my throat, and nodded. "I do. Just promise me..." They waited, clearly ready to promise anything, "...don't kill each other while I'm gone."

They didn't say anything, but I could see in their eyes that they understood, and that they would obey.

"I only need a few minutes," I said, standing and making my way past them toward the bedroom that I knew was through the door on the other side of the room. "I won't be long," I said. "We have more to discuss when I get back."

The bedroom was pitch black. Haden had thick black curtains that blocked out even the tiniest sliver of light. With the lights off, the room would have been just as dark in the middle of the day as it was at that moment. I focused my eyes, and it only took a few seconds to see clearly enough to cross the room—an advantage of being a vampire.

I sat down on the bed and enjoyed my drink, then I set the empty glass on the end table and lay down. I held the stone and cross in my hand, trying to focus on what Dohiyi must be like—trying to see if I could control my visions enough to take me there, but it didn't work. Eventually I gave up, too tired to continue trying. I rolled to my side and tried to relax into the stiff mattress.

23

I had only intended to close my eyes for a few minutes, but I fell into a deep sleep, and my dreams were vivid. Sharper than they had been in a long time.

I was sitting on a hard wooden-chair: the folding kind that the Council brings out when we have sector-wide meetings. There were rows of empty seats in front of me. Floor-length pleated curtains draped the walls, and the room was decorated with flower arrangements and potted plants. The scent was overpowering, and I started to feel lightheaded. I heard a muffled cry, but when I looked around I was alone.

"Hello?" I called out, but no reply came.

I felt paralyzed, trapped in my seat. I'm not sure how long I sat there before I heard them talking.

"She is stronger than you give her credit for," I heard someone say, from somewhere beyond the doors behind me.

"She's just a child," another voice pleaded, a woman.

"Give her time. She will heal. And so will you."

I shook off the sensation of paralysis and stood up and walked toward the large carved wooden door at the back of the room. I gripped the iron door-handle and pulled, but it was locked. I thought about knocking, but something inside me didn't really want to leave—couldn't leave. I turned my back to the door and walked slowly up the aisle between the rows of chairs.

"One. Two. Three," I counted the rows as I walked, staring down at the floor in front of me. "Four. Five. Six." The tension mounted with every step, but I had to continue. "Seven. Eight. Nine. Ten." I glanced up then, only five more rows until I'd be at the front of the room.

Ahead of me, there at the very front, surrounded by flowers, were two simple but elegant mahogany boxes with shiny brass handles along the sides. One box was longer than the other, but except for that they were identical.

"15." I stared at the wooden boxes and ran my fingers across the top of the smaller one. It was as smooth as ice, but warm to the touch. Something inside my mind was telling me I had been there before, that I knew this place—this room—but I couldn't find the words to understand what was happening, or what I was feeling.

"You can learn to bridge the divide between the past, the present, and the future."

This is the past. My past, I thought definitively.

"We will remain, as long as you need," they had said.

"Zelina? Ciara, are you there?" I called, hoping they could somehow hear me. "I need you, please." I waited, but no one came. I reached to touch one of the brass handles on the longer box.

"Not that one."

I turned, and there were young Ciara and Zelina, now in simple but beautiful black dresses. "You came," I said, relieved.

"Of course we came. And I see you got my present," young Zelina said.

"Present?"

"The cross," she said, nodding toward the necklace that hung loosely at my throat.

"Yes, I..." I started back down the aisle to them. But Zelina held up her hand for me to stop.

"It's time," she said.

"Time for what?"

"Time for you to let me go," Ciara said, a single tear running down her cheek.

I turned back, suddenly realizing who was in the box—the casket. "No," I said, as the tears filled my eyes. "It isn't true. It can't be true."

"You already know that it is," she said, guiding me back to the front of the room and placing my hand on the cold, brass handles along one side of the smaller box. "It was her death that allowed you to truly open yourself to your destiny. Although she is gone, she will always be with you, in you."

I turned to look at her, but she was no longer standing beside me. I looked around, but both girls were gone. I turned back to the mahogany casket. Slowly, I began to lift the lid.

"What are you doing?" A startled voice called out from behind me.

I quickly let go of the handle, and the lid dropped back into place. I spun around.

"I was..." I stopped. I was face to face with the red-haired woman. "Mary?"

From the look on her face I realized I had said her name out loud, and not in my head like I had thought. She rushed up the aisle toward me, and just as she was wrapping her arms around me, I woke up.
Alone.

24

I sat up in the darkness of Haden's room, wondering if I should try to fall back to sleep or join him and Jabari in the living room where I could hear them whispering. Another benefit of being a vampire is that there isn't much I can't hear if I focus. I was trying not to focus.

Looking down at the internal monitor on my wrist, I was surprised to see that it was 07:00. I had slept through the night, something I hadn't done in a while. I hadn't even realized I was that tired.

Iris must be worried, I thought. I went into the bathroom and splashed a little water on my face to help wake me up, straightened out my hair, and went into the living room.

Jabari and Haden were there, as I expected. But they weren't alone. In fact, it was a full house. Iris sat at Jabari's side, talking quietly with Teagan and Hudson.

I guess Iris isn't as worried as I thought. Or she was, and that's why she's here.

I hadn't seen Hudson since the last moon cycle, and hadn't spoken to him since our first moon cycle. I had assumed he was ignoring me, or was just afraid of me. Professor Gunner, the man who taught me to fight, was standing with Haden, and they appeared to be involved in a heated discussion. What I did not yet know was that Professor Gunner was the pack leader, the Alpha, of the second largest wolf pack in Sector C.

"She is too young to be a pack leader, Haden."

"You think I don't know she's young? You think I asked for this?"

I could feel the heat rising in my cheeks as I took note of each of the people in the room. They didn't even notice me when I walked in.

"What are you all doing here?" I asked, and the muffled whispers abruptly stopped. "Haden, why are they here?"

"Zelina, you're awake," he replied.

"It's seven o'clock," I said. "Why are they here?"

"Zelina," Iris said, stepping forward. "We were just discussing the events of last night."

I never took my eyes off of Haden. He had said that pack business stays within the pack, but Teagan and Hudson were lions, and Iris was a Tiger. Professor Gunner was a wolf, but he wasn't part of our pack. At least he hadn't been in the crowd the night before.

"I'll ask again. Why are they here?" I asked.

Haden hesitated, sucking his lips in, and then clearing his throat. "Teagan brought Hudson— apparently, he is a member of your pride."

I glanced up, my eyes meeting Hudson's, and he nodded. I returned his questioning eyes with a smile.

"And the others?" I asked.

I was just getting to that," Haden said, turning back to Professor Gunner. "Have you come to challenge her?"

Challenge me? I knew what that meant. If he had come to challenge me, he'd kill me. I'd never stand a chance fighting Professor Gunner one on one, wolf to wolf. He'd eat me alive, literally.

"No. I have not come to challenge her. She's a child—"

"I'm not a child," I corrected him.

"You are a child," he said, not even looking back at me. "She is too young to be a pack leader, but I won't kill a child. I'm not a monster."

Monster... No, I didn't believe he was a monster. I had seen a real monster just weeks before, and I didn't have any desire to see another.

"Then why are you here?" Haden asked.

"Because a few of her pack members came to me last night, seeking refuge within my pack."

"They what?" Haden barked. "Did you allow it?"

"I did," he said, nodding. "And I will allow any others to join as well, if that is what they want."

"Have you come here just to boast, then?" I asked.

Professor Gunner finally turned to look at me, to really look at me, and I could see in his eyes the man I had known for so many years. He had never been a hard man. He cared about his students. Sure, he was a tough teacher, strict even, but only because the lessons he was teaching us were a matter of life and death, literally.

He stepped toward me and reached out, placing his hand on my shoulder. Haden edged a little closer to me too, instinctively.

"A…that is, Zelina, how long have you known me? Have you ever known me to boast?"

"No sir," I said, slipping back into the role of student as if it was the most natural thing in the world.

"I haven't come to boast, nor do I like it that you are losing pack members, but I can't leave them to wander."

He had a point, whether I liked it or not. Besides, I knew I shouldn't take their leaving as a reflection on me. Change is hard for anyone, and although I was trying, I wasn't completely comfortable with this change either.

"Then why have you come? If not to challenge her, if not to boast? Why?" Haden asked.

"Because I like Zelina," he said, matter-of-factly. "She was my best student, and although I believe she is too young to take on the burden of being pack leader—and it is a burden—" he said, turning to me, "I also believe that in time, given the right guidance, she will make a great leader."

Haden squared his shoulders, and when he spoke his voice was deeper than before. "She has me to guide her."

"And me, if she would like my guidance," Professor Gunner said mildly. He wasn't ignoring Haden's aggressive stance, but he wasn't reacting defensively either.

Still, it was a standoff. Neither of them seemed to know where to go next with this. It was Teagan who intervened. She stood up from the couch, motioning to the others to stay seated, as if to say, "No need to make more of this than necessary."

"And me," said Teagan, stepping forward. "I was the only Leaena in Sector C until now. She will need my guidance as well. Besides," she continued, looking back at Jabari and then Hudson, "she has already begun to build her pride, and from what Jabari tells me, it is many strong."

My eyes met Jabari's, and he nodded in agreement. I had seen their eyes, golden and shining in the darkness of the tree line, but I hadn't been able to tell how many there were.

"I would suggest a uniting of our two wolf packs." Gunner said, first addressing me and then Haden.

"A uniting?" I asked. I knew my charge had been to unite the vampires and the lycanthropes, but somehow, this didn't feel right.

"Yes, with me as the Alpha and you," he continued, turning to me. "You would be my—"

"No!" I said, not letting him finish. I wasn't sure if he was going to declare me his Luna, his Beta, or just another member of his pack, but whatever he was about to say, I knew it wasn't right. "I have my own pack, and I am committed to them. It wouldn't be right for me to declare our packs united, not without their input, and not with you as the Alpha." I felt the heat radiating from Haden as he stepped closer behind me.

They were all watching me, waiting to hear what I would say next. I wasn't sure what to say. I agreed with Professor Gunner, that I was too young, but that didn't change the fact that I was the new pack leader and a new Leaena.

"I will accept your help and your guidance," I said. Professor Gunner moved to interrupt, but I stopped him. "But not your offer to merge our packs. Don't think that just because I am young I am not capable of making decisions on my own. I learned a lot from you as a child, but I am not a child anymore. Guidance is one thing, and I will take it, but trying to lead through me will not happen. I fully support unity—bringing the packs together along with the lions and all the other lycanthropes, and even the vampires—to work together cohesively as one. This I will support, even work toward and fight for. But I will not give up my rightful place as pack leader to do so. If you will not step down, then I will find another way to unite our people. Do you understand?"

No one answered.

"Did I make myself clear?" I asked everyone in the room.

"Yes," Haden finally said. "We understand." The others nodded. I could see on their faces that they were both surprised and impressed by my show of power. I didn't care. I knew the rules that governed the lycanthropes. If I failed as a leader, someone within my pride or within my pack would step up and try to take my place. I wasn't going to let that happen.

I looked down at the monitor in my wrist, a constant reminder that even though there is a whole world out there, I'm only part of a very small portion of it: Sector C. "It's almost eight o'clock. It's Saturday, and I have things I need to do. I'm sure you all have places to be as well, and by the looks of it most of you have been up all night." I waited, expecting them to say their goodbyes and start gathering their things to leave, but no one moved. So I did.

I shrugged and went to the door, and I simply opened it and left, pulling the door closed behind me. It felt incredibly empowering, until I looked up and saw that I was not in the hallway of Haden's building.

25

A tall oak tree cast a shadow on a patchy, unkempt lawn, and a cool breeze from the back seemed to urge me forward toward the old rusty gates of the Fort Hood Veterans Cemetery. I had never been inside the cemetery gates, and, as far as I knew, no one had been buried there since long before the war of 2082. I took a few steps forward, then a few more, and eventually found myself weaving in and out of the scattered gravestones. At first, many of the gravestones were laying on their sides crumbling with age, and hidden under fallen leaves and broken tree branches. However, the further I walked the newer and more beautifully kept they appeared to be.

I wasn't sure where I was going, but I felt myself being drawn deeper and deeper into the graveyard. It felt vibrant. Healthy green grass covered the earth, trees in full bloom swayed in the gentle wind, and flowers of every kind were on display in vases by the gravestones. Staring into the distance as I walked, I almost stumbled over a young brown-haired girl who was lying on a blanket on the ground, clutching a small teddy bear to her chest. I stopped just short of her, but she didn't move for a while.

When she finally did look up, I saw that silent tears were streaming down her face.

"Do you know who I am?" I asked.

"No," she said quietly, wiping her tears away.

"I'm you," I said.

"You are?"

I nodded, and I could see her trying to process this new information. "Are you OK?" I asked.

She shook her head, and I could feel the weight of her pain as if it were my own. "They're gone," was all she said.

The earth below my feet was still misshapen, bulging, and topped with freshly laid sod. There was something shimmering on the ground, reflecting the sunlight. It was a new granite gravestone, half covered with leaves and a freshly cut flower bouquets. When I knelt to brush the leaves away and set the flowers aside, I saw that the gravestone was larger than I had expected.

Two names, side by side, filled the top half of the stonework: William Remington and Ciara Remington. Under William's name were the words, *Remy—Col., U.S. Army / Devoted husband and loving father / May 4, 1962-July 11, 2017.* Under Ciara's name the words read, *Gone too soon, but forever in our hearts / September 19, 2010-July 11, 2017.*

"Ciara?"

I read the gravestone at least a dozen times, but it didn't make sense.

"Remy?"

"My sister and my daddy," she said. "They're gone," the little girl said again, not looking up.

The date of deaths was July 11, 2017. This was my past. The grave marker looked new, and the sod had just been rolled out: you could still see the lines where the patches had been cut. knew it hadn't been long since the funeral.

Why do I keep getting thrown into the past when I 'm meant to unite the factions of the future? I wondered.

I traced their names, Remy and Ciara, with my finger. The granite was colder than I expected.

"Ciara Remington," I read aloud. "Remington. Remy." *It could be a coincidence,* I thought to myself. *It* must *be a coincidence,* I told myself.

"They exist in both worlds, having gotten from one life to the next the way most do, through life and death. But, their energy signatures remain constant."

I knew it wasn't a coincidence. I knew in that moment that Ciara, my sister, had died long ago. I knew that her energy remained, traveling from lifetime to lifetime, like so many others, just as my father's life energy must have been traveling from one life to the next. But just because William Remington had been my father in that past life, that didn't make him my father in this one. *Or did it?* I wondered.

"I'm sure Ciara was probably a popular name back in…" I read the gravestone again, "…2010." Doing the math in my head, "That would make her…" I looked up, but the little girl was gone.

"Wait. Where did you go?" I called out, as I stood up to look for her, brushing the dirt off the knees of my pants.

"Who are you looking for?" Haden asked, from somewhere behind me. When I spun around, he was standing in the doorway of his apartment staring out at me.

"What?" I asked, confused, until I realized where I was. I was back in the hallway. Old carpet covered the floor and grey paint covered the walls. One of Haden's neighbors was leaning out her doorway, staring down the hall at us.

"You just yelled, 'Where did you go?' Who were you talking to?" Haden asked. He looked concerned, maybe even more so than I was feeling.

"Where did you go..." I repeated, stalling. "Right. I was talking to myself. Actually, I was talking to Merick, but he's not here. I wasn't really expecting an answer. It was more like, thinking out loud," I said, trying to reassure him.

He stepped into the hall, pulling the door closed behind him. "I know that all of this must be overwhelming, but you are not alone in this."

"I know."

"As your Beta, I am here to help in any way I can," he said. Then, through mind-speak, *"Anything you need, all you have to do is ask."*

"I need to get to Dohiyi," I said. Jabari and I had already explained everything to Haden, so he had an idea of what or where Dohiyi was, which was probably why he hesitated. *"Please, I can't go alone."*

"Then I will go with you. Just tell me when."

"Just like that?" I asked, surprised at his willingness to go without asking any questions.

"I told you, anything you need."

He went back to the door of his apartment, "Are you coming in? Everyone else is already here."

"Yeah, I'll be right in." I glanced down at the monitor in my wrist, 15:32: seven and a half hours since I had left that morning. *How is that possible? Where had the day gone? Where had I gone?*

26

I took a deep breath, because that always seemed to help steady me when I was feeling nervous, and I followed Haden back into his apartment. I wasn't sure who, or what, I was expecting to find, but it certainly wasn't a hospital room.

Mary was standing on the far side of the bed, and at the foot of the bed a tall man in a white lab coat was holding a clipboard, reading something written there. Amelia was standing off to his side, looking very young in her pale blue hospital scrubs.

"What is all this?" I asked, but they didn't answer.

Then I saw Haden. He was standing on the right side of the room, wearing some sort of uniform: dark pants with narrow gold stripes down the sides. The matching jacket had brass buttons, and the jacket front was decorated on both sides with gold badges and rows of small folded ribbons in all colors. At his side he held a matching cap with a narrow black visor and a gold crest centered in the front. Something about those brass buttons on the jacket seemed so familiar, but I couldn't put my finger on why.

Everyone was looking at whoever was in the bed, but I couldn't see who it was.

I took a few steps into the room, closer to the bed, and saw Nash sitting in the left corner of the room, with his head resting against the wall. He was asleep, but his face seemed red and puffy, as if he had been crying.

"What is he doing here?" I asked. When no one answered, I asked again, this time louder. "I said, what is he doing here?" Still no one noticed. Their focus stayed on the bed.

I moved to the edge of the bed. It was the young Ciara, lying peacefully, as if asleep, her red hair spread across the pillow.

"Ciara?" I said, grabbing her arm, but she didn't wake up.

"You're saying, there's no chance?"

"I'm sorry, Mary," the man in the lab coat answered. "There is no brain activity. She's already gone."

"She'll never wake up?" Mary asked, tears streaming down her face. "First my husband and now my baby girl?"

"I'll give you time to say your goodbyes." He said it gently, then he hung the clipboard on the end of the bed and left. Amelia quietly followed him out. I thought about following them, to try to get some answers, but I couldn't leave Ciara behind, not like that. I needed to understand why I was there, why I was meant to see this moment. I already knew she was dead. I had seen her casket, and I had sat by her grave. Why did I have to see this too? And why were

Nash and Haden there? How were they connected to my past?

"Mary, your husband was a good man and a great leader. We're all so sorry for your loss. If there is anything we can do—" Haden had joined Mary, and stood across from her at the bedside.

"No. I'm sorry, I appreciate your kind words, but there isn't anything anyone can do. I can't even…" She lowered herself into a seat next to the bed, never letting go of Ciara's hand. "I don't even know where to begin. I can't breathe, and I feel like…" She clasped her hands on the bedrail, and her knuckles were white. "My son won't talk to me unless he's yelling," she said nodding toward Nash.

Son?

"My other daughter can't stop crying. They…" Tears were pouring down her face, but her eyes stayed firm and focused on Haden. "They had to sedate her, in a room down the hall, just so she could get some sleep. I'm not even sure when the last time was that I closed my eyes, let alone slept. Every time I try, I see their faces. I just… I can't… I can't do this. I don't know how."

I took a few steps back. I had never seen anyone so overcome with emotion, and it felt wrong, somehow, to be watching like this. I slipped out the door and down the hall. I peeked into each room I passed until I found the right one. There in the bed, fast asleep, was the little brown-haired girl. A clipboard hanging at the end of the bed had a single piece of paper clipped to it. Only two words were written there, printed in dark black marker: Zelina Remington.

27

When I opened my eyes, I was sitting in the lobby of Remy's office.

Another vision? Or is this reality? It was getting harder and harder to tell *when* in time I was. I wondered when, if ever, I was going to find my way back to my own timeline, or maybe I already had and I just couldn't identify it any more. I knew I had the power to control it, the little girls had told me that much, but I had no idea how to actually do that.

Calliope was pounding away at her keyboard. She seemed to be busying herself just so she wouldn't have to speak to me. When her phone rang she picked it up quickly—another welcome distraction—but it didn't last long.

"You can go in now," she said, glancing up at me only briefly as she hung up the phone.

"Thank you," I said, as I passed by her desk and pushed open the door. She looked surprised, and maybe she should have been.

Remy sat behind his large wooden desk looking out the window, watching sector residents passing by, and seemingly thoroughly preoccupied by his thoughts. I wondered if his mind ever wandered the way mine did, but I was doubtful.

Remy… Remington.

"You know," he said, evidently not so preoccupied after all, "it isn't an easy job keeping everyone safe, keeping you safe, keeping everything running smoothly in here." He still hadn't looked up. His focus was on something out the window, or maybe even further away than that.

"No, I wouldn't think it would be."

With a deep sigh, he finally turned to look up at me. "Was there something you needed, Zelina?" he asked.

Well, at least I now know I'm the one who wanted to meet. He hadn't called me to his office. That little piece of knowledge gave me the courage I needed. I wasn't going to let this moment pass without finding some answers.

Then I saw it, something about him seemed different, less commanding. His shoulders slumped forward slightly, his eyes seemed tired or sad. If I didn't know him better, I'd say he seemed defeated.

I realized I had been watching him from the doorway, and I quickly moved to approach his desk, and he gestured for me to take a seat.

"I just wanted to let you know—"

"Is this about last night?" he asked, cutting me off.

"Last night?" I had lost track of time between all my recent visions—travels. I was having a hard time determining what was real and what wasn't, or should I say what was happening in Sector C and what was part of my past life. I had been to the cemetery, the hospital, the… *the meeting with the wolf pack.*

"I've been told that you are the new Alpha to Haden's pack. I was glad to hear you did not take the position by force. Haden is a valuable asset to our internal security, and I would have hated to lose him."

A valuable asset? He talked about him as if he was property and not another living being. I shouldn't have been surprised. Most of the vampires did see the lycanthropes as lesser beings, just as the lycanthropes viewed the vampires.

"And your Leaena," he continued. "I hear she has already begun to form a pack."

"A pride," I corrected him. "Werewolves form packs, werelions form prides."

He was watching me closely. It was no secret that the conversation made him uncomfortable, or maybe it was disappointment I was seeing. Whatever it was, it was written all over his face, and he didn't even try to hide it.

"Of course, a pride. Either way, it is very impressive how much you've grown in the short time since your transformations."

Impressive? His choice of words made me wonder if what I had seen in his expression may have been something other than disappointment.

"Thank you, sir. That means a lot, coming from you." I cleared my throat, "The reason I wanted to see you was actually about Ciara—"

"Yes, *Ciara*." He looked away as he said her name, and for an instant I felt the need to reach out to him. I stopped myself, and he continued. "We haven't located her yet," he said, shaking his head.

"No, I know, and you won't. That's why I'm here."

That got his attention. He stood to meet me, eye-to-eye. "Explain *won't*." He didn't seem angry, but more intense.

"She's gone." Saying the words out loud hurt more than I had expected. They felt more final than I could have imagined.

"What do you mean, she's gone?"

"You've been looking for her outside the wall, and that's where she has been, until now. Now she has left the guarded twenty-mile guarded border outside the wall. Now she's gone." I knew that telling him she had left would give me up as an accomplice, but I decided it didn't matter. If he wanted to punish me, then so be it. At least I would have helped my sister escape.

Besides, Jabari's words kept running through my head, and I prayed I could trust they were true. *"Your leader, the one you call Remy. He is not who you think he is. He has been working with the Resistance, from within the sector."*

"Gone? Are you sure?"

I nodded. I couldn't tell if he was relieved or disappointed.

"Then she is probably dead," he said, matter-of-factly.

I knew that was a possibility, but it had been her choice, and I had to respect that. Besides, with Isaac, Merick, and the others there to protect her, I knew they had a fighting chance. "You might be right, but I'd rather believe she's out there somewhere, living her life the way she wants to. And, I'm happy just knowing that is a possibility, even if it is a small one."

"Then you're living in a delusion."

"Maybe I am. Maybe I'm not." I wondered if there was more truth to what he had said than even he could know. "There's something else," I said.

"What?" he asked, almost hesitant.

"She didn't kill Wyatt." He was watching me closely. "She had been bit, by a water moccasin. Wyatt was trying to save her. Then, while she was still too weak to help him, he was attacked. It wasn't her who killed him, but it was your endless pursuit of her that forced her beyond the wall. Forced her to leave the safety of the sector. It was your orders that led the guard to hunt her down, pushing her to seek alternate refuge."

This time, when he looked up and met my eyes, I could see an unspoken question dancing on the tip of his tongue.

"I think you already know," I answered, before he asked.

"Dohiyi?" he asked, lowering his voice to a mere whisper.

"Dohiyi," I answered, with a nod. I watched him carefully, looking for any signs of anger, but what I saw was his shoulders relaxing as he leaned back in his chair.

"So, you know?" he asked.

"I know a little, but that's why I'm here. I'm hoping you can help me fill in the gaps."

"I..." he started, but stopped himself. He sat there for a few moments as his expression changed to something more like sorrow. Then he shook his head slightly, and got up and went to the wet bar on the other side of the room. He poured two glasses, taking a sip from the first, and holding the other one out to me. A few minutes later, we were sitting in the comfortable club chairs in front of the wet bar, with a small table between us. He finished his drink, and set his glass on the table.

"I will help, with what I can," he said, nodding his permission to ask what I wanted to know.

So many questions, I thought to myself. *Should I ask about Dohiyi? Should I ask about the Resistance? Should I ask about Councilman Ash?* A thousand questions ran through my mind.

"I saw your grave," I said. "I know you're my father. I know Ciara is my sister, and Nash is my brother. I know my mother was a breeder, then a donor, and now a vampire."

He stared at me for what felt like forever before leaning back in his chair. "Do you have a question?" he asked.

"Yes," I said, and suddenly I felt like a child staring up at a father who could scold her at any time. "Did you really die?"

"No," he said, flatly, and my heart sank. "I've been around a long time, Zelina. Long before the sectors were established. Long before the war that brought light to the presence of vampires and lycanthropes."

I wondered how old he really was, but I wasn't going to ask. The gravestone had his birth date as May 4, 1962, but now I was guessing it had been long before even that.

"Then why did you leave us? Why did you let us believe you were dead? Ciara died, and you left

Mary to take care of me and Nash all on her own. Why?"

He turned away, grabbing at the nape of his neck, a gesture I recognized in Nash. "I'm not proud of what I did, but I had no choice," he said.

"We all have choices."

He turned, and his eyes met mine. He nodded. "Perhaps we do. But I had lived through the centuries, from a time when vampires were believed to be made-up creatures of the night to a time when small clans, like mine, were finally able to coexist peacefully with humans. However, that didn't last long. Rogue vampires—possessed by something more sinister than I can explain—began to disrupt that harmony, destroying what trust we had gained from small pockets of human society."

"In the mid-20th century, I became a respected leader in the military. I lived two lives: one among the humans and one among the vampires. I led a small clan of vampires, right here where Sector C now stands. We lived in hiding, but we survived, together. At that time, I hoped that one day we would be strong enough to abolish the—"

I waited as he struggled to find the right word.

"Monsters," I said, finishing his thought.

"Monsters? Yes, that is fitting. At the time, we had no name for them. Eventually their disruptions brought light to the fact that vampires and lycanthropes had lived among the humans for centuries. Then the war began, and society was all but extinguished. Vampires, lycanthropes, and a few thousand humans were all that remained. The High Council was established, and they created the sectors. The humans became breeders, helping us to regrow the population. From the very beginning, the High Council's intention—their ultimate goal—was to create a stronger race of vampires and lycanthropes, a race strong enough to defeat the *monsters* if they ever returned."

Doesn't he know that the monsters are living among us? I wondered.

"I know you sent Merick away," I said, abruptly. "Why did you do that?"

"He was no longer safe here."

"Why?" I asked. I wanted him to say the words. I needed him to recognize that the monsters were living among us.

"His connection to you made him a target for others within our community."

"You mean Ash."

He quickly turned, scanning the empty office as if Councilman Ash could somehow have heard what I said. "You mustn't make accusations you cannot prove."

"But I—"

He silenced me, with a simple gesture. "Trust me."

28

"Trust—?"

Before I could finish my question, Remy was standing beside me, and his large but gentle hands were at the sides of my head. I braced myself for the pain I knew was about to pierce through my skull, but it never came.

"Just let go," were the last words I heard. Everything happened so quickly after that.

You know how people say that right before you die, your life flashes before your eyes? Well, I'm not sure about the dying part, but my life—lives—did flash before my eyes. It started with recent memories: of Merick and me sitting on a blanket having a picnic; of Ciara and me studying and laughing on my upper bunk in the selection student barracks; of Merick and me running the selection course; and of staring down at my tablet taking a test in Professor Kade's class.

Slowly, the memories began to grow blurred, as if I was watching them through foggy glass. And then there came events that I myself didn't remember: I was old, rocking back and forth in a rocking chair on a porch somewhere; I was walking hand-in-hand with a man I didn't recognize; I was in labor, giving birth, with the same man standing at my side. Then I was young again, in a classroom full of other kids, then swinging in a tire swing that hung from a branch of a large oak tree. The memories came at me quickly and in no particular order.

Then I was running on a beach, chasing the little red-haired girl, with water splashing up at my legs...

"Hey, wait for me," yelled a little boy from somewhere behind me. I turned around and saw that it was Nash. He was maybe five or six years old, but I would have recognized him anywhere, with his bouncy blonde curls and bright blue eyes. For so long I had been angry with him because he had worked for Councilman Serenity as her spy, informing on Merick and me. But seeing him there, calling out to me, I felt...love. I wanted to protect him.

Then the memory was gone. I was spinning around and around. I could hear myself laughing, but I couldn't see anything. It was dark... No, my eyes were closed. When I opened them, Mary stood watching young Ciara and me playing outdoors on the grass. We held hands and spun around and around, faster and faster, until we flew apart. "Again! Again!" Ciara cried, laughing almost as hard as I was. We grabbed hands again.

I was in a car, sitting in the back seat between Ciara and Nash. I didn't remember ever having been in a car, but there I was, as if it was the most natural thing in the world. Remy was driving, and Mary was in the front seat next to him.

"Just look...please!" Nash was saying over and over.

"I'm driving," Remy said, but he turned back anyway. His eyes were only off the road for a few seconds, but that's all it took. I turned to look out the window to my left, and Ciara smiled at me. She didn't even see the enormous red truck that came speeding through the intersection toward us.

I heard screams, felt the car tumbling down into a ditch, and then everything went dark.

"I can't get a pulse."

I heard sirens in the distance, people moving around me, then I felt myself being lifted and placed on a solid hard surface, but I couldn't open my eyes.

"This one's D.O.A." someone said. I wasn't sure who they were talking about, but it couldn't have been me. I wasn't dead.

I couldn't tell how many people were there with me, but hands were suddenly all over me: someone was wrapping my leg, someone was holding my head still, someone else was...

OUCH! I wanted to scream as a sharp pain pierced my arm, but there was something down my throat. I couldn't move...I couldn't breathe...I couldn't speak...I couldn't see. All I could do was lie there, listening to them hustling around me.

"Push another amp, start bagging!"

Something was placed over my face, and a rush of air pushed through my lungs.

"Clear!"

Something cold and hard was placed on my chest and side, then a painful shock of electricity hit me all at once. A constant high-pitched beeping filled the room, then a hum.

Silence.

"Damn it, I'm not losing another one today. Push 70 of Mannitol."

A burning sensation grew in my arm where they had stuck me.

"Clear!" And again with the electric shock, and suddenly I could breath, or rather, I was choking on whatever was down my throat.

"She's choking... Get the tube out, she's choking on the tube."

As soon as it was out, I started feeling better. It was as if nothing had happened. I opened my eyes, and I was sitting there in Remy's office as he watched me.

Just a vision? I wondered.

"What was that?" I asked, as I looked up at Remy.

"I think you already know the answer to that question," he said.

I nodded.

"Why didn't you tell her?" I asked.

"Tell wh—"

"Mary. My mother. Why didn't tell her you survived the accident? Why didn't you tell me?" I could feel tears filling my eyes, but I didn't feel sad. I was angry. "We had already lost Ciara. We thought you were dead. Why didn't you tell us?" I was standing, pacing, and I didn't give him a chance to answer. "How many years did you wait? How long did you wait for her to die so you could find her again and recreate your little family? How well did that work out for you? Is this the life you always wanted us to have?" I stopped briefly to catch my breath.

"No. No, this isn't the life I wanted for us," he said, standing, and again gazing out the window. "I had hopes for so much more for us. But your mother was innocent and naive. She didn't know who or what I really was, and there would have been no way to explain—medically—how I could have walked away from that accident. If I had survived, my vampire clan would have been exposed. I had to protect my clan. I knew that Mary could protect you and your brother, but my clan had no one except me."

"So, you just left?"

"I was never far, but yes, I did leave. I had to, to keep them safe. But know this. It wasn't an easy decision, Zelina."

"Where is she now?"

He took a deep breath, one he hadn't needed in centuries. He turned from the window, and met my eyes. "Mary knows who and what I am now. I've shared with her our history and she has accepted the choices I had to make."

"Where is she now?" I asked again.

"She is safe."

I knew instantly what he meant. He had sent her on to Dohiyi. Just when I discovered who she was, she was just out of reach.

"And Nash?"

"What about him?"

I wasn't really sure what I wanted to know. Ciara and Mary were safe in Dohiyi, as was Merick. Nash was my brother, although he didn't know it, and even though he had never treated me like a friend, much less family, I still cared. "Will you protect him too?"

"If it is the last thing I do," he said, nodding.

"The last—"

"Now that you know…" he cleared his throat. "I tried to keep all of this from you, for as long as I could. However, now that you know, there is little I can do to protect you. *He* will find out," he said, whispering. "And when he does, I will not be long for this earth. There are so many more of them than there are of us."

I knew who he was talking about: Councilman Ash and his army of monsters.

He stepped toward me, and held out his hands. "I'm so sorry," he said, and I took his hands without thinking. He pulled me into his chest and wrapped his arms around me, and for a moment I felt safe. Then I heard him whisper softly, "It's time to wake up."

29

When I opened my eyes, I was alone, lying in a hospital bed and covered with a thin white blanket. There were framed photos on the bedside table and on a wall shelf, and there were vases of flowers that looked like they had been there a while. There were 'Get Well Soon' signs taped to the walls. The sun was shining through slits in the window shades, and even the small amount of light was too much. I pulled myself up, covering my eyes to allow them to adjust. I leaned back against the pillows. My throat burned, my breathing was labored, and my entire body felt stiff. I felt different: more human and frail.

There was a glass next to my bed, and I reached for it. I was hungry, and the cold water that hit my lips didn't satisfy my hunger. I reached up my fingertips searching for my fangs, but they weren't there.

What is happening to me?

I swung my feet off the edge of the bed and went over as close as I could to the window—which wasn't all the way because of the tubes and wires that were connected to me. Judging from the distance to the ground, I had to be at least five or six floors up. The parking lot below was full of cars, people moving about, and a few ambulances just pulling in, lights flashing.

Where am I? I wondered. Suddenly my arm started to burn. I quickly lifted the sleeve of the thin blue gown and watched as the glowing sphere appeared just beneath my skin. The burning subsided and all that remained was the familiar tattoo I had received from the sphere of light—my activator.

I was still standing there, my hand caressing the tattoo as I stared out at this new world in awe—and fear—when the door opened behind me. I heard something crash to the floor, and...

"Zelina? Oh my God, Zelina, you're awake. How?"

I was moving slowly, but when I turned around Mary was standing there with coffee on her blouse and a broken mug on the floor at her feet. She didn't even seem to notice as she rushed into the room and wrapped me in her arms and sat down with me on the bed. She was crying, and hugging me tighter than I've ever been hugged. I glanced over her shoulder and noticed a young man—tall, with short, wavy blond hair—standing in the doorway.

"Nash," I whispered, without realizing I had spoken his name aloud.

Our eyes met, but he just stood there outside the doorway. He didn't come inside, not right away.

"Nash, get the doctor!" she cried. "Tell them she's awake!" Nash didn't move, and Mary looked up at him. "Go!" she whispered.

He must have done what she asked, because a few minutes later the room was overrun with nurses and doctors. At least three people checked my pulse and my blood pressure, one nurse poked at my arm taking vial after vial of blood, and another was examining a clear bag attached to the side of the bed—and me—saying something about, "…and her urine output looks good."

Urine output?

I felt as if I didn't have time for this, but I knew from what the little girls had told me that I needed to spend "awake" time in both lives in order to keep the bridge of energy strong. I knew I wasn't out of time, not in this timeline or the next, so I resolved to be patient and try to interact with these people—my family and friends who were somehow asleep to the realities of the world. Sleepwalking through their obliviousness.

Amelia finally came in, wearing her flowing black slacks, red blouse, and white lab coat.

"Amelia," I said, at the same time she called out to me.

"Zelina, do you know where you are?"

I nodded. "The hospital," I said.

"The base hospital," she corrected me.

Base hospital? That was new.

For the next hour, I sat there with Amelia, Mary, and Nash, and learned the truth, their truth. It was amazing, and I was grateful for the answers our conversation provided.

My family lived—lives—in Texas: Fort Hood, Texas, to be exact. My father, Remy, was a Colonel in the U.S. Army. I even attended school there on the base, before the accident, that is.

Amelia had been a medical student at the time of the accident. She had been driving behind us when

the red truck hit our car. She told me how she had
rushed out to help. She had been the first person at
the scene, and the one who had called the
ambulance. She had helped my mom and Nash first.
Then, with my mom's help, she had pulled me out of
the car. I had a broken leg, and was unconscious, but
she had thought I would be all right.

Mary, my mom, only sustained some minor
injuries, and Nash, my younger brother, wasn't injured
at all unless you counted a few scrapes and bruises.

"When the ambulance arrived," she said, "we
realized the man driving the truck was already dead."

This one's D.O.A., I remembered hearing.

"And your father—"

"Remy?" I asked.

Amelia looked up at me, surprised. "Yes, he—"
she started, but it took her a few moments to
continue.

"He also died. He sustained the majority of the
truck's impact. Even if he had been breathing, there
was nothing the doctors could have done. There was
just too much damage to his lungs and heart," Amelia
explained.

That's not true, I thought. I knew Remy had
lived long past the day of the accident. I thought about
telling them, but I decided it was probably best not to.
He had made his decision, chosen to leave his family,
it wasn't my place to bring him back. Besides, he had
been a vampire in a world where vampires and
lycanthropes were still creatures of movies and make-
believe.

"What about Ciara?" I asked, although I
already knew.

"Her injuries were extensive. Because the truck hit directly into her side of the car, she suffered major damage to her rib cage, two of which were broken and had punctured her lung. The glass had shattered, cutting up her face, neck, and arms, and she lost a lot of blood before we made it to the hospital. She had significant swelling in her brain, and by the time we got her to the hospital there was no brain function." I looked up to find Mary wiping away tears, and Nash sitting quietly off to the side, his hand behind his neck pulling at the back of his hair. He looked sullen...defeated. In that moment, I could see the resemblance between him and the Remy I knew in Sector C.

Amelia explained, without saying it in so many words, that they ended up pulling the plug on Ciara later that night, after it became clear that she would never wake up again.

I didn't want to ask, but I had to. "And me?"

"Your leg was broken, and you had a slight concussion, but other than that you were all right...or we thought you were, for a while."

"What do you mean, for a while?" I asked. I'm not stupid, I knew something had been wrong with me, otherwise I wouldn't still be in the hospital. But I also knew something they didn't know—how necessary it was for me to be in the coma.

"After the funeral, we couldn't calm you down," Mary said. "For weeks you wouldn't eat more than an occasional cup of broth, you wouldn't talk, you wouldn't sleep. You just sat on Ciara's bed and cried. The doctors suggested a sedative to help you rest."

"You had a reaction to the sedative. I still can't explain it." Amelia said. "We think your immune system must have been compromised prior to the accident."

"What kind of reaction? What aren't you telling me?"

"You started seizing, and then..." She looked up, took a deep breath, and said the impossible. "You died."

"I...died?"

"Technically, yes. But we were able to revive you. After we got the seizures under control, we discovered you had developed encephalitis. It's an inflammation of the brain. Your doctors made the decision to put you in a medically induced coma to give your brain time to heal."

Mary and Amelia shared a look. I couldn't tell what it meant, but I was sure it wasn't good.

"And?"

"And, until today, we haven't been able to wake you, not fully. You've come in and out of the coma a few times over the years, but only for a few seconds—minutes at most—before you'd slip away again. This is the longest and most coherent you've been."

"Will I—"

"You should be fine. Your vitals are all good. Your blood work has come back normal. There is nothing to indicate that you won't—"

I stopped listening for a moment. This news alarmed me! I wasn't done! I wasn't near done! Unification was years away—maybe even decades away! Had I gone through all of this only to fail? To be stuck in the past, destined to live through the very wars that had destroyed my past and cause the future divide that I was so desperately trying to fix?

Without thinking, I said, "What about Merick?"

At that, Nash looked up. "Your imaginary friend?" he asked, then glanced up at Mary.

"Imaginary friend? What are you—"

"Merick was the name of your imaginary friend when you were little," Mary explained.

When I was little?

"You really believe that Merick was just an imaginary friend?" I asked.

"Of course," she said.

I wondered if it was possible that in this timeline, as a child, I had somehow connected with the Merick I know from Sector C. My tattoo tingled just under my skin and I knew it was true. Merick had been real all along. *They* just couldn't see him.

"I know he was," Nash answered, matter-of-factly. "I remember you playing with him, and talking to him. Except you were the only one who could see him and hear him. Ciara and I always pretended to see him, but he wasn't real."

"He was real, even if you couldn't see him," I thought to myself.

"What?" Nash asked.

OK, maybe not to myself.

I looked at him, eye to eye. *"Can you hear me?"* I asked.

I watched as his eyes widened with the realization that I was talking in his head, not out loud.

My excitement soared, as did my pulse rate, which was confirmed by the rapid beeping of a monitor at the side of my bed.

Mary and Amelia were instantly alarmed. Amelia rushed to the side of the bed, pushing buttons and checking the charts on the screen. "She needs to rest," she said.

Mary quickly got up to leave, gesturing for Nash to do the same.

"I'm OK, I'll calm down," I assured her. "You two go, it's fine, but please let Nash stay. We have a lot to talk about. I promise to rest."

They both looked as if they were about to protest, so I added, "It's just nice to have the company. I want to catch up."

They smiled gently, and Nash eased back into his chair, cautiously.

"We won't be far away," Mary said. "If you need us, send Nash."

"I will."

As the door closed, I contemplated how I was going to explain the unexplainable.

"How did you...?" he gestured to his head, with a questioning look on his face. He wasn't afraid, but he was curious.

"I'm not sure," I said, honestly. "But I have a theory."

He pulled his chair closer to the bed and leaned in. "How long have I been here?" I asked. "In this coma."

He shook his head, and I couldn't tell if he was doing the math or just didn't want to tell me. "I was in first grade when… That makes it just over ten years, almost eleven."

Eleven years? "That makes me, seventeen or eighteen, right?"

He nodded. "You just turned eighteen a month ago."

"The same age I am in Sector C."

"Did you say, Sector C?" he asked, hesitantly.

"No, I thought Sector C. You're just listening in on my thoughts."

"What? No I'm not," he said, defending himself.

I laughed. "I'm kidding. It's fine. I'm not sure how it's carried over into this timeline, but we seem to have a—"

"Connection," he said, finishing for me.

"Yeah, a connection." I cleared my throat, suddenly nervous. "Have you heard of Sector C?" I asked.

He nodded. "In a dream, or a memory of a dream."

My tattoo tingled again, and I knew there was more to our connection.

"How often did you come see me? Here in the hospital, I mean."

"We're here every day, Mom and me. Sometimes she just sits in the hallway. It's been hard on her. But I usually come in and do my homework here with you."

Homework? I looked around the room, and there on the ground next to his chair was a black backpack stuffed full of books and papers. "Do we ever talk?"

He furrowed his brow. "No, not until today."

I mean, did we ever talk?" I asked, this time in his mind. "Did we ever communicate, like this?"

"I'm not sure, maybe." He grabbed at the sleeve of his jacket, and adjusted himself in his seat.

"What can you tell me about Sector C?" I asked, taking a stab in the dark. I was assuming he knew more than he thought. If my theory was right, we had been communicating all along. And if young Zelina and young Ciara were correct, I was pretty sure he had been one of my guides, helping to keep my connection between the past and the future open. He may not have even been aware that he was doing it.

"I don't know. It's more like a feeling than anything else. I know life there isn't like here. There are different rules. Its stricter. Lonelier, too."

I nodded. I hadn't thought about it that way, but he was right. Life in Sector C could be very lonely.

I fluffed the pillows behind me, making myself more comfortable as I set in to tell him a story. I wasn't exactly sure where to start, but a sudden tingling sensation on my arm guided me.

I pulled my arm out from beneath the blanket, and slowly raised the sleeve of my hospital gown. "You aren't going to believe this…" I began.

His eyes widened in disbelief as the colors of my tattoo danced just beneath my skin.

"What is it?" he asked.

"An activator."

He stood up, reaching out to touch my arm. As soon as his hand rested on my arm, I could feel the energy floating through me and into him. I'm not sure what he saw in the minutes that passed, but when he finally opened his eyes and pulled his hand away, he had an identical sphere of swirling colors just beneath the skin of his palm, and one more player had become…Awake.

"Is it real?" he asked.

"Yes."

"You have to go back, don't you?"

"If I'm going to finish what's been started, then yes."

"But, why you?" he asked, fighting back tears.

"I have to change our story, Nash. I can't leave things the way they are there. It isn't the future I want for you and it isn't the future Dad wanted for you either."

He gasped, in shock. Maybe sadness. "Dad? Is he there with you too?"

I wasn't sure how much I should tell him, how much him knowing could affect this past. "He is." I watched as the tears overflowed. Losing Remy had been harder on him than anyone, and now to know he still existed, even if in another timeline, it was like ripping open an old wound. "Nash, can you keep a secret?"

He nodded.

"He's here with you too." I watched as his eyes widened, his pupils expanded. "I don't know where, but I know he isn't far. I can't tell you how to get in touch with him, I'm not even sure you can, but he survived. He survived the car accident."

"He survived?" he asked, and I could see not only pain but anger beginning to build inside of him.

"Nash, he isn't the same, not like you remember him. He's different. He's…" *How do you tell your brother your father's a vampire? How could he ever understand?*

"A vampire, like in Sector C," he said. It wasn't a question, but I answered him anyway.

"Yes."

He didn't say anything, not for a long time. Neither did I. I knew he needed time to process everything and I wanted to give him as much time as I could. When he finally looked up, something had changed in him.

"When will you go?" he asked. I could see the pain in his eyes as he tried to accept the fact that he would be losing me—again.

"I'm not sure, but soon, probably."

"Should I get Mom?"

"No, she wouldn't understand. Besides, I think it's best if this stays our secret, at least for now."

He nodded. "Will I see you again?"

I smiled. "Don't worry, I'm never far. And, if I'm right, now that you know the truth…" I took his hand in mine and traced the tattoo on his palm with my finger, *"it should be even easier for us to stay in touch."*

"You think?" he asked, using mind-speak for the first time.

"I believe you just answered your own question."

It was his turn to smile. He leaned forward and gently kissed me on the forehead. "I love you," he said, and everything faded away.

30

I gasped for breath as I sat straight up in bed. The question burned in my brain. *How*? How was I going to fix everything?

"Another nightmare?" Ciara asked, popping her head up on the side of my upper bunk.

Nightmare?

"A, are you all right?" she asked, quietly leaning in so no one else could hear.

"I'm…" I glanced around, surprised to find myself back in the selection student barracks. "Where's Merick?"

"Merick? Who's that?" she asked, looking more confused than I felt.

"Umm…where's M?" I asked, and a wave of nostalgia swept over me. I looked around the room at my fellow selection classmates, who were busying themselves with last-minute studying, or just getting ready for the day. I pulled back my blanket, and I was dressed in the all-too-familiar selection student grey sweatpants and top.

Ciera looked around the large room. "M! Come here a minute. A is looking for you."

What is happening to me? I had made it back to my timeline, but things weren't right. I was still a selection student. I grabbed for the necklace beneath my shirt, hoping it was still there. It was. I held my half of the broken vision stone and the cross tightly in my fist, I may be starting over, but at least this time I know the truth. *Maybe if M still has his half,* I thought to myself, *maybe he'll remember.*

"Hello, Earth to A. What's going on in that brain of yours?" Ciara asked, as she pulled her long red hair up into a ponytail.

I jumped out of bed, grabbing them both by an arm, and dragged them with me into the bathroom.

"You know this is the girls room, right?" Merick asked, as the door shut behind us.

"Yes, I know." I pushed them into a shower stall and closed the door behind us.

"What is going on, A?" Ciara asked.

"I finally understand," I whispered.

"Understand what?" Merick asked. I smiled to myself. *He would understand a lot sooner this time.*

"The prophecy," I said.

"Are you ok?" Ciara asked, as she put her hand on my forehead, checking for a fever. "What prophecy? What are you talking about, A?"

"Don't call me that," I snapped. "My name is Zelina. You're Merick, and you, you're Ciara."

"Ciara," she repeated. "I kind of like that."

"I have been to the past, and the future."

"The—"

I didn't let him finish, "The prophecy is coming true, right now as we speak, and I know what it means," I said, as I raised the sleeve of my grey sweatshirt. The glowing sphere was still there, and I heard them gasp when they saw it. The present from the two little girls. The present from the past to the future.

I took a deep breath—one that I very much needed. Here was Ciara, my true sister. Here was Merick, my soulmate. It was time to begin, and only three people were missing: the one who had come to be my most trusted advisor, my Beta, Haden; Jabari, the first lion of my pride; and Nash. This time I'd make sure my brother was on my side. "We have to find Haden, Jabari, and Nash," I said.

The End

Also by Nina Soden

The Blood Angel Series

What if everything you thought you knew about yourself and the world turned out to be wrong? The Blood Angel Series is set in a world very much like our own, yet Atlanta isn't just an ordinary city and Alee Moyer isn't just an ordinary girl. Having barely survived her childhood, it will take the death of her father for the truth of her bloodline to come out. Even if it means losing her identity or even her life, she won't be able to escape her true destiny as the first surviving dhampir in history. Surrounded by a new world where the horror films she grew up watching have become reality and the most unlikely characters have become her lifeline, Alee must find herself and her purpose if she hopes to survive.

http://www.ninasoden.wordpress.com
http://www.twitter.com/Nina_Soden
https://www.amazon.com/author/ninasoden